I glanced to the right . . .

Richie Monroe was headed the other way, carrying a cooler that someone had asked him to stow.

Richie was what I would charitably call dumpy. Tattered jeans, raggy T-shirt, scuffed sneakers. He wasn't anywhere near as tall as Levi, and he had a paunch that didn't surprise me. According to what I'd heard, when Richie wasn't doing odd jobs, he was downing cases of beer at home or bellied up to one of the island's many bars.

He stared at the cooler in his hands. "I'm allowed to be here." The rain fell harder, and Richie lifted his chin and sent a laser look in Mike's direction. "Until I move away from this pit, I'm allowed to be anywhere I want. It's my island, too."

"Yeah, if you don't blow up the whole place one of these days."

Mike pushed past Richie just as lightning split the sky directly overhead and thunder blasted loud enough to make my collarbone vibrate.

I darted to my right, eager to get on dry land, too, and I would have done it if a couple things hadn't happened all at once.

A blast of wind slapped against my back.

Another streak of lightning turned the inky blackness so blinding white that I squeezed my eyes shut.

Waves made the boats all around me bob and slap against the dock.

And Richie Monroe screamed for help.

He was in the water.

A Tale of Two Biddies

Kylie Logan

BERKLEY PRIME CRIME, NEW YORK

THE BERKLEY PUBLISHING GROUP
Published by the Penguin Group
Penguin Group (USA) LLC
375 Hudson Street, New York, New York 10014

USA • Canada • UK • Ireland • Australia • New Zealand • India • South Africa • China

penguin.com

A Penguin Random House Company

A TALE OF TWO BIDDIES

A Berkley Sensation Book / published by arrangement with the author

Berkley Prime Crime Books are published by The Berkley Publishing Group.
BERKLEY® PRIME CRIME and the PRIME CRIME logo are trademarks of
Penguin Group (USA) LLC.

For information, address: The Berkley Publishing Group,
a division of Penguin Group (USA) LLC,
375 Hudson Street, New York, New York 10014.

ISBN: 978-0-425-25776-0

PUBLISHING HISTORY
Berkley Prime Crime mass-market edition / February 2014

PRINTED IN THE UNITED STATES OF AMERICA

10 9 8 7 6 5 4 3 2 1

Cover art by Dan Craig.
Cover design by George Long.

For librarians everywhere
who foster the love of reading and
the importance of books

ACKNOWLEDGMENTS

You might be reading *A Tale of Two Biddies* at any time of the year. But I finished writing it at the end of summer and I've just returned from a visit to South Bass Island, where the League of Literary Ladies mysteries are set. I got the chance to enjoy island hospitality and island life, from the ferry ride to and from the mainland (always one of my favorite parts of the trip), to motoring around in a golf cart (the preferred island mode of transportation), to enjoying some of the fabulous wine produced by local wineries.

South Bass is a vacationer's paradise set to the beat of Jimmy Buffett songs. There's history around every corner. In fact, the island is close to the sight of Commodore Oliver Hazard Perry's famous victory at the Battle of Lake Erie during the War of 1812. He's the one responsible for the famous quote, "We have met the enemy and they are ours."

Acknowledgments

In winter, a couple hundred hearty souls remain on the island, but it's summer when most of the action happens, and it's summer that *A Tale of Two Biddies* celebrates. No, as far as I know, there's never been a Bastille Day celebration on the island, but hey, islanders are always looking for a little fun. Maybe they'll start a new tradition!

As with every book, there are people I need to thank including my husband, David, and my brainstorming group—Shelley Costa, Serena Miller, and Emilie Richards—without whom there would be no Guillotine! Thanks, too, to the folks over at Berkley, to my agent, and to my Airedale, Ernie, who patiently listens when I talk out plot problems and hardly ever interrupts.

❦ 1 ❧

"It was the best of thymes, it was the worst of thymes!" I was mid-munch, a shrimp dripping cocktail sauce on its way to my mouth, and I needed one second to grab a napkin to keep the spicy sauce from landing on my new yellow T-shirt. While I was at it, I focused my eyes from the bunch of gloriously green herbs that had just been thrust in front of my nose to the other bunch of dried-out herbs next to it, and beyond, to the ear-to-ear grin of Chandra Morrisey.

"Get it?" Chandra was so darned proud of her little play on words, she hop-stepped from one sandal-clad foot to the other, those small bouquets of thyme jiggling in her hands like maracas. I swear, I thought she'd burst out of her orange capris and the diaphanous lime green top studded with sequins. "Do you get it, Bea? It was the best of thymes . . ." She held the freshest bunch of herbs at arm's length. "It was the worst of thymes." She flashed the other bunch. "You know, just like the first line of *A Tale of Two Cities*."

"I get it!" I grinned, too, because let's face it, it was a balmy evening in the middle of July and I was sitting on a dock on an island in Lake Erie with the women who were once just neighbors and were now my friends, enjoying the Monday-before-a-huge-tourist-week celebration for merchants and residents that had been organized by the local chamber of commerce. What was there not to grin about?

I finished off that piece of shrimp and popped out of the folding chair where I'd been lounging. Of the four of us in the League of Literary Ladies—South Bass Island's one and only library-sanctioned discussion group—Chandra was the least likely to actually read one of our assigned books. I didn't hold that against her. What Chandra lacked in literary ambition she made up for in sheer exuberance, a wacky take on everything from her wardrobe to her love life, and a skewed look at the world that included crystals, incense, and tarot cards.

That's why I was careful to keep the skepticism out of my voice when I asked, "So, what do you think of Charles Dickens?"

"Best of thymes, worst of thymes." As if it would hide the fact that her answer was as evasive as the look she refused to give me, Chandra stuck out each hand again, and the pungent, woody scent of thyme fragranced the evening air. *Dawn in Paradise*. That's how Rudyard Kipling had once described the aroma of thyme. I couldn't say if he was right or not; I only knew that I'd lived on the island for six months since escaping an ugly stalking incident in New

York, and things were going well. Just as I'd once dreamed of doing, I'd turned my life not just around, but completely on its head, and created a new career and a new, peaceful existence for myself. My bed-and-breakfast—Bea & Bees— was booked every weekend from now until the end of summer, and I'd settled into a life that was slower paced and far more satisfying than the mile-a-minute stress mess I'd lived in New York. For me, relocation was the right choice. For me, South Bass Island was Paradise.

Even if once in a while, there were reminders that even Paradise had its perils.

A blast of wind off the lake snaked its way up my back, and in spite of the heat, I shivered. One murder does not a Paradise destroy, I reminded myself. Just like I reminded myself that, thanks to me and the other Ladies, the murder that had happened a couple of months before had been solved, the perp caught, and order restored to Paradise.

It wasn't going to happen again, I told myself. This was the heartland, not the big city, and I was grateful for that.

Just like I was grateful that Chandra had remembered to bring the thyme from her garden. I gave myself a swift mental kick to get my thoughts out of the past so I could concentrate on the present and the party atmosphere that enveloped the docks and spilled over into DeRivera Park across the road. Except for the boat slip right next to Luella's, which was empty, our fellow islanders were everywhere, chatting, unwinding, and gyrating to the beat of the steel drum band playing near the entrance to the dock. People milled around us, comparing notes about the tourists and how good (or bad) their business had been so far that summer. They shared plates of the food, and recipes when they were asked, along with a camaraderie that could only be forged on a four-mile-long spit of land three miles north of the Ohio mainland.

Party, I told myself, and took a deep breath. Paradise, I reminded myself, letting that breath out slowly. This wasn't the time to think about murder, and it sure wasn't the place. Just to prove it to myself, I grabbed the good-looking bunch of thyme from Chandra, stripped the elfin leaves from their stems, and sprinkled them on the salad I'd brought as my contribution to our potluck dinner.

"Did I hear someone say it was time to eat?" Luella Zak jumped off her thirty-foot Sportcraft boat and joined us on the dock. "Kate's coming," she added, glancing over her shoulder toward the fishing charter she captained. "She's just opening the wine."

"One red." Like Chandra had with the herbs, Kate held out the bottle for us to see and joined us around the folding table we'd set with a cheery red, white, and blue cloth and red acrylic dishes and glasses. "One white. Both from Wilder Winery. I hear they make some darned good wine."

Kate ought to know. She was a Wilder and owned the winery.

"Oh no, you know the rules!" If Kate wasn't holding those bottles, I think she would have swatted Chandra's hand when Chandra eyed up the salad and reached for a plate. "Toast first. Eat second."

"Toast first." I handed around glasses and Kate filled them. "What are we toasting?"

"The chance to relax a little before another busy week,"

Luella said, and raised her glass. Luella was in her seventies, and as tough as any skipper I'd ever met. She was short, wiry, seasoned by the lake on the outside and as gentle as a lamb on the inside. Of all of us, she was the one who loved books and reading the most, and she'd willingly joined the League, not been coerced into participating like the rest of us had. "I'm always grateful for fishermen, but I'm just as grateful to be on dry land once in a while and let my hair down."

"You got that right, sister!" Chandra squealed with delight. She spun around, taking in all our fellow revelers, and raised her voice. "Here's to a great party!"

"And the opportunity to enjoy good wine." Kate lifted her glass. "And good food."

"And good friends," I added. A few months ago, their reactions would have been predictable. Kate would have rolled those gorgeous green eyes of hers. Chandra would have looked as sour as if she'd bit into a lemon. Luella was as steady and predictable as the lake where she made her living was not; then, like now, she simply would have nodded. Fortunately, things had changed since the days when Kate, Chandra, and I were hauled into court for our neighborhood bickering and sentenced to a year of discussing books on Monday evenings. I, for one, was grateful. "Here's to the way things have turned out." I glanced around the circle and smiled back at the friendly expressions that greeted me. "Things are different and I'm so glad."

"To friendship," Luella said, and we clinked our glasses, sipped our wine, and filled our plates. Before I had a chance to dig in, though, Gordon Hunter stopped by to chat. Gordon lived on the mainland but had a summer cottage not far from Put-in-Bay, the island's one and only village. He was a mover and a shaker who'd been hired by the chamber of commerce to fill in for an employee out on maternity leave, and if this party he'd organized was any indication, he was going to be good for business.

"Le fait de s'amuser?" No, Gordon wasn't French. At least I didn't think he was French. What he was, was the driving force behind the Bastille Day celebration planned for the rest of the week. Bastille Day on South Bass Island? Of course, it's not an official holiday, but islanders are always looking for a way to cook up some fun, and tourists are always looking for any excuse to join in. It was a stroke of genius on Gordon's part, and the reason, of course, that the League of Literary Ladies had chosen *A Tale of Two Cities*, the Dickens classic about the French Revolution, as our latest read.

Gordon gave Chandra a friendly poke. "That's, 'Are you having fun?' for those of you who haven't been to Paris lately."

I had been to Paris. Just about a year earlier in fact, but my French was as rusty as my wanderlust. I took his word for the translation and offered Gordon a glass of wine.

He wasn't a sipper. He took long, quick drinks. Something told me that was the way Gordon attacked all of life. He was a little older than middle-aged, with salt-and-pepper hair, and as suave as a toothpaste salesman. While the rest of us were dressed casually and comfortably, Gordon was decked out in khakis, a white shirt, and a navy blazer with brass buttons. He didn't look as much like a PR guy as he did an admiral.

Maybe he knew what I was thinking because when the guy who owned what was advertised as "the longest bar in the world" came by, Gordon gave him a crisp salute.

"It's going to be a helluva week," Gordon said. He reached for a shrimp and dragged it through cocktail sauce. "Everybody ready for the crowds?"

"I've got charters every day," Luella said.

"And we're doing winery tours and tastings every afternoon and evening," Kate added. "I put the notice online a couple weeks ago and we're packed for every single one of them."

"My rooms are filled," I put in. "Thanks again for sending the band my way," I told Gordon.

With the wave of one hand, he acted like it was nothing. "Folks around here tell me you're from the Big Apple, Bea. I figured if anyone could handle a rock band called Guillotine, it was you. They check in yet?"

"Tonight," I told him, and reminded myself I'd have to be back at the B and B by then. "Apparently, rock musicians aren't early risers."

Gordon refilled his glass before he moved on to the next boat and the next group of partiers. Watching him, Luella shook her head. "Can't blame the poor guy for drinking. You heard what happened last night?"

I hadn't, but that was no big surprise. My B and B was on the outskirts of what was officially considered downtown, and I was often the last to hear the latest gossip.

This time, though, apparently Kate and Chandra hadn't heard, either. As one, we pinned Luella with a look.

"Gordon let Richie Monroe help him out on his boat."

Kate's mouth dropped open. Chandra gasped. After six months on the island, I knew Richie well enough. He was fifty years old or so, the guy people called when they wanted small jobs done. Richie shoveled snow in the winter. He ran errands for tourists. He sold ice cream out of a cart on weekends. He carried bags at the grocery store.

I looked from one woman to the other. "I've had Richie do some things for me around the house. He pulled the weeds in the front flower beds. And he cut the grass the weekend my lawn service guys couldn't make it because of a funeral. Richie's reliable."

"Reliable, maybe." Something told me it was no big secret—what is on an island this size?—but Chandra leaned forward and lowered her voice. "But he's not exactly careful."

"Wasn't careful last night." Another head shake from Luella. "He slammed Gordon's boat into the dock. The way I heard it, he did some damage."

Automatically, my gaze traveled down the dock to where Gordon was chatting it up with Alvin Littlejohn, the magistrate who'd sentenced us to be a book discussion group, and his wife, Marianne the town librarian. "Gordon doesn't look especially upset."

"He's a trouper," Luella said. "And he knows he's got to put on a good show tonight. He put a lot of time and effort into planning this Bastille Day event. He can't let it fizzle. But the way I heard it, he was madder than a wet hen last night. Can't say I blame him. If it was my boat he'd damaged, I would have threatened to wring Richie's neck, too."

"Is that what he did?" It seemed so out of character for

debonair Gordon that the comment caught me off guard. "You don't think he'd really—"

"I'm surprised Richie's still alive and breathing, anyway." Chandra's bleached blond hair was chin-length and blunt cut. When she swayed her head from left to right, it stroked her cheeks. "You'd think by now, Mike Lawrence would have gutted Richie like a walleye."

I wasn't so far out of the loop that I hadn't heard this story. Though it had happened the autumn before I moved to the island, Richie's monumental screw-up had already reached the status of island legend. "You mean because of how Mike hired Richie to turn off the gas in that fancy new summer cottage over at the other end of the island," I said.

"And how Richie wasn't paying attention to what he was doing, as usual," Kate added.

Just thinking about it made Luella wince. "And how Richie left the gas line open instead of shutting it."

"And that big, fancy summer home . . ." Chandra put down her wineglass long enough to slap her hands together. "Kaboom!"

"Poor guy who owned that house," Kate murmured.

"Poor Mike," Luella commented, and when she looked down the dock, we all did, too, and saw that Mike Lawrence wasn't partying with his neighbors. In fact, a boat neared the empty slip next to Luella's and he got ready to help the dockmasters get the boat berthed. "What with the insurance claim and the owner of the home suing him and the government after him because he was paying Richie under the table and not paying Social Security taxes for him, Mike has lost just about everything he owned—including his contracting business. He's picking up every odd job he can get his hands on, and he's living in a trailer over near the state park. Imagine living in a trailer with a wife and three little kids."

I could imagine it, and what I imagined was cramped and uncomfortable. I made a mental note to see if I could come up with some work for Mike around the B and B. It wouldn't solve all his problems, but it might help.

"Well, look who's here! One of the guests of honor!"

I didn't know there were guests of honor for the week's festivities, so Luella's comment surprised me. That is, until I turned away from watching Mike work and saw who was headed our way on the dock.

Alice Defarge—or was it Margaret?—and talk about a legend! The Defarge twins had lived their whole lives on South Bass and they owned the island's only knitting shop. As far as I'd heard, neither of the ladies—seventy-five if they were a day—had officially been named a guest of honor, but the Defarge reference was lost on no one. At least no one who knew anything about the Dickens book. In *A Tale of Two Cities*, Madame Defarge is the iconic figure who sits knitting in the shadow of the guillotine.

Thankfully, our own Defarges were far less ghoulish. In fact, the sisters—who I'd met at various potlucks and island functions—were as sweet and as friendly as can be. This one—whichever one she was—sure enjoyed the reference to being the guest of honor. Her smile was as bright as her snowy white hair.

I adjusted my black-framed glasses on the bridge of my

nose. "Alice or Margaret?" I asked Kate out of the corner of my mouth when the old lady neared.

"Alice." As subtly as she could, Kate pointed, indicating Alice's white cotton pants and her sky blue, short-sleeved shirt. "Margaret always wears something pink."

I'm sure I'd heard that before, but this time, I told myself not to forget it.

"Isn't this great fun!" In the light of the setting sun, Alice twinkled like a prom queen. Just like her sister, she was a tiny woman with a neat, poofy hairdo and a spring in her step. "I only hope . . ." Her gaze moved past us to the lake. "There are some pretty dark clouds out there. I hope the weather isn't going to spoil our celebrations this week."

"There's a chance of rain tonight," Luella told her. "But nothing for the rest of the week. Will you and Margaret join us for dinner?"

Another blast of wind kicked up over the lake and brought with it the distant rumble of thunder. "Thank you, but . . ." In no time at all, Alice headed back the way she'd come. "I'd better help Margaret get our picnic settled over in the park. Just in case it starts to rain and we need to pack up in a hurry."

"Nice lady," I said when she was gone.

"A real sweetheart," Chandra confirmed. "So's her sister."

"And you'd better be really careful every time either one of them is around," Kate advised, then laughed when she saw the look of disbelief on my face. She grabbed my arm. "I'm just saying. Hasn't anybody told you? The Defarge sisters—"

"Are the biggest gossips on this or any other island," Luella said. "There are a lot of people around here who believe that's why they opened their knitting shop in the first place. You know, so they'd have a ringside seat right downtown and they could keep an eye on everyone and everything that happens around here."

"They know your business before you know your business," Chandra added. "And there's nothing they like better than telling the world."

By the time they were done with their warnings, my smile was tight. "Then it's a good thing I don't have any business worth discussing."

"Right." Kate split the word into two syllables. That is, before she grabbed her dinner dish and took it with her when she went to a nearby boat to chat with its owners.

"Anything you say." Chandra had already finished her plate of food, but when she walked down the dock to visit with some of our neighbors, she took the bottle of red wine with her.

"Good luck with that," Luella said, and she, too, walked away, leaving me alone on the dock and wondering what had just happened.

For like a half a second.

That was when I realized I wasn't alone, and the reason they'd all pulled up stakes and fled was suddenly all too evident.

Where Levi Kozlov came from, I don't know, but my guess was the other Ladies had seen him coming and decamped to give us some alone time. I'd mention it to them later, along with the fact that as far as Levi was concerned,

I didn't need alone time. Yes, he was tall, honey blond, and gorgeous. Yes, there were sparks that flew between us like the quick flashes of lightning I saw far out over the water. Yes, I was attracted in a way I hadn't been attracted to a guy in a long time.

But . . .

"Hey." Levi had a bottle of beer, and he raised it in greeting. "What's up?"

I clutched my wineglass in both hands, grateful acrylic was strong and I couldn't snap the thick stem. "Not much. With you?"

He shrugged. A normal enough motion, except when the person gesturing happens to own a pair of Greek god shoulders that moved effortlessly beneath the navy T-shirt that advertised his bar. "Been busy?" he asked.

"Yeah. Busy. You?"

"Busy."

I swear, we could have gone on like that for hours, side-stepping anything that even remotely resembled a conversation and sounding like two idiots in the process. I told myself to get a grip. After all, even though Levi had admitted to me in the spring that he knew the story I'd told around the island—the one about how I was the widow of a rich antiques dealer from New York—was a total fabrication, as far as I knew, he'd kept my secret. *Why* was another matter.

Maybe it was the why that made me so nervous.

I pulled in a breath to steady the rhumba beat inside my ribs. "Have you had dinner?"

"I had a sandwich at home." That didn't stop him from reaching over and grabbing a handful of pita chips Kate had

13

brought along with a bowl of her homemade hummus. He munched on a chip. "It sounded like a hassle, packing up food and bringing it down here." He looked over our little buffet. "Though as usual, it looks like you're being the perfect hostess."

"It's not my party." I stepped back, distancing myself from the idea, and at the same time giving him better access to our table and the food on it. "We all contributed, and no one will mind if you share. We've got ribs."

Levi's blue eyes lit. "Luella's ribs?" He reached for a plate and dug in. "You know, I've been trying to convince her that she should quit the fishing business and come to the bar and be my barbecue cook. She's a genius."

I had to agree.

"And the salad's yours," Levi commented, taking some of that, too. "I'm not a mind reader, I can just tell. It's fresh."

"So you're telling me I'm fresh?"

He drizzled lemon caper dressing on his salad at the same time he gave me a sidelong look. "You're different."

"Different good or different bad?" I could have kicked myself the moment the question fell out of my mouth. Not only was I opening myself up to a subject that might be construed as too personal, but I realized that Margaret Defarge was now standing at the end of the dock (white pants, pink shirt), and yes, she was watching us carefully. The last thing I needed was to be the subject of island gossip.

On the off chance that a serious Bea Cartwright would short-circuit island rumors quicker than a friendly, grinning one, I wiped the smile off my face.

Apparently Levi took my expression to mean we were back to superficial. "Business has been good this summer."

I was grateful for what amounted to cocktail party chatter. I'd had my fill and more of cocktail parties back in New York. I could bullshit with the best of 'em.

"For me, too. I've been pretty much booked solid since Fourth of July. I'm making it work," I said, and instantly regretted that I'd let myself sound a little too smug, a little too proud. Emotions were revealing, and sure to open the door to deeper conversation. "That is, I'm glad I moved here." That was no better, and I took a sip of wine. "It's been busy, which is why—"

"I know, I've been busy, too." Finished with his ribs, Levi wiped his hands on his napkin and polished off his salad. "That's why I haven't seen you around much."

It was a better excuse than the one I would have been forced to give if I was up against a wall. I'd come to the island for peace and anonymity, and I couldn't get involved in a relationship—with anybody—and put that at risk. I'd seen Levi around. Of course I had. And each and every time, I'd been careful to sidestep, dodge, elude, and avoid.

"Thyme." Levi swallowed a bite of salad and smiled his approval. "Nice addition."

"I'm lucky to have Chandra and her herb garden next door."

Another rumble of thunder punctuated my words and Levi set down his plate and looked up at the thick gray clouds that raced across the lake, headed our way. He already had the chips and the hummus in his hands before he asked, "You want help cleaning this up?"

15

I wanted to tell him no, but my other neighbors were scrambling, too, to get their tables and their food stored, and I figured they knew more about weather on the lake than I did. I nodded and grabbed the salad and the peanut butter brownies Chandra had brought along, and together Levi and I hurried onto Luella's boat. Most of the deck was open to the evening air, but the steering wheel (is it called a steering wheel on a boat?) and other controls were under cover, and we set the food there. When the table was empty, Levi brought that aboard, too, and we loaded all the food back on it.

Another blast of wind hit, along with a wave that made the deck of the boat bounce, and Levi propped his fists on his hips and drew in a lungful of electricity-charged air. "A storm on the lake and a cozy place to drink wine and watch it happen."

Was this an invitation?

And would I accept it?

I held my breath, waiting for the question as well as for an answer I wasn't sure of.

"Unfortunately . . ." He moved back to the open deck. "I left windows open at home. You going to be okay getting back to the B and B?"

I assured him I would be. It was getting darker by the moment and the wind was getting stronger and steadier. "Chandra's got her van. I'll drive back with her, and the food is safe enough for now, so we don't have to lug anything with us."

When Levi got off the boat, I did, too, just as lightning ripped through the clouds overhead and lit the dock. In its eerie glow, I saw a man jump off the boat that had just docked next to Luella's. With his baseball cap pulled low over his forehead, the collar of his windbreaker turned up, and his chin to his chest, he raced past me, heading for dry land.

That's when a whole stream of people closed in on me, including Mike Lawrence, who led the way, and Luella and Kate, who each had hold of one of Margaret Defarge's arms to help her along. Chandra waved to me to hurry up. Gordon Hunter was right behind them, and he yelled something about the gazebo in the park.

Just as the first fat raindrops plopped against the dock, I stepped back, waiting for Mike and the rest of them to pass, only to realize that he'd frozen in his tracks a few feet to my left. When he stopped, everyone else had no choice; they did, too.

I glanced to the right. Richie Monroe was headed the other way, carrying a cooler that someone had asked him to stow.

"What the hell are you doing here, you idiot?" Mike grumbled like the thunder that shivered in the air.

Richie was what I would charitably call dumpy. Tattered jeans, raggy T-shirt, scuffed sneakers. He wasn't anywhere near as tall as Levi, and he had a paunch that didn't surprise me. According to what I'd heard, when Richie wasn't doing odd jobs, he was downing cases of beer at home or bellied up to one of the island's many bars.

He stared at the cooler in his hands. "I'm allowed to be here." The rain fell harder, and Richie lifted his chin and sent a laser look in Mike's direction. "Until I move away from this pit, I'm allowed to be anywhere I want. It's my island, too."

"Yeah, if you don't blow up the whole place one of these days."

Mike pushed past Richie just as lightning split the sky directly overhead and thunder blasted loud enough to make my collarbone vibrate.

I darted to my right, eager to get on dry land, too, and I would have done it if a couple things hadn't happened all at once.

A blast of wind slapped against my back.

Another streak of lightning turned the inky blackness so blinding white that I squeezed my eyes shut.

Waves made the boats all around me bob and slap against the dock.

And Richie Monroe screamed for help.

He was in the water.

❰ 2 ❱

"Bea, that was amazing!" High praise, indeed, especially coming from Kate, but I would have gladly shrugged it off if her arm wasn't around my shoulders in a sort of half atta girl/half congratulatory hug, and if Chandra wasn't stationed directly in front of me, her mouth hanging open and her eyes wide with amazement. This girl did not like to be the center of attention, and what with the folks gathered around Richie in the middle of the octagonal gazebo in the park and the ones who pressed around me from every side just a few feet away . . . well, center of attention was the name of the game.

I cringed.

And thanked my lucky stars that the *Gazette* hadn't gotten wind of Richie's accident. Or my involvement in fishing him out of the drink.

"With all the wind and all the rain and all the people running back and forth on the dock and yelling and trying to figure out what to do to save Richie . . ." Kate was so hopped up on adrenaline, she gave me a shake that made my teeth rattle. "You were the only one who thought to dump out the contents of that cooler he'd been carrying and toss it in the water for him to use as a flotation device. It was brilliant!"

"It was a gut reaction." Honest, I wasn't trying to be modest, I just wanted to brush the whole thing off and get out of the limelight. "Besides, Luella was the real hero. She was the one who grabbed that fishing net with the long handle from her boat so Richie could hold on to it and we could pull him onto the dock. Good thing, too. That cooler would have started taking on water sooner or later, and it would have dragged Richie down with it." I didn't dare to think what might have happened then.

"Good work, ladies!" On his way over to where Richie stood trembling in the puddle of lake water that dripped from his clothes, Hank Florentine, the local police chief, gave us a thumbs-up. He'd brought a blanket from the red, white, and blue SUV he'd parked nearby, and in the pulsing red lights he'd left flashing, I saw him drape the blanket over Richie's shoulders and ask if Richie was all right.

"I . . . I am now." The temperature had dropped since the storm blew through and Richie's teeth chattered. "But . . . but Hank—"

"Yeah, yeah, just a sec." Hank turned away from Richie and honestly, I wasn't surprised. Near-death experience or not, Richie Monroe was easy to ignore. He might always be around, but in his own way, Richie was invisible.

Hank wormed his way over to me and I found myself wishing he'd brought along another blanket. My T-shirt and capris were soaked from the rain, my dark, curly hair was plastered to my head. I used one finger to wipe the worst of the rain spatters off my glasses, plunked them back on the bridge of my nose, and wrapped my arms around myself just as Hank nodded. I knew that from him, that was praise pretty much the equivalent of a tickertape parade.

"I heard you moved fast, Bea. Back at the station, they're already calling you a hero."

"Just like in that movie!" In the effort to think exactly what movie *that movie* was, Chandra jumped up and down and waved her hands. "You know, Bea, that movie based on the book from that writer you don't like, the one you're afraid to read."

"FX O'Grady." Luella supplied the name and I bit my lip to stifle a groan. "Bea might be quick-thinking and brave when it comes to lake rescues, but she's scared to death of FX O'Grady's horror stories," Luella told Hank so he'd know what we were talking about.

"Can't say I blame her," he said. "The last time I finished one of his books, I couldn't sleep for a week. The guy has some serious psychological issues. And a freaky imagination."

"But he did that." As if it would explain both the *he* and what *he* did, Chandra pointed across the road to the dock and automatically we all looked that way, too. Six months on the island, and I was learning that storms like the one we'd just experienced were nothing unusual. Lake Erie is the most shallow of the five Great Lakes and when the wind picks up, the waves can turn treacherous in no time at all.

Add a dose of summer heat and humidity and it's the perfect recipe for a quick-hitting thunderstorm. As fast as it struck, though, the storm was over, and now lightning flashed over the mainland to our south and the rain that had been driving and furious simply pattered against the gazebo roof.

"He did that," Chandra said again. "That guy in the movie. You know, the hero of the story where the vampires rise from their underground kingdom. The hero was trying to save his friend who fell in a lake and he tossed a closed cooler into the water." Chandra's excited expression melted. "Of course, the guy who got saved ended up getting sucked dry by the vampires later in the movie, anyway."

"Well, I guess what that proves is that FX O'Grady and I have the same sort of freaky imagination." I managed a smile and hoped that would put an end to the topic. I didn't like being thought of as a hero, almost as much as I didn't like being associated with the King of Horror. "It just seemed like the most logical thing to do and the only thing I could think of at the moment."

"Well, it worked, and that's what matters." Hank backed away. "EMS is on its way," he said, almost as an aside to Richie. "They're going to check you out."

"But, Hank!" Richie's clothes streamed water and he'd lost one of his sneakers. When he stepped out of one puddle and moved forward, a new puddle formed around him. "You have to know, Hank. We gotta talk."

Hank scratched one hand through his buzz-cut hair, and even if Richie didn't get the message, the rest of us did. Our police chief might be pretending to be patient and profes-sional, but now that he'd made sure Richie was okay, Hank had other things to do. Other things more important than Richie Monroe.

Hank's words were clipped by his clenched teeth. "So tell me, Richie. What do we have to talk about?"

I take it back. I guess Richie did get the message because he raised his pointy chin, and beneath the blanket, his scrawny shoulders shot back. "How about the fact that some-body just tried to . . . to kill me?"

Kate stood on my left, and astonished, I glanced at her. Chandra was to her left, and looking just as skeptical as I felt, Kate turned that way. Luella was over on our right, and as one we all looked at her and saw her roll her eyes.

Hank, though? Hank was stonefaced. "Is that so?" He tugged his left earlobe. "Somebody tried to kill you, huh? How do you know?"

Richie's bottom lip quivered. "Know? Well, I . . . I . . . I just know, is all. I mean, there I was out on the dock, mind-ing my own business, and then everybody started runnin' around and talkin' real loud and it was thundering and light-ning and—"

"And that's how you know somebody tried to kill you?" Hank asked.

Richie scrubbed one finger under his nose. "I know because I felt a hand on my back. I know because I know what it feels like to get shoved. And I got shoved. Right into the water."

"All righty then." Hank let out a long breath before he hauled a little notebook out of his back pocket and flipped it open. His pen was in his shirt pocket and he pulled that out, too. "Who was it, Richie?" he asked, pen poised over paper. "Who tried to make you into fish food?"

"Well, I . . ." Richie blinked and his shaggy brows dropped low over eyes that were as pale as the single anemic light that hung from the center of the gazebo ceiling. "I dunno. It's not like I saw the person or anything."

Hank flicked his notebook closed.

"Now wait a minute!" Richie put out a hand to grab Hank's arm. At the last second, he thought better of it and froze. "Just 'cause I didn't see who it was, that doesn't mean it didn't happen," he said. "There was lots of people around. Somebody must have saw something." He glanced around the circle of people in the gazebo. Island residents, every single one of them, and like the other Ladies and I, they'd already made up their minds: Richie was being Richie, and everybody knew that Richie Monroe liked attention almost as much as he liked to make up stories in which he was either the one being picked on by uncaring and unreasonable people, or he was the hero. Same tune, different words.

One by one, the folks around us turned and wandered away.

The other Ladies and I might have done the same thing if we'd been quicker. Unfortunately, before I could move, Richie's eyes met mine. "Tell him, Bea! You saw what happened. You were right there."

One of Hank's eyebrows lifted. "Were you?" he asked me.

"Right there? Sure I was. But . . ." I went over the scene again in my head. *Chaos* just about described it, and in that chaos . . .

"Richie came by carrying the cooler," I explained to Hank. "He talked to Mike Lawrence, but—" When I saw the way Richie's eyes lit as if he was ready to glom on to that bit of

info and convince Hank to slap the cuffs on Mike, I was quick
to add, "But by the time Richie fell in the water, Mike was
already gone. I'm sure of it."

"You're not sure. You can't be sure." Richie gave me a
testy little click of the tongue. "If you were, you'd tell Hank
how you saw somebody push me."

"But I didn't," I told Richie, then turned to Hank. "I can't
say if it did or didn't happen. I can say I didn't see it. But
then, I was scrambling, just like everyone else. I didn't realize Richie was in the water until he called for help."

"It was pretty confusing." Luella confirmed my version
of the story. "There was a lot going on, and a lot of noise."

Hank took this in, then glanced at Kate. "You have anything to add?" he asked, and when she didn't, he closed his
eyes for a second—no doubt praying for strength—and
asked Chandra the same thing.

"I think we have a mystery on our hands," she announced.

A muscle twitched at the base of Hank's jaw. "That's not
what I asked."

"But it's true. I can feel it." Chandra swayed like a snake
charmer. "The aura of the island has changed."

"And there's a disruption in the Force." Hank's sarcasm
wasn't lost on anyone, not even Chandra.

"You shouldn't ask for the truth if you can't handle it,"
she snapped.

"You shouldn't start talking nonsense," Hank shot back.

And I stepped forward before things could get any more
out of hand. See, Chandra and Hank had once been married,
and as strange as it seemed when they started in on each other
like this, I knew they still ended up in bed together once in a

25

while. This did not mean that they were inclined to be friendly at other times. Like this one. In fact, Hank went out of his way to make fun of Chandra's belief in all things woo-woo, and because he did, Chandra took every opportunity she could to throw her oddball theories in his face.

"How about we all just sleep on it," I suggested, taking in not only Chandra and Hank, but Richie, too. "I bet after we've all had a chance to warm up and relax, we'll remember more of what happened. That would be good, wouldn't it, Hank?"

He got my message. If there was any hope of us escaping Richie's crazy talk and Chandra's New Age babble, it was time to put the subject to rest. "Yeah, yeah." Hank headed out of the gazebo. "I'll keep all this in mind," he told Richie, even though none of us standing there believed it was true. "And if any of you remember something, feel free to stop by the station and let me know." Hank didn't waste a moment, and a few seconds later he roared out of the park in his SUV.

"Proof!" Richie puffed out a breath of annoyance. "How can I have proof when I was the one getting pushed? Bea, are you sure—"

"I'm not sure of anything," I said. "I wish I was. I wish I could help."

"Well, here's something that will help." Margaret Defarge had obviously been listening to the entire exchange. She stepped out of the shadows behind Richie, and how she happened to be so well prepared, I can't imagine, but Margaret had a thermos in her hands. She poured and handed a cup of steaming liquid to Richie.

"It's tea, dear," she said when he accepted the cup and downed it. "And there's plenty of sugar in it. It'll warm your insides and that will help clear your head. Then you'll remember that the next time there's a great deal of commotion near the water, you need to be more careful."

Richie's bottom lip jutted out. "I'm always plenty careful," he said, and no one had the nerve to mention the blown-up summer cottage, or Gordon Hunter's boat. "I was plenty careful tonight."

"Of course you were." It was a little out of character for Kate to be diplomatic, but then, I knew Richie sometimes helped out around the winery. She knew him better than the rest of us did. "But that doesn't mean someone didn't bump into you accidentally and—"

"It wasn't an accident." Richie stomped one foot and water spurted from the puddle and splashed us all. He didn't apologize. "It was real. You're all standing around acting like it's no big deal, but somebody just tried to kill me."

"There, there." Margaret handed Richie a second cup of tea. "You'll feel better after you've had some time to relax and recover."

Richie snuffled and took the cup out of her hands. "Thank you, Margaret," he said, and maybe he was finally coming out of the shock; his gaze snapped to hers. "Or are you Alice?"

Margaret's silvery laugh was as gentle as the pitter-pat of the raindrops on the roof. "Don't be silly, dear. You've known me all your life. You know exactly who I am."

"Yeah," Richie said. "Yeah, I do."

With Richie sipping tea and Margaret clucking over him

27

Kylie Logan

like a mother hen, the Ladies and I had a chance to turn our backs and exchange looks.

"You don't think—"

Kate hushed Chandra's question with a well-placed elbow to the ribs.

"Well, it's only natural to ask," Chandra hissed. "Mike was on the dock, and Mike can't stand Richie."

"And Gordon was around, too. And now . . ." Luella stood on tiptoe and glanced around the park. "I don't see him anywhere. He disappeared. Just like Mike did."

"Oh, come on!" It wasn't unusual for me to be the voice of reason. After all, I was the one who tried to talk these ladies out of investigating a murder just a few months before. Of course, that hadn't worked.

The realization sat on my shoulders, as real as my clammy clothes. I knocked it away with a twitch.

"You don't really believe any of what Richie's saying, do you?" I whispered. "Nobody would try to kill somebody in front of so many people. And even if they wanted to . . . well, they wouldn't want to. Nobody's trying to kill Richie. Sure, he's screwed up some things, but I'm sure Gordon has insurance on his boat, and I know that big summer house on the other end of the island is already being rebuilt. Nobody would actually want Richie dead because of any of that."

"Except maybe the guy whose house he blew up," Kate said.

"Or the guy whose boat he damaged," Chandra added.

"Or Mike," Luella said. "He lost everything, remember."

I cut her off before she could go any further. "Okay, I get it. So lots of people are mad at Richie. But murder?" I scrubbed my hands over my face. "If you wanted someone dead, there are plenty more efficient ways to get it done than to push someone in a lake."

"Listen to her!" Chandra screeched her approval, then remembered that we were supposed to be keeping our conversation under wraps. "You do have a freaky imagination, Bea. Just like FX O'Grady."

"Thanks for nothing." I gave her what I hoped was an intimidating look. Since Chandra went right on grinning, I guess it didn't work. "Just because we caught one murderer doesn't mean there are others lurking around every corner."

"No one said there are," Kate conceded. "But it does seem mighty coincidental, don't you think that Mike was on the dock. And so was Gordon. And then Richie—"

"Tripped and fell. Or slipped and fell. Or wasn't watching where he was going. Or was in such a hurry to stow that cooler he was carrying, he moved too fast. Or he—"

"Bea's right." Luella patted my arm. I had a feeling it was more to make me keep quiet than because she bought into what I said. "We all know Richie can be a little over-emotional. Once he calms down, he'll forget all about what happened and he'll be as good as new."

"But I told you. Somebody pushed me!" Richie had a new audience, a group of well-wishers who'd come over to see how he was doing, and his lament filled the gazebo.

"Of course, you've got to ask yourself how good 'as good as new' is," Kate whispered, leaning my way.

I didn't have a chance to consider it. There was a commotion at the dock and, grateful for a break from the Richie drama, we all looked that way.

"Well, that proves it. The storm is officially over," Luella said. "One of the jet ferries is here from the mainland, and by the look of things . . ." She craned her neck. "Looks like lots of new visitors."

"Including my rock group, I bet." I groaned. I hadn't forgotten that the members of Guillotine would be checking in to Bea & Bees that evening; I'd just been a little too busy saving Richie's life to care. "Chandra, can you drive me back to the B and B?"

Chandra wasn't listening. But then, I guess I couldn't blame her. Like her, my attention was suddenly caught by a flurry of activity over near the cinder block building that housed the public restrooms, where a group of a dozen or so women emerged from what little protection they'd been able to find from the rain under the eaves. As near as I could tell from this distance, they were all about Chandra's age, that is, close to fifty. You wouldn't have known it by what they wore.

Miniskirts.

Leg warmers.

Acid-washed jeans.

Fishnet gloves.

Shoulder pads.

Lots and lots of shoulder pads.

"A Madonna convention?" I asked no one in particular.

"More like a flash mob stuck in a 1980s time machine." Kate stepped back to watch the action. "They're headed for the ferry."

Kate was right. The women ringed the dock, and when the first passengers stepped off the ferry, they started to squeal like teenagers.

"You're kidding me, right?" I had to raise my voice to be heard over the excited wails.

"Guillotine has fans?"

"Weird, 1980s fans," Chandra pointed out.

I pictured the posters hung all over the island to advertise the big Saturday night Bastille celebration here in the park that would feature a concert from Guillotine. In the picture, the five members of the band were dressed in faux French Revolution style. Tight trousers, shirts with puffy sleeves, hair pulled back in ponytails. None of this meshed with the eighties throwbacks jumping up and down and yelling their lungs out.

But then, when five long-haired guys stepped off the ferry, suitcases in hand, I had to admit they didn't exactly live up to what I'd been expecting, either.

Kate's expression was sour. "They're old!"

"And overweight," Chandra added.

"And my goodness, aren't they loving the attention!"

Luella was right. The women closed around the smiling rockers, who dropped their suitcases and offered handshakes and kisses like they were stumping for votes.

With their groupies right behind them, Guillotine swaggered through the park.

"I've got to get back home," I said. "Luella, if you leave everything from dinner, I can come back later and help clean up."

She held up one hand. "No worries. I've got it covered."

By now, the five members of Guillotine were close to the gazebo. They smiled and waved, and I reconsidered my plan. If I raced home, it would only look rude when they realized they'd already seen me in the park and I'd left as soon as they arrived. I'd introduce myself, and offer them a ride.

I stepped forward just as the guy leading the way—middle-sized, and with a round beer belly and a mullet so dark I knew there was no way the color could be natural—stepped into the circle of light thrown by a nearby lamp.

"What the hell!"

Behind me, I heard Richie Monroe grumble and, surprised, I turned to see what he was talking about.

I shouldn't have bothered. Richie was gone, so fast that he left behind that blanket Hank had brought him. It was soaking up that puddle of lake water.

❮❖ 3 ❖❯

If there was one thing I'd learned to appreciate over the last six months, it was having a routine.

Back in New York, see, I didn't have one at all. Sure, I worked, but I also partied and jetted from one place to another on a frantic schedule that included more work and more parties, plenty of schmoozing, and lots of stress. It was all good in its own weird way, and I'm not complaining. Working like a madwoman back then allowed me to live the life I was living now. But as exciting—and profitable—as it all was, my hectic schedule never left me with enough leisure to develop a day-to-day, make-it-a-habit, sit-back-and-enjoy routine.

No way I would ever go without again.

I reminded myself of all this when I grabbed my first cup of coffee on Tuesday morning and, just like I did every day, took a deep breath of sun-kissed air and headed out to the front porch for a few minutes before my guests stirred and breakfast was served at nine. From the white wicker couch with its floral pillows in shades of teal and purple that matched the colors of the house, I could watch the never-ending changes in the lake across the street, listen to the gentle whoosh of the waves against the shore, and savor these special, quiet moments.

That day, I was fully prepared to do it all over again. After all, that's what a routine is all about.

I would have fallen right back into the comfortable habit if a couple things didn't happen the moment I stepped outside.

Number one: I caught a glimpse of the hindquarters of Jerry Garcia, Chandra's cat, just as he leapt over the front porch railing—and out of the flower box where he'd no doubt been continuing his lowdown dirty ways by peeing on my pink geraniums.

And number two . . .

Well, number two left me stunned and frozen in place just outside my front door. Otherwise I would have made at least a symbolic stab at chasing Jerry and reminding him (as I did every morning) that he was one very bad pussycat.

"There's a guillotine on my front porch." Yes, this was me talking to myself, but let's face it, it's kind of hard not to say something when you suddenly find yourself staring at a six-foot-tall instrument of death.

I edged around the dangerous-looking thing, checking out the honed-to-a-deadly-edge blade that hung at the top and the ghastly red wooden frame that held the stocks where a victim's head could be locked into place.

"There's a guillotine on your front porch."

When Chandra spoke from down on the front lawn, I shrieked and pressed a hand to my heart.

"Sorry." Her sandals slapped against the front steps. "I was just coming to say good morning and—"

"Hey, there's a guillotine on your front porch."

Out on the street, Kate beeped her car horn. Since it was a beautiful morning, she had the top down on her BMW convertible.

"A guillotine!" As if I wasn't capable of seeing what was three feet in front of me, Kate waved and pointed. "There's a guillotine on your front porch!"

I gave her the thumbs-up to make it perfectly clear that I realized this, and when she drove off, I took the time for another once-over of the guillotine.

As much as I wanted to, I couldn't take my eyes off the head chopper. "Coffee?" I asked Chandra.

"I brought some tea. Japanese red glossy ganoderma." She stuck her mug under my nose and I sniffed and made a face. "It's great for detoxing," Chandra said, "and I figured after what happened last night, that couldn't hurt. I mean, at this point, the detoxing is only for me, but at least that's a start. First me, then the rest of the island. I need to find a way to dissipate the prevailing aura."

It wasn't easy, but I forced myself to look away from the guillotine. "And which prevailing aura would that be?"

"The one of impending doom, of course!" Chandra took a

gulp of tea and I guess it didn't taste any better than it smelled because she made a face, too. "First there was the storm."

"A perfectly natural occurrence, especially at this time of year."

"Then there was the attempt on Richie's life."

"Which may or may not have happened but probably didn't."

"And now this?" With her mug, Chandra indicated the guillotine. "You don't think it's coincidence, do you?"

"I think I need to figure out what this monstrosity is doing on my front porch. And how to get rid of it."

Alas, I didn't have the chance. Because two vans pulled up and stopped, and suddenly the street in front of the house was filled with women in miniskirts and fishnet gloves.

"Uh oh." Chandra said what I was thinking. "The fan club is back."

I watched the women unload signs.

I ♥ you, Dino!
Jesse for President!
Scotty, Paul, and Nick Forever!

"Whatever they're up to," I called back to Chandra, automatically starting down the front steps, "they sure aren't going to do it at my B and B."

I intercepted the bad fashion posse just as they were coming up the front walk.

"Excuse me?" Remember, I used to live in New York. Like every Manhattanite worth her (or his) weight in salt, I was perfectly capable of giving those two little words all the oomph of a full-out rant. "Where do you ladies think you're headed?"

Leading the way, a woman with bright blue eye shadow and very big hair looked at the woman next to her, but before that miniskirt-clad woman could speak, a lady in a pleated cheerleader skirt stepped out from the middle of the pack.

"I'm Tiffany Hollister." She said this in a way that made me think it was supposed to mean something, and when it was obvious I didn't get it, Tiffany tugged at the ponytail she wore over her right ear. "I'm president of the International Boyz 'n Funk Fan Club."

"That's . . ." I searched for a word and came up with, "terrific," even though I was pretty sure I didn't sound like I meant it. "What are you doing here?"

"What are we doing?" Tiffany snapped her gum and raised her voice to a decibel level that hadn't been heard on the island since the night before when thunder rattled the rafters. "What are we doing here, girls?"

They all started up on cue, chanting to a singsong beat.

> *We're here because we love Dino,*
> *and Scotty and Paul, too.*
> *We're here 'cause Nick is awesome,*
> *and Jesse's awesome, too.*
> *We love them to the max,*
> *they're totally tubular hunks.*
> *We're here because we love 'em,*
> *Boyz 'n Funk!*

Honestly, I think they would have started up again if I didn't hold out both hands like a traffic cop. "That's enough." I emphasized my point by shooing them toward the street.

"This is private property and if you want to conduct a protest of some kind—"

"Did you hear that, girls!" Tiffany squealed with laughter. "She thinks we're here to protest!"

"What we're here to do is worship at their feet," the woman with the blue eye shadow said, and sighed.

"And to let them know they'll always be number one in our hearts," another one crooned.

"We love them to the moon and back!" Tiffany assured me.

I hadn't had a chance to take as much as one sip of my morning coffee, so in an effort to kick-start my brain, I glanced toward my house. I looked back at the so-eager-I-thought-they'd-burst middle-aged ladies. And I had to ask. "Guillotine?"

My perfectly logical question was greeted with even more shrieks of laughter.

I closed my eyes, and prayed for strength.

When I opened them again, Chandra was beside me. "Boyz 'n Funk," she said, as if this was supposed to make things clearer. "Come on, Bea. You're a baby, sure. But even you must have heard of them."

Some distant memory stirred in my brain, along with a vision of a girl named Jennifer, my long-ago babysitter who these days would be about the same age as the women on my front lawn. In my pre-pubescent eyes, Jennifer was the epitome of teenage glamour, leg warmers and all. When she showed up at my house, she always had her boom box with her, and the way I remember it, her boom box was always playing the latest and the greatest by the hottest eighties group this side of New Kids on the Block: Boyz 'n Funk. The pieces clicked into place, even if they didn't quite mesh with the five middle-aged, overweight, and very tired-looking guys who'd piled into the B and B the night before. "The boy band?"

"*The* boy band!" Tiffany assured me. "Still going strong after all these years!"

"But if they're still going strong," I pointed out, "why are they—"

"Guillotine?" Tiffany had an endless supply of giggles and she threw them around with abandon. "It's a charity thing. Didn't you hear? Dino and the boys, they wouldn't normally do a gig like this in the middle of nowhere. I mean, why would they when they used to sell out stadiums all over the country? They're doing this for charity. Because—"

"They're wonderful!" the woman behind Tiffany said.

"And so giving and caring," another one put in.

"They'll always be number one in our hearts," a third assured me, and she emphasized the point when she jumped up and down.

Pretty soon, the rest of the ladies joined in. Oh, it was a sight, all right. Especially when a couple of the women needed to stop mid-squeal to catch their breath. Bad enough, but the noise only got worse when the front door popped open and the man who'd introduced himself as Dino Lucci when he checked in the night before stepped outside.

"Dino! We love you!" Tiffany screamed and waved the sign she was holding. "Come on." She waved him to the front lawn. "Pictures! Please. Pictures!"

Dino started down the steps and I knew if I didn't take things in hand, I'd never have a chance. I herded the women out to the street.

"Public property!" I pointed down at the pavement. "And I can't do anything about what you do out here. But that . . ." I pointed back at my front lawn and the house beyond. "You don't step one foot there or I call the cops. You got it?"

I think maybe they did. But then, the closer Dino got, the more intense the swooning. I left them at it, and more anxious than ever for coffee, not to mention a little peace and quiet, I turned back to the house just as Richie Monroe pulled his beat-up pickup truck into the drive. He was right on time with the delivery of fresh croissants I'd had flown over from the mainland for this morning's breakfast.

Croissants, café au lait, brioche, fruit.

After all, this was the week of the Bastille celebration and I was all for joining in the fun. Besides, Luella's daughter, Meg, who usually took care of breakfast at Bea & Bees, was on vacation. Having the food brought in from a reputable—albeit expensive—bakery on the mainland was the most logical choice.

I said good-bye to Chandra, waved to Richie, and told him to bring the food around the house to the back door. When I headed inside to set the table, Dino and I passed each other in the middle of the lawn. What with the waves of adoration coming from the curb, I thought for sure he'd look as smug and puffed up as he had the night before when he realized his fans were waiting at the ferry dock, so I was surprised to see him glance toward the driveway and stop dead, his face folded into an expression as grim as a thundercloud.

I stopped, too, and turned to find Dino with his fists on his hips and Richie opposite him. And what with all the uncontrolled—and very loud—screaming coming from the Boyz 'n Funk fans, I couldn't hear what Richie said. I could not, however, fail to catch on to the fact that he was angry.

Richie's jaw moved up and down like the pistons on an engine going full throttle. His fists were clenched. His cheeks were the color of flame. I heard snatches. "You gotta lot of nerve!" ". . . scumbag, no good—"

And Dino? He listened. For maybe half a second. Then he tossed that glossy black mullet, turned, and strutted out to the street where he was instantly enveloped by his adoring fans.

There were two things I wanted to talk to Dino about, but with the five members of Guillotine (aka Boyz 'n Funk) munching their way through a dozen and a half croissants and what seemed like a couple gallons of coffee and juice, I didn't have a chance.

Have no fear, I wasn't about to let Dino disappear right after breakfast the way his bandmates did. Not until I had some answers.

He'd just downed the last of the brioche and there were crumbs on both of Dino's chins, but I didn't bother to point this out. Instead, I started to gather the dirty plates and eased into what I thought might turn into an uncomfortable conversation. "When Richie came over this morning to bring the croissants . . ."

Dino gulped down the last of his coffee. "Who?"

"Richie. Richie Monroe." Not that it would explain anything because Richie was long gone, but I looked out the dining room window in the direction of the driveway. "This morning when you were going out to talk to your fan club. He brought—"

"Oh, the delivery guy." Dino pushed back from the table. "What about him?"

"He said something to you."

As if trying to remember, Dino scrunched up his eyes. "Did he?"

"He didn't look happy."

"Poor sucker!" He trotted around to my side of the table. "The sun is shining, there's a beautiful woman in the room with me, and Boyz 'n Funk are back together again for what's going to be a kick-ass concert. What's not to be happy about?"

"I thought maybe you could tell me."

He took a moment to think about it. "You mean about the delivery guy."

"He was angry."

Dino's left eye twitched. "He said something about something." Another pause for thinking. "Blah, blah, blah. It didn't make sense. None of it. If you ask me, he must have had me mixed up with someone else."

"I am asking you."

Dino grinned. This close, he smelled like cigarettes and I hoped he remembered I had a strict rule about not smoking inside the house. "He had me mixed up with someone else."

Maybe I wasn't getting answers because Dino was right and he didn't know who Richie was or what he'd been blathering about. Or maybe . . .

42

I thought about the night before and the way Richie had disappeared the moment Guillotine got off the ferry and showed up in the park.

"You didn't used to live around here, did you?" I asked Dino.

"Never set foot on the island before. Though if I'd known there was a chick as cute as you around . . ." He sidled closer.

I stepped away.

If ever there was a time to change the subject, I knew this was it. "There's a guillotine on my front porch," I told him.

"Isn't that the coolest thing you've ever seen!" Dino's eyes lit. Apparently, there was nothing like head-chopping mayhem to make a guy forget his lame come-on. He strolled out to the front porch and, ignoring the new squeals of adulation that started up out on the street, he waved a hand at the guillotine like Vanna at the letter board. "It's for the act. You know, the concert on Saturday night. What do you think? It's a killer, eh? Killer? Get it?"

I got it.

"But what's it doing here?" I asked. "And when will it be moved?"

Dino groaned. "Oh man! I thought a babe like you would be way cooler about something this awesome."

I reminded myself that he was a paying customer. "I'm plenty cool with it, except . . ." A couple golf carts—the island's preferred mode of summer transportation—whirred by and I saw drivers and passengers point and stare. "This is a quiet neighborhood," I said, in spite of the fact that with Tiffany and her troops out on the street, it was anything but.

"Well, it's usually a quiet neighborhood, and I don't want to cause a commotion. And you . . ." I glommed onto an idea and rode it like a Kentucky Derby winner. "You don't want to ruin the surprise for Saturday night, do you?"

It was obvious Dino was so excited about his toy, he hadn't thought of this. He started out slowly and, little by little, his nod picked up steam. "I was thinking it would start a buzz, you know? I never figured—"

"As if you need buzz!" Yes, I could sound sincere, even when I didn't mean it. Remember all those cocktail parties and all that schmoozing I talked about? Schmoozing is good practice for dealing with once-upon-a-time rock stars. "Besides . . ." As if it were a snake, coiled and ready to strike, I gave the guillotine another look. "It would be terrible if something happened and someone got hurt. My insurance rates are already through the roof, and if somebody was injured—"

"Not going to happen, honey!" I guess the pat on the back Dino gave me was supposed to make me feel better. The way his hand lingered on my shoulder definitely did not. "It's a gag. You know, a toy. The whole guillotine thing, it's a magic trick. I can prove it. Go on." He gave me a nudge. "Kneel down. Put your head in there. I'll show you."

I locked my knees. "No way. You can talk magic all you want, you're not going to get me to do that."

"Come on." Another nudge from Dino. "You're not scared, are you?"

"Yes." And I wasn't afraid to admit it. "Even if you're right and this thing can't hurt me, just putting my head in it . . ." I shivered and took a step back. "Sorry! My imagination's way too good, and what I'm imagining scares the bejabbers out of me. I'd never get close to that thing. Not in a million years."

"Spoilsport!" If Dino expected this assessment of me to change my mind, he was wrong. "Hey, I'm going to do it, baby, and if I've got the guts, you should do it, too. On Saturday night right before intermission at the concert. I'm going to kneel down, and ol' Jesse's going to pull this. Here, just like this." He reached for a lever at the top of the contraption and gave it a tug, and the blade flashed down.

I gasped.

Dino laughed. "I'll let you in on a little secret. That's exactly when all the lights are going to go out at the park. Just for a minute. Just to get people all worked up. And then when the lights come on again . . . get this, this is going to be so freakin' cool! When the lights come on again, there's going to be this basket here at the front of the guillotine, see. And inside it is going to be a dummy's head!"

Yes, it was on the tip of my tongue to mention that if Dino's head was in the basket, of course there would be a dummy involved.

But remember what I said about being the hostess. And about Guillotine paying for a week's stay.

"So how does the dummy's head—"

"I'm going to slip out of the guillotine," he answered even before I finished the question. "You know, when the lights go out. And that's when we'll throw the dummy's head in the basket. It's great, right? People are going to love it!"

I wasn't so sure. "What if it doesn't work?"

Dino's eyes were the color of a Hershey's dark chocolate bar, and he raised them toward the porch ceiling just long enough to let me know he couldn't believe what a party pooper I was.

"Nothing's going to happen!" he wailed, arms out at his sides as if he were singing the last notes of an aria. "Nothing bad, anyway. It's all just a sight gag. Quick." As if he actually expected this to produce results, he snapped his fingers. "Get me something that I can put in here and chop."

I will admit that my first inclination was to refuse, but in spite of myself, I was intrigued. My second thought was to look around for Jerry Garcia, though truth be told, if push had come to shove, I wouldn't have actually had the heart to use the cat in the demonstration. Instead, I went inside for one of the cantaloupes Richie had brought along with the croissant delivery.

"Perfect!" Dino said, and he grabbed the cantaloupe and licked his lips with delight. He propped the melon in the stocks, raised the blade, and once again, pulled the lever.

I let out a gasp that turned to an "oh" of amazement when I saw that the cantaloupe was intact and unharmed.

"See, I told you." Dino was as proud as if he'd invented the crazy trick himself. "It looks real enough, but it's nothing but a prop. It's a magic trick! This guillotine couldn't hurt a fly!"

❖ 4 ❖

Elephants pounded through my head. I was pretty sure they were wearing heavy boots. With tap cleats on them.

My breastbone vibrated.

As if some sinister dragon had its lair in the basement of Levi's bar, the floor under my feet pulsed with the creature's every breath.

It was Wednesday night, and Guillotine was giving a one-time-only abbreviated preconcert show.

"You know, to get people all revved up for Saturday night," Dino had told me before he and the other boys in the no-longer-boys boy band left the B and B earlier that evening.

If this was what revved up was all about . . .

I clutched the bar and watched ripples in my glass of Wilder Winery Reisling vibrating to the driving bass beat. That is, right before an earsplitting chord crescendoed, dragged on (and on), and ended with wailing feedback from the amplifier. Dino screamed his thanks and told the packed audience the band would be back after a short intermission.

I was so relieved by the moment of silence between the last echo of the music and the sounds of the crowd coming back to life and talking too loud—because by now, we were all hearing impaired—my spine accordioned and my breath whooshed out of me.

"Enjoying the concert?" Honestly, I was so intent on keeping my sanity, I hadn't even noticed that Levi was behind the bar and directly across from me. He poured a beer someone had ordered and grinned. His voice was too loud. But then, I'd bet any money his ears were ringing, too.

"I'm not sure 'enjoying' is the right word." I shook my head and wondered if this was how Quasimodo felt when he screamed, "The bells! The bells!" Someday, I would suggest to the League that we read *The Hunchback of Notre-Dame*. Since Kate, Luella, and Chandra were all at Levi's that night, too, they would no doubt understand. "'Tolerating' is more accurate. Something tells me the music will be better in the park on Saturday night. More open air. Less—"

"Pain?" Levi said what I was thinking, and though I didn't ask him to, he topped off the wine in my glass.

"They're great! Aren't they great?" Gordon Hunter came up behind the stool where I sat. Kate had been perched on the one next to me until just a few minutes earlier when ferryboat captain Jayce Martin walked by and invited her outside while he had a smoke. Kate is not a smoker. And she claims she's up in the air when it comes to reciprocating what were unspoken but clearly emotions-of-the-undying-adoration kind from Jayce. Still, she didn't waste a moment taking him up on his offer.

A man in a Cleveland Indians T-shirt had already taken Kate's place, and he scooted over to let Gordon squeeze in.

"Luckiest bar owner in Put-in-Bay!" Gordon pounded the bar and looked over to where Levi had gone to take orders. I glanced that way, too, and saw Levi step back to let Mike Lawrence by with a couple cases of beer. It looked as if Levi had beat me to the punch when it came to finding some extra work for Mike.

When Mike got nearer, Gordon ordered a lite beer, and Mike set down the cases and got it for him. "Lucky dog, Levi won the chance to host this little mini-concert," Gordon told me. "You know, in that chamber of commerce promotion I cooked up earlier in the summer."

I did know, and according to Luella, who always had the inside scoop on what our fellow merchants were up to, I also knew Levi had been reluctant to enter. His bar had been open less than a year and it already had a reputation with islanders and visitors alike as a spot for good food, cold beer, and a comfortable and quiet place to sit and watch island life go by. Levi didn't want—or tolerate—customers who partied too hearty, and he didn't need—or court— publicity. He wasn't thrilled with the prospect of hard-drinking rock fans, but he knew he had to participate in the promotion so the other merchants wouldn't think he was some kind of elitist.

I certainly wouldn't have thought that.

But then, when it came to Levi, I wasn't exactly sure what to think.

As if he was reading my mind, Levi came back to my end of the bar and tipped his head toward the door. "Need some fresh air?" he asked.

I could have admitted that I needed the fresh air but was reluctant to be alone with him, but honestly, how immature would that be? We were both adults, and we didn't have to be best friends—or anything else—to pass a few blissfully quiet moments together.

I was sure my wineglass would be cleaned up by the time I got back, so I took one more sip, slid off my barstool, turned, and nearly slammed right into Tiffany Hollister.

"Okay, so it's not exactly their old music like they used to play their old music when they were playing their old music," she told the big-haired woman next to her. "But they're still awesome." She caught my eye and I don't know if she recognized me as the woman whose privacy she had invaded the morning before or not. That didn't stop her from beaming. "Aren't they awesome?"

"Awesome," I said, more because I wanted Tiffany to move so I could get by than because I believed it.

"And so wonderful!" Tiffany nearly swooned. But then, that might have had something to do with the Long Island Iced Tea she was drinking. I had a feeling it wasn't her first of the night. "They're doing this for charity, you know," she said, as if she hadn't already told me this the day before when she and her rabid friends descended on the B and B. "You don't think they'd be pretending to be this crazy Guillotine group for any other reason, do you? It's not like they need the publicity or anything. I mean, really, why would they? They're Boyz 'n Funk!"

The guy in the Indians T-shirt had apparently been eavesdropping. "Who?" he asked.

Eyes flaming like a missionary bent on converting a new soul, Tiffany closed in on him and I saw my opportunity. I sidled my way over to the front door where Levi waited for me.

"Charity, huh?" He'd obviously heard what Tiffany had said because his mouth pulled into a one-sided smile. "The way I heard the story, the only charity these guys are interested in is their own. They took this gig because they couldn't get work anyplace else."

"So now they're Guillotine." Before we stepped outside, I took one more look over my shoulder at the gruesome guillotine. Yes, I remembered what Dino had said about how the device was all part of an elaborate magic trick. And yes, I remembered his demonstration and how my cantaloupe had remained unharmed. In fact, I'd served it that Wednesday morning at breakfast. That didn't keep a shiver from crawling up my spine.

Though the air-conditioning was cranking inside Levi's, it felt cooler outside with a breeze off the lake and room to move and breathe. There used to be an empty shop to the left of the bar, but earlier that summer it had been leased by a hair salon, which was closed and quiet this time of night. I headed that way, far from the smokers who all seemed to have gathered to the right, between Levi's and the souvenir shop that abutted that side of the bar.

"Remind me never to enter another merchants' concert promotion," Levi said once we were out of range of any of his customers' hearing.

So, he assumed we'd still be talking again some time in the future.

While I tried to decide if this was a good thing or a bad thing, my attention was caught by a commotion across the street right in front of the closed storefront that used to house the Orient Express restaurant. It was the scene of the murder the other Literary Ladies and I had investigated earlier that year, and because of that—and the still-disturbing fact that we'd been the ones who'd found the body of Peter Chan, the restaurant's proprietor—I usually avoided the place.

That wasn't so easy now because I could see two guys who were obviously feeling no pain jawing with a short, thin guy in tattered jeans, a dirty T-shirt, and new sneakers.

"Richie," I groaned, and since I knew two against Richie automatically meant trouble, I started across the street.

"Hey, Richie!" I called out when I was halfway there. New York, remember, and I'd learned early on that there is no better way to diffuse a tiff than to pretend ignorance and get the warring parties separated. "I've been looking for you, Richie." Like it was the most natural thing in the world, I stepped between Richie and the two men.

Have no fear, Levi was right behind me, and though I might not know what he really thought of me, how he'd discovered that the story I'd told my friends about a dead husband who never existed was a lie, or how I was supposed to handle the waves of electricity that cascaded through me every time he was around, I was pretty sure I could trust him to have my back.

How right I was! Levi didn't say a word; he simply planted his feet and crossed his arms over his chipped-from-marble chest. He was taller than both the strangers by a head, and the set of his shoulders and the tilt of his chin pretty much screamed what he didn't have to say—he wouldn't put up with any nonsense. One look from him and the two strangers backed off and headed toward the park.

I turned my attention back to Richie who, in spite of the fact that he'd been doing his best to hold his own against the two guys, watched them leave with what was clearly relief etched on his face.

That relief turned stony when Richie looked my way and his mouth twisted. "You didn't need to save me. I can take care of myself."

I shrugged like it was no big deal. "I'm sure you can." As casually as I could, I glanced the way the two guys had gone just to make sure they weren't stupid and decided to double back. "Friends of yours?"

Richie snorted. "Drunks." He twitched. "They were being punks, that's all. They wouldn't move out of my way when I wanted to walk by."

"Well, seeing you here worked out well for me," I told him. "Because I've been looking for you." For what? I asked myself the question at the same time I came up with the answer, so I didn't insult Richie by making him think I'd only come across the street to save his skin. Even though it was true. "Richie, I wondered if you could do some work for me around the B and B."

Richie's expression melted into a grin. "Don't need no work."

Levi stepped forward. "Come on, Richie. Bea's being generous, and you're always looking for work."

"Maybe you didn't hear me." Richie's gaze darted from one of us to the other, his eyes bright with excitement. I'd seen him at Levi's earlier in the evening, and I knew he'd had a couple beers. But this wasn't alcohol talking. Richie was jazzed. "I said I don't need no work. Don't need nothing around here anymore. Not dumb jobs pulling weeds or selling ice cream. Not putting up with weekend drunks who don't know how to act." Richie's gaze flashed across the street toward Levi's. "I don't need none of it no more. I'm gonna have plenty of money soon. And when I do, I'm leaving."

"Leaving? When?" I asked him.

"Leaving." Richie marched across the street. "And I'm never coming back."

Side by side, Levi and I watched him go inside the bar.

"Diffusing a drunken brawl wasn't exactly what I had in mind when I asked you to step outside," he said.

"I know." I didn't. I mean, I assumed diffusing a drunken brawl didn't figure into it, but honestly, I didn't know why he'd asked me to come outside. Or why I accepted. Not that I couldn't imagine both Levi's motivations and my own. But what I imagined shouldn't be what I was imagining, anyway, so the way I saw it, I shouldn't be imagining it in the first place. "It wasn't exactly a brawl," I pointed out instead.

"It could have turned into one." He gave me a quick, sidelong look. "What would you have done then?"

I pursed my lips. "I don't think of myself as a superhero, if that's what you're worried about. And I'm not especially brave. I could see that it wasn't really serious. Richie's an easy target, that's all. A couple guys with a few too many drinks in them and Richie. As soon as I realized what was going on, I knew it wasn't a good combination."

"So if things got out of hand, you would have gone in with fists swinging?"

In spite of the fact that I'd told myself a couple thousand times that where Levi was concerned, I had to curb my emotions, I laughed. I held my arms out at my sides. "Do I look like a fighter?"

Bad move, because Levi took the opportunity to take me up on my offer and check me out thoroughly. His eyes were blue, and more than a time or two, I'd felt their icy touch. That night, though, they were as warm as a summer sky. He looked over the black shorts I wore with a top the color of ripe strawberries. His gaze moved up to my face and I hated myself for it, but I found myself holding my breath.

"We've been avoiding each other all summer," he said.

"Not avoiding. We've been—"

"Avoiding."

Since he was right, I didn't bother to argue.

"It's because of what I said, right?" I knew what was coming. Which would explain why I sucked in another breath and held it until my lungs felt as if they were on fire. "When I told you I knew you were never married."

Across the street, the crowds that had been outside during intermission slowly snaked back into the bar, and I took the opportunity to watch them while I considered what to say. I decided on, "I could ask how you found out."

"You know it's not that hard. Modern technology and all that. It's easy to dig up information on just about anybody."

I turned back to him. "Then maybe I should ask why you cared enough to look."

He tugged his left earlobe. "Now that's the real question!" Levi took a step closer. "What if I told you I couldn't help myself? After everything that happened last spring, I was interested in you. Heck, more than interested. I was intrigued."

"So you decided that instead of getting to know me better, you know, by stopping by for coffee or asking me out on a date, you'd do some Internet snooping."

I thought he might be offended, but he laughed. "Let's call it research."

"Let's say that what you found out isn't something I want other people to know about."

Levi tipped his head back toward the bar where I knew Chandra, Luella, and Kate were waiting and where, no doubt, they'd pepper me with questions about what had happened when Levi and I came outside. "Your friends?"

"Know what I've told them."

"And you've told them . . ?"

"What I want them to know."

"Fair enough." As if he were facing a firing squad, he held his arms close against his sides. "But as long as we're being truthful—"

"Hey, Levi!"

Whatever Levi was going to say, he didn't have a chance. Mike stepped out of the bar and waved to us, then stabbed his thumb back toward the bar. "Getting busy in here," Mike yelled.

And Levi got the message.

Too bad I didn't. While we walked across the street so Levi could get back to work, I wondered what he'd been about to confess. *As long as we're being truthful . . .*

I suppose it was just as well he never had the chance to finish.

As long as we were being truthful, the last thing I wanted Levi to find out was that no matter what, I couldn't be completely truthful with him.

Not without revealing the secrets I'd come to the island to hide.

A couple more songs from Guillotine and I was well and truly done for the night. Yes, there was supposed to be a short fireworks show at the park as soon as the concert was over, but I swear, the way my head pounded, I wasn't sure pyrotechnics were the right remedy.

Since we'd arrived together, I looked around the bar for Kate to tell her I'd had it for the night and was heading back home. But the place was so crowded, even a flaming redhead was impossible to find.

Guillotine started another song and I did another swing through Levi's. Richie Monroe was in one corner not far from the stage. His arms crossed over his chest, his eyes narrowed, he stared at the stage as if he wanted to make it go up in smoke.

But then, maybe Richie's ears hurt, too.

I spotted Kate over near the front window and I'd just turned to head that way when the guitars stopped and Jesse, the Guillotine drummer, crashed a stick into his cymbals.

Like everyone else in the bar, I looked at the stage to see what was happening.

And stifled a curse.

Three guys from the audience had jumped onto the stage. One of them carried a watermelon and he held it up over his head and yelled something about how they were going to see if the guillotine prop would really work.

Dino's face paled, and I guess I couldn't blame him. No doubt he'd seen his share of rowdy fans before. Heck, he'd dealt with Tiffany and her crew and actually seemed to enjoy it. But if these guys made it over to the guillotine with their melon, they'd ruin the big surprise he had planned for Saturday night, the one Dino was sure was so freakin' cool it would get everyone talking about Guillotine.

Automatically, I glanced at the bar and saw Levi moving through the crowd, heading to the stage to take control of the situation.

It wasn't easy.

People surged toward the stage, somebody called out, "Off with its head!" and the crowd took up the chant.

The guys who'd interrupted the concert were more determined than ever, and not about to be stopped by five middle-aged band members.

While two of them held back Dino and the others, the one with the melon raced over to the guillotine and positioned it in the stocks, and I actually found myself feeling sorry for Dino. He'd been so proud of his little trick, and he was going to be so embarrassed when, like my cantaloupe, that watermelon faced certain death and made it through without a scratch.

Levi made it to the stage just as the guy pulled the lever and the blade shot down.

It plonked into the watermelon with a sickening thud that made the crowd let out a collective gasp.

A second later, the front half of the watermelon neatly fell away from the back half.

And red juice splurted out of the melon and spilled across the stage.

❖ 5 ❖

It's all fun and games until a magic trick goes very, very wrong and puts an end to the revelry—and the rock concert.

One look at that sliced-in-half watermelon, and Dino's face turned the color of ashes. It took him a moment to catch his breath, but once he did, the first thing he did was declare that the concert was over and wave his bandmates off the stage.

And the second?

It was that second thing that had me wondering, because right after he growled, "We're getting the hell out of here," Dino shot a look into the audience that I swear could have melted steel. Coincidence? I couldn't say. I only knew that it was aimed right at the spot where I'd last seen Richie Monroe.

"What did I tell you? There's an aura of impending

doom!" Chandra's comment made me regret that I'd mentioned what I'd observed inside the bar. Now that the concert was over, we were standing outside Levi's with Luella and Kate. The mini fireworks show wasn't supposed to officially begin for another half hour, but with the concert being cut short, town officials and the folks from the fireworks company scrambled to get things started sooner. From here, we might not be able to see everything, but we could watch at least some of the show and we wouldn't need to contend with the crowd that streamed into the park.

I glanced Chandra's way. "I think it was more like an accident," I said.

"You can think anything you want, that doesn't make it true." She wasn't supposed to carry her lite beer out to the sidewalk with her, but Chandra had it in a paper cup and figured no one knew. She downed a gulp. "You said so yourself, Bea, Dino and Richie had a fight in your driveway yesterday. Obviously they hate each other. And I bet Dino tried to kill Richie the other night. You know, when he got pushed into the lake. That's why Richie retaliated today and fixed the guillotine so it would cut off Dino's head. Admit it, it all makes sense. And it explains why Dino sent a death-ray look at Richie after the guillotine incident. You know, to let Richie know he was onto him and that paybacks would for sure be a bitch."

As usual, following Chandra's train of thought was a trip through Convoluted R Us. I didn't even bother to mention that when Richie went into the water on Monday night, Dino wasn't even on the island yet. Or that tonight the guillotine was just for show; Dino wasn't scheduled to put his head in it until the Saturday night concert at the park. What was the use? Instead, I concentrated on the meat of her argument.

"It wasn't exactly a fight," I told her, because the more I thought about what had happened in my driveway when Richie delivered the croissants, the more I realized it was true. "It was more like Richie laying into Dino and Dino acting like he didn't have a clue what Richie was talking about. Richie was madder than a wet hen, but not Dino. He just stood there and acted like he didn't care about whatever it was Richie said. And later, when I asked him about it, he said he didn't know who Richie was. In fact, he told me he'd never even been on the island before. Dino said Richie must have mistaken him for someone else because he didn't know Richie, so he couldn't possibly know what Richie was mad about."

"Then it's just like in *A Tale of Two Cities*." Sure of her theory—whatever that theory was—Chandra nodded. Kate, Luella, and I? We stared at her in amazement.

"Don't act so surprised!" Chandra finished her beer and tossed the cup in the nearest trash can. "If you ladies were reading the book like you're supposed to be—"

"What's amazing is that you are."

Chandra twitched away Kate's comment with a lift of her chin. When she pulled back her shoulders, she looked like a kid giving a book report in front of the class—if a kid giving a book report wore purple shorts; a tie-dyed top in swirls of purple, pink, and orange; and sandals with two-inch-high platforms. "In *A Tale of Two Cities*," she said, glancing from one of us to the other and daring us to criticize her take on the book, "there are two guys who look alike. One guy's name is Sydney . . . er . . ."

"Carton," Luella said. She'd obviously read at least some of our assignment.

Chandra grinned. "That's right, Carton, and he's a lawyer. And there's this other guy named Charles Dubray—"

"Darnay," Kate corrected her.

"That's right." Chandra's smile froze around the edges, but she accepted the correction with good grace. "Darnay. Charles Darnay. He's French, and Sydney is English. And the two of them—Charles and Sydney—they look an awful lot alike. Darnay is being tried as a spy and a witness says he can identify him for sure, only when the time comes, he can't tell Darnay from Carton, who's also in the courtroom, and that's how Darnay gets off. And Darnay and Carton are both in love with the same woman, and later, when they're going to chop off Darnay's head with the guillotine, Carton changes places with him." Sighing didn't seem to fit into Chandra's book report, but sigh she did. "Sydney sacrifices himself for love."

It was as apt and economic a synopsis of *A Tale of Two Cities* as I'd ever heard, and I told Chandra so.

She blushed. "Well, some of us take our reading assignments seriously."

"Yeah, some of us do. Which is why I can't believe—"

With the lift of one hand, I cut Kate off. There was no use for the two of them going at each other, and I knew if I didn't put an end to it, that's exactly what would happen. The League of Literary Ladies had come a long way since the day we were sentenced to discuss books for the next year, but I had no illusions. If we weren't careful, if we didn't remember that our problems were in our past and that we were all friends now, our neighborhood bickering could erupt again at any moment. I wasn't going to let that happen. Not when for the first time since college, I had real friends I could trust to stand at my side, thick or thin.

Besides, we had more serious things to worry about than who was reading what. Like who messed with the magic guillotine, and why. Kate must have been thinking that, too. "So what do Sydney Carton and Charles Darnay have to do with Dino and Richie?" she asked.

I thought I understood what Chandra was getting at so I explained. "Richie went after Dino. Dino says he doesn't know Richie. That means Richie thought Dino was someone else, and he wouldn't have thought that if Dino didn't look like someone else. Like Sydney Carton and Charles—"

"Darnay." Chandra was proud of herself for remembering the name. "And don't you see, it explains everything. That's why Richie yelled at Dino at your place yesterday, Bea. Mistaken identity."

I gave Chandra's theory another few moments of thought. It was a little out there, but then, so was messing with a magic trick that was designed to be harmless. "So whoever messed with the guillotine might have done it because he thought Dino was someone he's not. If that person knew the guillotine was only going to be used as a prop tonight, then rigging it like that was designed to send a message. But if that person thought Dino was actually going to do the guillotine trick tonight, if he thought Dino was going to kneel down and put his head in the stocks and Jesse was going to pull that lever . . ." I couldn't make myself finish the thought.

I didn't have to. Kate did it for me. "That could have been Dino's neck in that guillotine."

"And it could have been Dino's blood splashed all around," Luella added.

"And it could have been Dino's head rolling around the stage like that half of watermelon," Chandra reminded us, though, really, she didn't need to. I'm pretty sure the way we all stood there, our arms wrapped around ourselves and our expressions twisted, we could imagine the scene for ourselves.

I shook away the thought because it was either that or collapse onto the sidewalk and whimper. Thinking like a detective was better than thinking like a horror writer. As the Ladies constantly pointed out, I do not have the stomach for that. "We don't really think that Richie would do a thing like that, do we?"

"Richie's not exactly what anybody would call normal," Kate said. "He might go after Dino if he hated him enough."

"Or if he hated the person he thought Dino was," Chandra added.

"Well, at least no one really got hurt," Luella said, and with a small smile, I thanked her for diverting the subject. Yeah, we were still discussing the guillotine incident. But without the gory details. "And I'd bet a dime to a donut those rockers aren't going to use that guillotine in their act on Saturday night."

I shivered. "I couldn't even put my head in that thing when it was on my front porch and Dino guaranteed me one hundred percent that it wouldn't hurt me. I can't imagine he'd have the nerve to do it on Saturday. Not after what happened tonight. Imagine . . ."

We all did, and as if we'd choreographed the move, we instinctively stepped closer to each other.

"Cold, girls?" Moving with far more energy than a lady her age should have, Alice Defarge trotted by, coming from the direction of the park. She had one cone of fluffy pink cotton candy in one hand, and a cone of blue cotton candy in the other.

Luella waved on behalf of all of us. "You're not going to watch the fireworks?"

With the pink cone of cotton candy, Alice pointed across the street to the knitting shop. I knew the cottage she shared with Margaret was behind it and across a small but neatly tended garden. "We can see just fine from the backyard," she explained. "Margaret's already got the lawn chairs out and I said I'd pick up dessert."

"Don't you know, Alice," Chandra called out. "It's not officially dessert if it's not chocolate!"

Alice laughed. "Not in our house." She scooted closer. "You know, back in the day they used to call me Chocolate Alice and they used to call my sister Vanilla Margaret. That's because Margaret hates chocolate with a fiery passion. She never eats it. Never even allows it in the house. No worries!" She gave us a conspiratorial wink. "I get my fill over at the fudge shop near the carousel, and Margaret is never any wiser. But when we're eating dessert at home . . ." Once again, she held out the cotton candy.

I had no doubt that the pink one was for Margaret.

"You are coming to the park on Saturday for the big

fireworks show, aren't you?" I asked Alice. "We're planning to get there early so we don't have to fight the crowd, and we'll save seats for you and Margaret if you'd like."

"That's so nice, dear." Alice backed toward the street. "I'll be sure to mention it to Margaret, but it will all depend on what time the reruns come on for *The Lawrence Welk Show*. Margaret loves Lawrence Welk. That Margaret, she can be such an old fuddy-duddy sometimes." With a sly smile on her face, Alice turned and headed toward home just as Levi walked out of the bar.

"Well?" I promised myself I wasn't going to bug him, but really, I couldn't help myself. All this talk of Richie and Dino and mistaken identities and heads being chopped off made my brain spin, and the only thing that was going to stop it was answers. "Did you find anything wrong with the guillotine?"

Levi wore a white apron looped over his neck, covering his jeans and T-shirt. It was spattered with red stains. "I'm no expert when it comes to magic tricks," he admitted. "I don't think I could tell if that thing was tampered with even if I looked. Besides, I didn't have much of a chance. Mike and I were too busy cleaning up watermelon guts."

"Guts. Ooh." Kate pressed a hand to her mouth.

I'd hoped for something more definitive as to the condition of the magic guillotine. "Well, we can always talk to the band," I suggested, and as if on cue, Nick, Jesse, Paul, and Scotty sauntered out of the bar. If the guillotine-trick-gone-wrong bothered them, they sure didn't show it. In fact, when their fans started to squeal, they stopped in the doorway, posed for pictures, then went over to the table that had

Kylie Logan

been set up at the other end of the sidewalk where the band was scheduled to sign autographs.

"No Dino," I commented.

"Probably swamped by worshiping women inside," Kate suggested.

And I found myself shivering.

Luckily, the thought was banished by the first *pop* from the park, and automatically we all looked up. A sparkling fizz lit the night sky above the trees. It exploded with a muffled *poof*, and crystal sparks the color of Margaret's cotton candy rained down.

"Come on. I want to see this up close." Jayce Martin zoomed by and grabbed Kate's hand, and together they hurried toward the park.

"Interesting," Chandra commented, watching them go.

"Fascinating," Luella agreed.

"And I'm staying out of this conversation," Levi said.

I turned his way to tell him I agreed, and I was just in time to see Dino slip out of the bar and walk over to the table for the autograph session.

Seeing an opportunity, I excused myself and headed that way, too.

"You're going to need to wait your turn," a woman in a *We Love Boyz 'n Funk* T-shirt told me when I approached the table from the front instead of the back of the line.

Really, I didn't think so. I mumbled something about being the band's landlady (technically true even if it wasn't relevant), and went around to the other side of the table to stand at Dino's shoulder.

"Hey, babe!" I might have tricked myself into believing

the greeting was for the so-excited-she-was-ready-to-self-combust woman at the front of the line if Dino didn't glance over his shoulder at me and give me a wink. "I figured you'd be here. Couldn't stay away, huh?"

"Couldn't pass up the opportunity to support a chamber of commerce event," I said as pleasantly as I could. My comment was punctuated by an explosion of golden stars above the trees in the park, and around us everyone made the appropriate oohing and aahing sounds.

I propped one hand on the table and leaned closer to Dino so I could whisper, "You told me that guillotine trick was one hundred percent safe."

His hand stilled over the picture he was about to auto-graph. It showed a smiling group of five teenagers, and automatically I went down the list. Aside from the fact that they were thirty years older and thirty pounds heavier, Scotty, Jesse, and Nick didn't look all that different. Paul had lost his crop of bushy hair completely. And Dino . . . I took another moment to study the dark and handsome kid in the photo, then looked at the man who was looking up at me. Hard living showed in every line of Dino's face, and his eyes had the hungry look of a man who'd tasted fame but had never gotten a big enough gulp to satisfy himself.

He dashed off the signature and handed the photo to the waiting fan. "It wasn't funny. Somebody's going to pay for that guillotine trick," he growled. The next woman moved to the front of the line. Excited, she danced from foot to foot. She never took her eyes off Dino once, not even when a shower of fireworks lit the street with streaks of green, orange, and purple.

I went for subtle. After all, nobody but me, Dino, and the people we'd shared the secret with knew that for tonight, the guillotine was supposed to be nothing but a prop designed to tease folks into going to Saturday's concert. "Somebody?"

Dino's gaze slid toward the front door of the bar, then back to me. "Don't you worry about me, babe." He patted my hand. "I know who it was, and there's no way the son-of-a—"

"Picture, Dino? Please!" The next woman in line jumped up and down and waved her smartphone. "Come over here and take a picture with me. Puh-leez!"

He did, and I took the opportunity to return to where Levi, Luella, and Chandra waited. My timing was perfect. The mini fireworks show ended with a mini grand finale. A dozen or so rockets all hit the sky at the same time, and along with the pops and the whirrs, the night sky lit up with flashes of white, puffs of gold, and twinkling yellow stars.

In the light, I saw Mike Lawrence hurry out of the bar and start down the street in the opposite direction from where Levi waited for me.

"I've got to get back behind the bar." Levi sounded almost apologetic and I didn't want to wonder why.

I settled back on the ol' reliable cocktail party talk. "It's late and I've got to get going, anyway."

No sooner had Levi gone back into the bar than I was surrounded.

"Oh, no!" Chandra looped her right arm through my left. "You're not going to run out of here now. Not when Levi's looking at you the way Levi's looking at you."

"He's not looking at me at all," I pointed out. Apparently

the fact that he'd gone inside and couldn't see me from in there was lost on both Chandra and Luella.

"You know what she means," Luella said. She grabbed my right arm. "You can't make the poor boy suffer."

"No one's suffering," I insisted, though if push came to shove, I would have had to admit that sometimes when I thought about Levi, I felt the pain. "He only talks to me to be polite."

"Uh huh." Chandra tugged my one arm. "And he's not the hottest thing on the island."

"Which has nothing to do with—"

"Sure." Luella tugged the other.

When they stepped back into Levi's, I had no choice but to go along, too.

Since most of the patrons who'd been there earlier had gone to the park and some of the others were still out worshiping the ground the former Boyz 'n Funk walked on, the place was just about empty and blessedly quiet. I knew that the members of Guillotine did their own setup and takedown (ah, how different from the days when the roadies did the grunt work), and since they'd walked off right after the watermelon surprise, their instruments were still on stage.

"Let's just hope they don't get the idea that anyone's looking for an encore," I mumbled, and I guess Chandra and Luella know exactly what I was talking about because they laughed.

Chandra scooted over to the bar. "I'm going to order another beer before it gets crowded in here again. What can I get you, ladies?"

Luella asked for ice water. Since I hadn't had a chance

to finish my last glass of wine, I opted for another Reisling. While I waited for it, I figured a quick trip to the ladies room was in order.

I never got there.

But then, that's because the restrooms were all the way at the back of the bar, past the makeshift stage and the pool tables that had been pushed against the far wall to make more room for the overflow crowd. Back there, it was darker and quieter than it was at the front of the bar. A few chairs were scattered around for those who'd watched the concert earlier, and all but one of them was empty.

Richie Monroe still sat in the corner.

It would have been rude not to say hello, considering Richie and I were the only ones around. "Hey, Richie!"

Except he didn't say hello back.

Just to be polite, I took a couple steps closer. "So what did you think of the concert? And the fireworks? Only maybe you didn't see the fireworks since you're still sitting here."

Richie had nothing to say.

I'm not sure when I realized that Richie was being anything but rude. I do remember I flagged down Levi. But then, I figured when something like this happens, a person should never be alone.

"What is it?" he asked.

I took a few more steps closer to Richie. As if it had been dropped, the glass he'd apparently been drinking from was shattered at his feet and there was a trickle of drool on his chin. His eyes were open. His mouth was twisted in an expression that reminded me of a silent scream. Richie's skin was the color of those pale fireworks that had lit the sky outside only a few minutes before.

Only, fireworks are hot.

And Richie?

Richie was one getting-colder-by-the-moment dead dude.

❖ 6 ❖

"What else did Hank ask you? What did he say? Luella and I were over at the bar and we didn't see anything and we didn't even realize what was going on until he got there and once he got there, he wouldn't let us over to where you and Levi were waiting for him and he cleared out the bar and made us leave along with the rest of the crowd and you were in there so long so I came home but I couldn't sleep all night, just waiting to talk to you, and it's all Hank's fault because he knows I could have stayed there. It's not like I was going to do anything, right? I mean, he already had a dead body on his hands. Poor Richie! The least Hank could have done was let those of us who knew Richie stay there with the body. He's impossible. I mean Hank, not Richie, because of course, Richie was impossible, too, but in a whole different way than Hank is impossible.

Only Richie isn't impossible anymore, and Hank knew that, and he knew I was there because he saw me when he walked in, and he could have let me in on what was going on. The man's as annoying as a mosquito in the bedroom in the middle of the night. He's—"

Good thing Chandra had to stop to catch her breath or I never would have gotten a word in edgewise. I decided on the very noncommital, "Well, you know Hank."

Understatement.

Hank was Chandra's husband number two, and just for the record, she never said much about either number one or number three. Hank, though? She had plenty to say about Hank. Then again, they both lived on the same four-mile-long by one-and-a-half-mile-wide island. I'm not very good at math, but even I know that's not a lot of square footage. Especially when it comes to tripping over an ex.

"Did he say—"

"He asked all the usual questions," I told her, and it's not like I was eager to get rid of Chandra or anything; it was just that she was so anxious to find out all the details of what had happened at Levi's the night before, she showed up at my front door not long after the sun came up. I'd been sound asleep when she started in on the doorbell, and now my hair was a fright, I'd left my glasses on the nightstand next to my bed, and I was dressed in my jammies, waiting for the coffeepot to fill. I hoped Chandra's arrival didn't disturb Dino and the other Boyz because I was in no condition to play hostess.

The coffeepot stopped dripping—hallelujah—and I filled one mug for myself and another one for Chandra. "Hank is very straightforward. You know that. He asked what I saw, how I found Richie, if I knew how long he'd been there."

"And you told him . . . ?"

I thought my shrug pretty much said it all until I saw Chandra's eyes still lit with the fire of curiosity. "I told him what happened. We were outside watching the fireworks. We came inside. I walked by on my way to the ladies room and found Richie." Not for the first time since the night before, the realization hit me somewhere between my heart and my stomach. "Poor guy. To die like that in a dark bar with nobody around."

"Unless there was!"

I knew it would come to this, given Chandra's tendency to let her imagination run away with her and all. In an effort to ignore the gleam in her eyes—and all that last comment of hers suggested—I kept myself busy getting ready for the day's breakfast. From what I'd seen the morning before, I knew my guests weren't early risers, but still, I promised breakfast at nine and I had to be ready by then, just in case. In keeping with the week's theme and the French tricolor, Meg had made some blueberry/cranberry muffins before she left, and I got them out of the freezer so they'd have plenty of time to thaw, then busied myself getting plates and bowls and silverware ready to go.

"Bea, don't tell me you didn't think the same thing."

I set down a handful of spoons and turned to Chandra, my back propped against the granite countertop. "I didn't."

"Except you did, or you would have asked what I was talking about."

I sighed. "There was no sign that Richie was murdered."

"Except somebody did try to kill him at the party the other night. Did you remind Hank about that?"

I didn't. Partly because Hank had heard it himself from Richie after we pulled him out of the lake. Mostly because I wasn't sure I believed the story in the first place. "There was no sign of foul play," I told Chandra. "Nothing more than a trickle of blood. It didn't look like there had been a struggle. It looked . . ." I wanted to say *natural*, but there isn't anything natural about dying alone in a dark bar. Though I would have preferred to forget the whole thing, I knew that was impossible, so I allowed myself to think back to the scene. I'd left Chandra and Luella near the bar and walked back toward the restrooms. That's when I spotted Richie, and that's when I said hello and he didn't say hello back.

"Richie's head was propped against the wall behind him," I told Chandra. "It was tipped to the left just a little. His elbows were up on his knees, and his fists were clenched. His expression was . . ." Again, I forced myself back to the scene. "Pained" was the only word I could think of. "His mouth was drawn out, but not in a smile. More like something hurt. Richie's jaw was clenched. Honestly, when I saw him, I thought he'd had too much to drink and just fell asleep like that. It wasn't until I looked a little closer . . ." A chill shot up my spine and I did my best to thaw it with a sip of coffee.

"That's when I realized he was dead. But honestly, Chandra, whatever else he is, Hank's a good cop." Really, I didn't need to remind her. In spite of the fact that she had a well-deserved reputation as the island crackpot, Chandra was as honest as the day is long. She was the first to extol Hank's

77

virtues. I mean, his virtues in addition to the ones he apparently showed off in bed.

I shook away the thought. "Hank saw all the same things I saw, and if there's anything fishy, you know he'll pick up on it. He'll talk to everyone who was at Levi's last night. He'll get the details. He did ask me if I knew if Richie had been sick. Or if he took any medications. So maybe he's thinking it was some kind of overdose. I'm afraid I couldn't help. I didn't know Richie all that well."

"I'm not sure any of us did." Chandra cradled her coffee mug in both hands. "And that's the real shame, isn't it? Here we are, all on this island together, and even though we see some people every day, it's like we're strangers." She plunked her mug on the counter and, shoulders back and head high, headed for the door. "I've got to light candles. And burn some incense. It's the best way I can think of right now to honor Richie's life."

I was not about to argue. Not at this time of the morning.

Instead, I followed her, pulled open the front door, and stopped cold. There on my front porch was a man with his hand raised; he'd been just about to knock.

I can't be blamed for staring. First of all, like I said before, it was way early. And as for the man . . .

Middle height. Middle weight.

Nothing unusual there.

But then there was the long frock coat, the narrow trousers, the plaid, double-breasted vest with its shiny metal buttons. Oh yes, and the cravat, a stiff, two-inch-wide piece of silk tied into a wide horizontal bow. He had a high forehead and poofs of hair over each ear, a bushy mustache and an unruly goatee trimmed long and squared off at the bottom.

"Good morning!" His smile was as bright as the sunshine that lit up the eastern horizon, and he had an English accent that struck me as more the community theater type than authentic.

"I do hope I am not calling upon you at too early an hour of the morning, but you see, I have had quite a challenging travel itinerary and this was the only time at which it was amenable for me to arrive." He glanced from Chandra to me. "I know from the signboard out front that I am in the right establishment, so I presume one of you must surely be the Miss Cartwright I am seeking."

If nothing else, the sound of my name snapped me out of my daze. I stuck out a hand. "I'm Bea. And this is my neighbor, Chandra Morrisey. You'll have to forgive the way I look, it's early and—"

"Nonsense!" The man stepped into the house and, eager to start the woo-woo mojo going, Chandra took the opportunity to leave. "You are the very picture of loveliness," the man said, "and I . . ." Since his back was to the open doorway, it was hard to say, but I'm pretty sure he blushed when he bowed from the waist. "I offer my deepest regrets again for discommoding you so. Ah!" He looked around the entryway of the house, at the chandelier that hung above the stairway directly behind me and the stained glass window on the wall above the door. "This will do nicely."

Really, I had an excuse; I hadn't finished my first cup of coffee. "Do what?"

He thought I was kidding. That's why he laughed. "Forgive

me." Again, he bowed. "I have not introduced myself. I am Charles John Huffam Dickens."

"Charles . . ." It took a moment for the words to sink in, and another for me to put them together into some sort of thought that actually made sense. "Charles Dickens. Of course! There's the Charles Dickens impersonator contest this weekend and the Dickens trivia event on Sunday. You're one of the contestants." In my head, I went over the list of the guests I knew were scheduled to check in that day. Only one said he might be arriving early. "You must be Gregory Ashburn."

He tipped his head to acknowledge the fact. "Gregory Ashburn, professor of nineteenth-century British literature, Columbia University. BA, Stanford. MA, University of Chicago. PhD, University of Pennsylvania. Yes, madam, there are those who know me by that name, though I would prefer if, for the weekend, you would call me Mr. Dickens. Or Charles. Or even Boz, if you feel inclined to such familiarity. It is a family nickname and a pseudonym I used early in my career. Authenticity. I am striving for authenticity. And I am sure there isn't another contestant who—"

"I do beg your pardon."

I had been so fixated on my conversation with Ashburn/Dickens, I hadn't realized another man had arrived on my front porch, and I turned to greet him and stopped dead.

Middle height, middle weight. Long frock coat, narrow trousers, plaid, double-breasted vest with shiny metal buttons. Stiff, two-inch-wide cravat, tied into a wide horizontal bow. High forehead, poofs of hair over each ear, bushy mustache, and unruly goatee. Need I even mention that it was squared off at the bottom?

"Oh!" I looked from one man to the other. "You must be—"

"Charles Dickens." The man stepped forward and extended his hand, and when I reached out to shake it, he took mine in his, bowed low, and brushed the briefest of kisses over my fingers. "I do hope I'm not interrupting," he said in an accent slightly less phony than my first guest's, and finally he took a moment to look at the other man who stood in my foyer.

The second Dickens's face paled. "Ashburn! You! How dare you—"

"Surely, sir, you must have me confused with someone else. My name is not Ashburn, it is Dickens," the first man told him. "And since I am that man, I hardly think you can claim that same celebrity. I was here first."

The second man's eyes narrowed and he cast a look over Ashburn. "First in terms of time, perhaps, but not in terms of perfection. The shoes . . ." The second man's gaze traveled up from those apparently offending accessories. "The shoes are all wrong."

"Wrong?" Ashburn lifted one foot, the better to show off his short ankle boots with the pointy toes. "Black, one-inch heel, laced closed. Perfectly acceptable."

"Black, one-inch heel, elastic sided." The second man showed off the shoes he wore. "Far more authentic to the eighteen fifties. If you were as much of a scholar as you claim—"

"You must be Timothy Drake." I interrupted and didn't feel the least bit guilty.

"Professor of nineteenth-century British literature," the man said. "BA, Harvard. MA, The Ohio State University. PhD, Cornell."

"You're here for the contest this weekend." It was so

apparent I didn't even bother to make it into a question. "I didn't expect you this early."

"A small mishap in the way of travel arrangements," Drake assured me. "I would have endeavored to find a different mode of transport and arrived at another time if I knew this early hour would attract the riffraff." With his top lip curled just the slightest bit, he looked at Ashburn.

I scrubbed my hands over my face and tried for logic. "It's going to be a long week, guys. Am I going to have to put an electric fence between your rooms?"

"He's staying here?" Ashburn asked with a look down his nose at Drake.

"He can't find a different hotel to accommodate him?" Drake shot back.

I threw my hands in the air. "A different hotel's not going to work because from what I've heard, every place on the island is booked solid for the rest of the week. So here's what we're going to do." I propped my fists on my hips. It might have been a far more intimidating stance if I wasn't wearing the white cotton jammies with the pink flamingoes all over them. "You're going to go up to suite six right now." I reached over to the table near the front door, grabbed the key, and slapped it in Ashburn's hand. "And you . . ." There were two more keys there and I got the one for suite four and gave it to Drake. "You're going to go to your room. You can both get settled while I get dressed, and if you come down in another thirty minutes, I'll have fresh coffee ready for you. How does that sound?"

"My dear, if you could give me a cup of tea to clear my muddle of a head I should better understand your affairs,"

Ashburn said, and added, "That's from *Mrs. Lirriper's Legacy*."

Not to be outdone, Drake stepped forward. "The privileges of the side-table included the small prerogatives of sitting next to the toast, and taking two cups of tea to other people's one." He shot an icy smile at Ashburn. "*Martin Chuzzlewit*," he added.

"So what you're telling me is that you both want tea." The men nodded. "Then tea it is, but not for thirty minutes. Got it?"

Another couple nods.

"And no bickering upstairs," I warned them. "I've got other guests, and they're not early risers."

"I do not suppose one of them just happens to be one of the judges of this week's little competition?" Ashburn looked hopeful.

"From what I've heard, there are three judges," I told him. "And every one of them is sworn to secrecy."

"Secrecy, yes," Drake mumbled. He and Ashburn started up the stairs together, stopped, and each waited for the other to move.

"Give me a break!" I moaned and turned to go into my private suite.

Which of them made it upstairs first?

What the dickens did I care?

Here's the bad news: For the first half hour that breakfast was on the table, the dueling Dickenses kept it up, taking turns at a Dickens character alphabet contest (Arabella

Allen, Major Joseph Bagstock, Sydney Carton, Dick Datchery . . .).

Here's the good news: Even two Dickens geeks going full throttle can't keep it up when five former rock stars racket down the stairs and proceed to discuss—with great passion and a whole bunch of expletives I hadn't heard since the last time I rode the New York subway—how their guillotine had been tampered with the night before.

If Dino and the Boyz thought Richie had something to do with the vandalism, they never mentioned it, nor did they say anything that made me think they knew Richie was dead. But then, they'd walked out of Levi's to sign autographs before the fireworks started, and if any of them went back inside after or put two and two together once Hank arrived, I couldn't say. I'd been a little busy, what with the whole dead body thing and all.

I refilled the muffin plate twice.

I made three pots of coffee and offered lattes to anyone who wanted them. The rockers told me they didn't bother drinking anything but high-test and that scalded milk and foam was for sissies. Only that's not the word they used. Like the stalwart Englishmen they were trying so hard to be, Ashburn and Drake turned up their noses at the very mention of anything French.

By the time they all went back to their respective rooms, I felt as if I'd just gone a couple rounds with naughty and overactive toddlers. I reminded myself to breathe and kept on reminding myself when I cleaned up the dishes, washed everything, and got it all put away. By that time, my blood pressure was back down where it belonged and I rewarded myself. Since I happen to love Paris and since I don't think there's anything sissyish about scalded milk, I made my latte an extra large.

No sooner had I stepped out on the porch with it, though, than a car pulled in the drive. My final guest, and I sped through my mental Rolodex.

"Dan Peebles," I reminded myself, and not for the first time, wondered why the name seemed so familiar. It didn't take long to find out.

"Big Dan Peebles, the Used Car King of Toledo. How ya doin'?" As soon as he stepped foot on the porch, Dan Peebles pumped my arm up and down, and I finally figured out why his name rang a bell. The Used Car King of Toledo was a mainstay on local TV and radio, with ads that were always too busy, moved too fast, and hit a decibel level I'd bet not even Guillotine could achieve.

Peebles stopped pumping long enough to give an over-the-shoulder look to a woman who trailed up the steps behind him. "This here's Didi. That's short for—" He threw back his head and let out a laugh that rang to the rafters. "Heck, I don't know what that's short for, but it don't matter, does it? She looks like a Didi."

She did, indeed. Though Peebles was sixty if he was a day, the blonde with him was at least a decade younger than my thirty-five. She was tall, thin, and so big chested, I had no doubt that cosmetic enhancement played a major role in her young life. If she took offense to Peebles not knowing what her real name was, she didn't show it. Then again, she was pretty busy tap, tap, tapping out a text message on a pink phone studded with rhinestones.

Peebles had a leather duffel in one hand and he dropped

it on the porch floor and fished in his pocket so he could press a business card in my hand. "My number," he said, and gave me a wink that I didn't take at all personally. After all, that overblown wink was his signature end to each of his TV commercials. "My private number. You give me a call when you're looking for a car and I'll take care of you. You have my promise!" It was another line I'd heard ad nauseam on those occasions when I wasn't fast enough to hit the mute button. "And you know what else I'll do for you?"

I was afraid to ask.

"After we seal the deal on that terrific pre-owned car I see you driving . . ." Looking out to the street, he stuck out an arm, angled his fingers into a viewfinder, and slowly followed the path of an invisible car, his expression euphoric. "After we seal that deal, honey," I got another wink, "we'll get your picture up on one of Dan Peebles's billboards. You'd like that, wouldn't you? Bigger than life! With some nice punchy line like, *Dan does it best!* Wouldn't that be great? Wouldn't your friends just love to see your face staring at them from some big ol' billboard over on the mainland?"

To me, it sounded like the definition of the seventh circle of Hell.

Fortunately, I didn't have a chance to point it out because Professor Drake strolled out of the house.

"Hey, lookee you!" Peebles stepped back to admire Drake's costume. "Don't tell me, let me guess." As if it would help him think, he snapped his fingers. "You're dressed like that What's-His-Name. What's his name, honey?" he asked Didi, but he didn't wait for an answer and something told me it didn't matter. "That guy. The one who wrote the books. Mark Twain, that's it!"

Drake had been basking in the attention, and now his smile fell like a bad soufflé. "Dickens," he said, and I think he sized up Peebles pretty fast because he knew he had to add, "Charles Dickens."

"Charles Dickens. Terrific." Peebles put a business card into his hands. "Wouldn't that be a great billboard! *Charles Dickens bought his car from Dan Peebles.* You remember that, Chuck." Honestly, I wondered if the man ever got tired of winking. "You think about that the next time you need a car."

Drake tucked the card into his pocket and looked at me. "I am going to have a turn around the island and allow some of the townsfolk to get a good look at me. After all, one of the judges might be about, and one never knows when one will have a chance to make a good impression. Furthermore, it will give your fellow citizens a chance to meet the *real* Charles Dickens."

Peebles watched him go. "Queer guy, huh, that Chuck? 'Furthermore'? Really? Who talks like that?"

"He's here as part of the Bastille Day festivities," I told Peebles because, after all, he was bound to run into Ashburn and Drake over the next few days and it was only fair to warn him. "So is one of my other guests. They're both portraying Charles Dickens. You know, because Dickens wrote *A Tale of Two Cities* and it's about the French Revolution."

When all I got from Peebles was a blank look, I knew it was all right to ask, "You're not here for the Bastille Day celebration?"

"Nah!" He grabbed his duffel and we headed into the house and I gave Peebles his room key. "Here to check out my property. Dang, I thought by this time of the year we'd be lying by the pool and keeping each other warm in the sauna room!" He pinched Didi's behind and she let out a squeal of delight. "But the new house, it's not finished yet. A real shame, too. Of course, it's not nearly as terrible as what happened to the other house last fall."

I had a bad feeling I knew where the story was going. "Your house, it's the one that—"

"Kablam!" His duffel hit the floor with a whack. "Yep, that was my place." His cheeks turned an ugly shade of maroon. "Some idiot here on the island didn't turn the gas off. Some idiot hired the idiot who was the idiot who didn't turn off the gas. Don't you worry, though." He slapped a hand to my shoulder so hard, I staggered forward. "I got my revenge. Took idiot number two to court and got him for all he was worth. As for idiot number one . . . well, I'm hoping I run into the little weasel this weekend, because I'll tell you what, I'm going to wring the guy's neck."

I didn't think this was the moment to tell him that the weasel in question was Richie, and that Richie was dead.

"You're rebuilding?" I asked instead.

Peebles nodded, and this time gave Didi a wink. "Foundation's poured, frame is up. Me and Didi, we're going to go out there and take another look just as soon as we get up to our room and make ourselves comfortable." This time he didn't bother with a wink; he poked me in the ribs with his elbow. "Comfortable, if you know what I mean."

She giggled again and led the way up the stairs, and I

realized that by now the latte I'd left on the front porch was probably cold. I stepped outside to get it just as Hank's patrol car stopped in front of the house. He slapped his cap on his head and strolled up to the house. I went down the steps and met him in the middle of the front lawn.

"Thought you'd like to know," he said, and believe me, I didn't take it personally when Hank didn't bother with small talk. He was that kind of guy. "It was a slow morning over on the mainland, autopsy's already done. I figured since you were the one who found Richie, it's only right you should know."

"They found a cause of death?"

Hank rolled back on his heels. "They found it, all right. And son of a gun, it looks like ol' Richie might not have been talking so crazy the other night when he said somebody pushed him into the lake."

A painful ball suddenly blocked my throat. "You mean—"

Hank shook his head. "Yup. Richie Monroe was poisoned."

❖ 7 ❖

"I told you, I told you, I told you!" I forgave Chandra the jumping up and down, but only because I knew she wasn't excited that Richie was dead, but that her theory that his death was the result of murder proved to be correct. "It's just like Richie said the other night. He said somebody tried to kill him."

"He did, didn't he?" It was later that same Thursday morning I'd heard the news from Hank, and though Kate was usually at the winery long before now, she told us she'd slept in a little that day. What with the crowds that had been coming to the winery all week for tastings and tours, she was exhausted. She was on her way to Wilder Winery, but like Chandra, she'd seen Hank's SUV and had to stop and find out what was going on. Luella had taken a fishing charter out bright and early, so now, Kate, Chandra, and I took a moment to share cups of coffee and munch fruit on the front porch. And to talk about Richie's murder, of course.

With her eyes narrowed in thought, Kate sipped her coffee. "Does that mean Richie knew someone was out to get him?"

"He sure didn't act like it, did he?" I spooned up the last of the raspberries in my bowl, then set it aside. "On Monday night when he fell into the lake, Richie was all about telling us how someone tried to kill him. But last night . . ."

I thought back to the mini concert at Levi's.

"Richie was in a good mood. In fact, when I asked if he'd like to make a few extra bucks, Richie said he didn't need it. He said he was going to have plenty of money very soon and that when he did, he was planning on leaving the island forever." I thought all this through while I took another drink of my latte. "To me, this doesn't sound like a man who was worried that someone was after him."

"But someone was." Chandra was still on that detoxing mission of hers, convinced that if she could make herself pure enough, that cleanliness would somehow flow to the entire island and get rid of the bad vibes caused by Richie's unfortunate demise. Something told me her Japanese red glossy ganoderma tea didn't taste any better this morning than it had the last time I'd seen her drink it. She sipped and made a face. Or maybe it was what she was thinking that caused her mouth to pucker. "Richie was right about someone trying to kill him. We should have listened."

"We couldn't have known," I said, though deep in my heart, I wondered if she was right. Could we have done something to change what had happened? "He was such an odd guy," I said, more to myself than to anyone else. "And odd guys who say odd things—"

"Don't get listened to." Kate, ever logical. "If you're feeling guilty about it, Chandra—"

"I'm not," she insisted, though the way her mouth drooped didn't exactly convince me. "But I am feeling a little responsible."

It was a disturbing thought, and rather than dwell on it, I got up from the wicker couch and started gathering dishes.

Besides, keeping busy was a great way to pretend I didn't notice that Chandra sat up just a little straighter.

Like she'd been zapped by electricity.

Or she'd just had what she thought was a great idea.

"I know one way we could make things better," she said. "We could—"

"No. We couldn't."

"Could what?" Kate looked at Chandra, then me. "Couldn't what?"

I knew a lost cause when I saw one, so I flopped back down on the couch. "Chandra thinks we should investigate."

"That's right." Chandra grinned. "And that must be what you're thinking, too, Bea. That's how you knew what I was going to say even before I said it. We're on the same psychic wavelength. You know when that happens, when two people think the same thing at the same time, it's a known fact that the two people involved should always do what they were thinking about. If they don't, then they're violating the laws of the Universe."

The aforementioned might have explained Chandra's

three marriages, but I wasn't buying it as far as a reason to investigate Richie's murder.

"We'd be sticking our noses where they don't belong," I told her, though honestly, I wasn't sure why I bothered.

"And getting in Hank's way," Kate pointed out. She finished her coffee and stood. "He's the professional, we need to let him do what he gets paid to do."

"Absolutely." I stood, too, but Chandra had already beat me to the rest of the dirty cups and dishes and she went into the house ahead of me with them.

Kate grinned. "Good luck," she said, and I knew I'd need it.

On my way past the dining room I checked on my guests. The Boyz had finished their breakfasts and were nowhere to be seen. Didi and Big Dan were looking deep into each other's eyes and sharing the last muffin. One bite for her, one for him. Drake was back from his earlier walk, and he and Ashburn . . . well, I can't say for sure, but it seemed to me their discussion had something to do with which Dickens character would make the most interesting one-night stand.

I shivered at the very thought.

And left them to it.

When I got to the kitchen, Chandra already had the sink filled with soapsuds and the water running to rinse the dishes. Even that wasn't enough to drown out the sounds of her sniffling.

"Richie was such a doofus. Everybody just felt sorry for him. But Bea . . ." She turned away from the dishes long enough for me to see that her eyes were red. "Of course we thought he was a doofus. Nobody knew him well enough to think anything but. We didn't treat him like a friend when he was alive. The least we can do is try to help him out now."

I grabbed a dishtowel and started drying. "I'm not sure how we can," I said, and stopped her before she could say what I knew she was going to say. "Kate's right. Solving Richie's murder is Hank's job. You've always told me that Hank is a good cop."

"Yeah, a good cop." She sniffed louder this time. "And a lousy husband."

"The good cop part is all we care about right now. That's all that matters as far as Richie is concerned."

Chandra reached over and turned off the water. "I went to high school with Richie. Back then, we were friends. If I don't do anything for him now—"

I put a hand on her arm. "You've already done what a lot of people will never do. You care."

A single tear rolled down Chandra's cheek. "But caring isn't enough. Don't you see? Maybe we could just . . ." She shrugged and the purple and pink dragon on the front of her T-shirt jiggled. "What if we just ask around? What if we just talk to some people, just ask some questions? It won't be like we're actually investigating, not like we did when Peter Chan was murdered. At least this way, the people we talk to, they'll know someone remembers Richie. His death will mean something. It won't go unnoticed."

As arguments went, it was a darned good one, and I told Chandra so. Of course as soon as I did, she knew she had me hooked. She finished up the dishes lickety-split and cleared the dining room for me, too, and when those dishes were all washed and everything was put away, she rubbed her hands together.

"Where should we start?" she asked me.

Being one of the island's newest residents, I was certainly no expert, but I had a pretty good idea.

Even with what passes for traffic on an island that has something like six hundred official residents and many times that number when summer visitors are counted, we got to downtown Put-in-Bay in just a couple minutes. I parked my SUV in front of Levi's and answered Chandra's question even before she asked it.

"No," I said. "I'm not going to talk to Levi."

Her smile was sly. "He likes you. And you like him, don't you?"

My words were clipped. But then, my teeth were gritted. "I thought the only questions we were going to ask were about Richie's murder."

"Oh, come on, Bea!" Warming to the subject, Chandra turned in her seat. "You know you're attracted to the man. Why not just come out and admit it? Or better yet, invite him for dinner, open a bottle of wine, and see what happens! It might be a whole lot of fun."

Not *might be*. *Would be*.

I knew that as sure as I knew my own name.

And as sure as I knew my own name, I knew I couldn't get entangled in a relationship.

Relationships—at least the good ones—are supposed to be built on truth and trust.

And I couldn't offer Levi either.

I shook the thought away and got down to business with a pointed look across the street at the Defarge Knitting Shop.

"Clever, Bea!" Chandra's attention was diverted, at least for now. "Very clever. If anyone knows anything about what happened last night—"

"It will be Margaret and Alice. They're the island busy-bodies. That's what everyone says, right?"

Chandra gave me a thumbs-up. "Only . . ." We got out of the SUV and waited for a van packed with tourists to pass before we crossed the street. "You don't think we're going to upset them, do you? I mean, they are little old ladies and I'd hate to give them bad dreams or anything."

I laughed. "Something tells me those little old ladies are way more savvy than any of us give them credit for," I said, and led the way over to the shop.

The knitting shop was one of a row of storefronts that included a place with the grand name of Emporium that sold T-shirts and sweatshirts, postcards, and sunscreen. Next door to it was the space that used to be the Orient Express restaurant, where one snowy evening the other Ladies and I found Peter Chan's body behind the front counter. The storefront had yet to be leased and it stood empty and dark, its windows like two eyes staring out at us, waiting for us to act on behalf of Richie the way we had for Peter.

I twitched away the thought and reminded myself not to let my imagination run away with me.

Questions.

We were here only to ask a few questions, to find out what Margaret and Alice might know, and then like the responsible citizens we were, if we learned anything that was even half-way interesting, we'd turn the information over to Hank.

I kept the thought firmly in mind and we closed in on the knitting shop.

In my months on the island, I'd been past the Defarge establishment plenty of times, but not being handy when it comes to things like needlework, I'd never been inside. Chandra and I walked up the two steps that led to the front door and I took a moment to glance into the display window.

Remember what I said about Margaret and Alice being savvy? Well, it showed in the bright, well put together front window where one mannequin wore a cream-colored cotton bathing suit cover-up that looked as if it had been crocheted, and another was dressed in a blue sundress and had a gossamer little knitted shawl in shades of blue, turquoise, and green around her plastic shoulders. Oh yes, this was the sort of eye-catching display that appealed to tourists, especially if they had the discretionary cash to add to their summer-time wardrobes, like the ones who were on the island that day for the boating regatta.

Both mannequins were surrounded by baskets heaped with yarn in summery sherbet shades of orange, lime, and lemon, along with bolts of unfurled quilting fabric printed with everything from beach scenes to frogs to smiling yellow sunshines.

The inside of the shop was not so brightly lit. In fact, it took a few moments for my eyes to adjust from summer sunshine to what I couldn't help but think of as Dickensian gloom. Unlike the upbeat front window display, the shop was timeworn and tired-looking, from the threadbare carpet that covered most of the hardwood floor to the walls painted a muted mauve. The color might have been the height of fashion thirty years ago, but these days it looked careworn. So did the shelves to my left. Some of them contained skeins of yarn, but many of them were empty, and there was a sparse selection of quilting fabric stacked against the opposite wall.

There was a rocking chair near the front window, its mauve and gray upholstery frayed. After what I'd heard about the Defarge sisters, I wasn't surprised to see a pair of binoculars on the floor next to it.

Alice was behind the front counter helping a man who looked a heck of a lot like Charles Dickens.

This Dickens was taller than Drake, younger than Ashburn, and though he wore the same sort of long frock coat, trousers, and vest, he hadn't shaved his hairline like both Ashburn and Drake had to get that characteristic Dickens high forehead. Maybe he figured it didn't matter what his hair looked like; there was a tall stovepipe hat on the counter.

"Chandra! Bea!" Alice waved us over. "Look who came to see me this morning. It's Charles Dickens."

"Not really." Like he actually had to add the disclaimer, the man blushed and scratched a hand through a goatee that had been glued on a little crooked. There were more whiskers on the left side of his chin than the right. "Just one of the impersonators. You know, for this weekend's contest," he said, without a trace of a phony English accent. "I've been reading Dickens all my life. When I heard about the trivia contest, I figured it was my opportunity to brush up on everything I know. Then when I read about the impersonators . . ." His smile was as wide as the bushy mustache that also sat a little askew. "I can't think of anything that could be more fun! Mason Burke." He stuck out a hand and shook ours, then ran a finger around the inside of his stiff shirt collar. "You'll have to excuse the costume. I'm trying to get used to it. You know, before Sunday. While I'm at it, maybe I'll get used to people staring at me, too!"

Chandra picked up a pair of knitting needles and one of two balls of brightly colored yarn that sat next to the hat. "I didn't know Dickens was a knitter."

Burke's expression fell. "Oh my, I can't say if he was or if he wasn't, and I suppose I should know that, shouldn't I? I hope one of you isn't one of the judges." He looked from me to Chandra, and when neither of us rose to the bait, he swallowed hard.

"I'd hate to think I'd been caught not knowing something I should know," he said. "If I'm going to be in a trivia contest, I should know everything there is to know about Dickens. But the yarn isn't for me. Or for Dickens. It's for my wife. You see, while we were loading the boat over at the yacht club in Cleveland, she tripped and twisted her ankle. Poor thing! She wanted to get out and about this weekend, and instead she's holed up back at the cottage. She's a knitter, and I promised I'd see if I could find her some yarn and needles to keep her busy. Thank goodness for Miss Alice here! You ladies must be knitters like my wife. That's why you're here this morning."

"Oh, I don't think so, dear." The wink Alice gave Chandra

and me confirmed all my suspicions. Alice might be a little old lady, but she was nobody's fool. "I have a feeling they've come to chat about something else. And we will," she promised us. "Just as soon as I finish ringing up this sale."

While she did, I took the opportunity to stroll to the back of the shop. Here, there was a display of patterns and magazines, and a rack of knitting needles and crochet hooks. One doorway on the back wall opened into a minuscule bathroom and another into an office that included a desk, two file cabinets, and no computer. I wasn't surprised. I bet Alice and Margaret liked to do things the old-fashioned way.

Between the two rooms was a short hallway, and at the end of it a screen door that was open to let in the summer air and a view of the garden out back and the cottage beyond. The scene was straight out of a picture book with its pink roses (Margaret's choice, no doubt), white daisies, and red geraniums, and the white cottage with its green shutters and trim.

While Alice put Mason Burke's purchases into a bag, I drifted back to the front counter, my attention caught by a framed drawing on the wall behind the cash register.

It was a reproduction in a heavy dark wooden frame, a pen-and-ink sketch of a man in Colonial clothing standing behind a wooden counter. There was another man in front of the counter, also in knee breeches and a tricorn hat, and a woman sitting behind it, a mobcap on her head and her attention on her knitting.

"It's lovely, isn't it?" Now that Burke had left, Alice came over and touched a finger to the picture frame. "I bought it at a garage sale years ago. Couldn't resist. Margaret wasn't thrilled." As if Margaret might be within earshot, Alice glanced all around and lowered her voice to a conspiratorial whisper. "I told her I paid five dollars for the picture and that really got her knickers in a twist. She said I wasted my money. What she doesn't know is that I really paid seven."

"You hung it in a place of honor, so you obviously love the picture. That's what matters," I told her. "And the lady knitting is just perfect for the shop."

When I glanced around again, Alice caught my look. She hurried over to the shelves where the yarn was displayed, patting and arranging. "It was a busy spring and I haven't had a chance to restock our inventory," she said, and I wondered what kind of businesswomen Alice and Margaret really were. Summer was—it had to be—the shop's busy season, what with the island packed with tourists. "Don't you worry," Alice said, as if reading my mind. "These shelves are going to be overflowing in a couple weeks. Take a look." She went back to the front counter, grabbed a yarn company catalogue, and flipped through the pages, pointing as she went. "I'm ordering this sock yarn in every color. And this . . ." She looked at a page that featured alpaca yarn in assorted natural shades of brown and cream and she nearly swooned. "And lots of sweater yarn, of course."

Alice's cheeks turned a color that Margaret would have liked. "And we're going to paint. And replace the carpet. My goodness, I'm so excited just thinking about it, I can barely sleep nights."

Chandra stepped forward. "Alice Defarge, have you turned to a life of crime?"

Alice's mouth dropped open. But just for a second. That

is, until she got the joke. Her laughter was as soft as the lightweight lime green cotton sweater she wore with black slacks. "You always were one to tease me," she told Chandra. "We're refinancing, dear. Just a couple more weeks until the papers are signed. And once the painting is done and the shelves are restocked, we're planning a grand reopening. You're both invited." She looked from Chandra to me and her smile disappeared. "But that's not what you're here to talk about, is it? Not the grand reopening or the party we're planning or how excited I am about the new yarn. You're here because of poor Richie."

"You've heard," I said.

Alice shook her head. "Didn't need to hear. Saw Hank Florentine walk by here this morning and knew from his expression that something was wrong. Man's got a face like a thundercloud when there's trouble. Then at the bakery . . . well, word is out about Richie and it confirmed what I suspected. I knew something was terribly wrong."

"We wondered, Alice," I said, "if there was anything you could tell us. Richie was over at Levi's last night. That's where he was found. Is your shop open late on Wednesdays?"

"Only until seven, and not much in the way of business after the dinner hour. Last night I closed up a couple minutes early, then Margaret and I had dinner. Beef stew. A lot of people say stew is a wintertime dish, but they've never tasted Margaret's. It's the best on the island, and we never get tired of it. After that, I went out to get dessert. You remember. You saw me outside before the fireworks started."

"With the cotton candy. Of course." I'd almost forgotten. "Did you see Richie when you were out?"

She thought about it for a moment. "Maybe yesterday afternoon. Or maybe that was the day before. I'm sorry." She grabbed the yarn catalogue and tucked it under the counter. "When you're my age, it's sometimes hard to remember things like that. I did talk to Richie recently, I remember that, and—"

"Alice!"

The voice shouting her name from the cottage interrupted her, and Alice sighed with exasperation. "You'll have to excuse me." She hurried around the counter and to the back door. "Margaret's a little hard of hearing so she thinks everyone else is, too. She's always yelling!"

"Alice, where's the peanut butter?" Margaret called out.

Alice answered just as loudly. "Where it always is. On the second shelf in the cupboard next to the sink."

She turned back to us. "She'll be happy now. At least for a while. Margaret's eating lunch early so she can take over here at the shop and I can go watch the regatta. Now . . ." She gathered herself and remembered our topic of conversation. "Richie. Yes, Richie. I knew him all his life. Margaret and I . . . we were his landladies, you know."

I didn't know that, and if Chandra did, it was something she'd forgotten to mention.

Alice went on. "Richie's parents . . . Lyle and Norma . . . they were the ones who rented our house from us. You know, back when Margaret and I moved here to the cottage so we could be closer to the shop. That was a long time ago, and the house had been in our family for years. We didn't have the heart to sell it. And Lyle and Norma were so nice, and they had little Richie and he was such a sweetie. It was the perfect solution to our problem and we were so grateful knowing there was someone there to take care of the house and love it the way we always had. Then when Lyle and Norma both died in that terrible accident . . ."

This was something else I hadn't known. I leaned forward.

Alice provided the details. "Richie was . . . how old do you think, Chandra? Maybe twenty at the time? He was living at the house with his parents and, I mean, my goodness, he was certainly old enough to take care of himself, so they decided to go on a vacation to celebrate their twenty-fifth anniversary. Hawaii, wasn't it?"

Chandra nodded. "I'd forgotten all about it."

"Helicopter crash," Alice explained. "You know, one of those tourist helicopters that flies over the island to show off the sights. Richie was an only child, and after his parents were gone, he was left all alone. He stayed on at the house, and Margaret and I . . . well, we tried to make him part of our family. We invited him for holidays, but he never came." Her shoulders sagged. "Poor boy lived all alone, and from what I've heard, that's how he died, too. Murdered. Who ever would have thought a thing like that could happen to Richie."

I dared to broach the subject we were there to talk about in the first place. "You're well-connected here on the island, and so observant." It was better than coming right out and telling Alice that she and her sister would someday have a statue in DeRivera Park with the words *Nosey Parkers* etched into its base. "Do you or Margaret have any idea who might have wanted Richie dead?"

Alice's mouth thinned. "Nobody! My goodness, certainly no one we know. It must have been some sort of accident, don't you think?" When neither Chandra or I answered, her face paled. "You think it was Mike Lawrence."

I wanted to tell her we didn't have enough information to think anything, but she didn't give me a chance.

"Or Gordon Hunter," Alice said. "I saw him at the party the other night and he was fuming about the damage Richie had done to his boat. Swearing up a storm. Which he really shouldn't have done, considering there were children around. Then there's that other man, of course, the one whose house—"

"Dan Peebles," I supplied her the name.

Alice nodded. "The Used Car King of Toledo. Oh, I remember that day last fall. Don't you, Chandra? I remember how mad he was when he came back to the island to take a look at the damage. Thought the man's head was going to pop right off his shoulders. And I hear he's back."

There was no use denying it. "He's checking on the new construction," I told Alice.

"Well, it must be him." To emphasize her point, Alice slapped a hand against the counter. "Because it couldn't be Gordon. He's been vacationing here on the island for years. And it certainly couldn't be Mike. My goodness, I've known Mike since he was a toddler. There's no way he would ever murder anyone." She smiled brightly. "I hope I've been able to help."

Chandra waited until we were back outside to say a word. "Well," she finally asked, "what do you think? Was she able to help?"

"Not really." I walked all the way down to the Orient Express before I started across the street. "Alice didn't tell us anything we don't already know."

"And what we already know is that if we take on this case—"

"We asked questions, just like you wanted to, Chandra. And now we need to step out of the way and let the professionals do their jobs."

Oh, if only things were so easy. See, once we crossed the street, we saw that sometime while we were in the knitting shop talking to Alice, someone had started a memorial to Richie outside Levi's front door. Already there were two bunches of flowers there, a single candle burning in a tall glass jar, and a photograph of Richie. If I had to guess, I'd say he was back in grade school when it was taken. It showed a goofy-looking kid with bushy hair and a gap-toothed smile. His ears were too big for his head and there was a scattering of freckles across his nose.

"Damn," I mumbled, and Chandra didn't have to ask what I was talking about. She knew. Just like I knew. And I knew the cold feeling in the pit of my stomach could only mean one thing—Richie might have been difficult. He might have been a loner. But we couldn't let his death go unnoticed. We couldn't turn our backs on justice.

We had no choice but to investigate.

❖ 8 ❖

When Levi came around from the side of the building, I had to clear the lump out of my throat before I could say, "Hello."

He strolled closer to the memorial and looked at the flowers and the flickering candle. "I'm going to need to move all this a little farther from the front door once the cops let me open for business again, but I'm not going to get rid of it."

"I didn't think you would." Not exactly true since I didn't know Levi well enough to know if he was sentimental. He didn't look like he would be, I mean, what with the wide shoulders, the chipped-from-granite jaw, and those incredible blue eyes. He looked more like an avenging Norse god than the warm and fuzzy type. It was nice to find out he had a heart.

Nice, but hardly relevant.

I told myself not to forget it.

"Oh, it slipped my mind completely! I need milk and bread and coffee." Chandra put a hand briefly on my shoulder. "I'm going to zip over to the grocery store. I'll be right back!"

I wanted to tell her that she didn't fool me, but she was gone before I had a chance.

Which left me alone.

With Levi.

"So you know what they found in the autopsy?" The island grapevine being what it was, I didn't think I had to ask, but hey, it was better than the two of us just standing there looking down at our feet and wondering what to say next. "You know Richie was murdered?"

"Are you kidding? That's all anybody can talk about." Levi moved away from the memorial and toward the walkway that wound to the back of the building. I knew there was a stairway back there and that it led up to the second-floor apartment where he lived, but it wasn't where he was headed. He walked right past the walkway to the souvenir shop next door, and rather than look like I was avoiding a conversation—even though I would have done anything to avoid a conversation—I followed along. "The bar is still officially considered a crime scene, so no one's allowed in," he told me.

As someone who depended on the tourist trade for a living just like Levi did, I knew if my business had been disrupted, I would have been upset. But Levi took it in stride.

I wondered why.

I gave him a careful look. "Bad timing, what with the weekend cranking up. You're losing a lot of business."

He considered this, but only for a moment. "I'll live."

"More than we can say for Richie."

"Yeah." His gaze wandered to the memorial, then back again to me. "Plenty of people have been by this morning. Even people who are just visiting the island. A murder creates quite a buzz."

"Poison." The word sent a shiver up my back. "It seems—"

"Impossible. And very—"

"Creepy."

There wasn't anything Levi could say to add to that, so he didn't say anything at all. Instead, he moved out of the way of a group of tourists heading into the shop and leaned back against the building, his long legs stuck out in front of him, his arms crossed over the green and white plaid cotton shirt he wore with butt-hugging jeans. Yeah, I know . . . not exactly the outfit of an avenging Norse god, but he looked plenty delicious anyway.

"You don't have any harebrained ideas about doing something about it, do you?" he asked.

I admit it, I was a tad touchy that morning. Then again, with everything that had been going on, I had an excuse. After all, I'd found a body just the night before, the Charles Dickens impersonators were piling up like leaves in an autumn windstorm, and my ears still rang with the not-so-harmonious melodies of Guillotine. I had a perfectly good excuse for flinching in reaction to Levi's question as if I'd been suckerpunched.

His use of the incendiary *harebrained* didn't exactly help.

I managed to control the spurt of anger that raced through my veins like wildfire. As for the sarcasm boat, that sailed the moment that one telltale word was out of his mouth. "Do

I think I can do something about it? You mean, do I think it's even vaguely possible for me to find out what really happened? That sounds like a challenge to me."

"Challenge?" He laughed like he never thought of what he'd said as anything more than a matter-of-fact comment designed to point out that I might have the desire to investigate, but in no way did I have the smarts.

And that only made me madder.

I pulled back my shoulders. "I did a pretty good job solving the case when Peter was murdered."

His smile disappeared. "You did," he admitted, and I was ready to forgive him until he added, "except for the part there near the end when you almost got bumped off by the murderer."

It was true, and not something I liked to think about because when I did, it gave me the heebie-jeebies. Naturally, the only practical way to deal with it was to get defensive. "*Almost* being the operative word in that sentence."

"All right, all right." He pushed off from the wall and stepped toward me. I stepped back. "I didn't mean to make you mad, I just thought that I should remind you that investigating crimes can be serious business. Correct me if I'm wrong, but I don't think a woman moves from Manhattan to an island in the middle of Lake Erie because she's looking to make her life more dangerous."

If only he knew how right he was!

Rather than point it out, I clamped my lips shut, and I guess he realized he wasn't going to get anything out of me because Levi went right on.

"Handling the bad guys, that's what the police are for. It's their business."

I agreed. Of course, I agreed. I'd said practically the same thing to Chandra not that long before. That didn't stop me from shooting back, "And why is it your business to think you need to remind me about police business? Or my business, for that matter."

He scraped a hand through his honey-colored hair. "Wow, I can't say anything this morning without stepping in it. Can we start again?"

I folded my arms over my chest and forced myself to take a deep breath.

It wasn't Levi's fault that Richie was dead and that I knew if I didn't try to figure out what happened, I'd feel as if I betrayed a fellow human being.

It wasn't Levi's fault I had difficult and demanding guests at the B and B and that I anticipated a week of running and fetching.

The electricity that zapped through my body every time Levi was around? Okay, so yeah, that was pretty much his fault.

His fault, and my problem, so really, it wasn't fair to take it out on him.

I sucked in another breath to still the frantic beating of my heart and gave in with as much good grace as I could manage.

"We can start again," I told him, then just so he didn't get the wrong message, I added, "depending on what you're going to say this time."

"I'm going to say . . ." Levi scrubbed his hands over his face. "I'm going to say that you were probably busy at the B and B this morning and I'd bet anything that you need another cup of coffee."

He was right, but he didn't give me a chance to admit it. He grabbed my arm. "If I invite you up to my place for some of my world-famous espresso, I'm afraid you'll bite my head off, so come on. The bakery has decent coffee and it's my treat."

I ignored the heat that built where skin met skin and scrambled to keep up with him all the way to the park, then down the street from there to the bakery. It was close to the lunch hour and busy with the regatta that day and the week-end right around the corner, but we found a table outside in the shade and Levi went for the coffee. A couple minutes later, he was back and he set a to-go cup in front of me and took the chair across from mine.

With thumb and forefinger, he flipped the top off his own cup of coffee. "Look," he said, "here's what I meant to say and I did a lousy job of it. I know you're an ethical person. You care about the truth, and about justice, and that's all really admirable. And I know you're smart, too. You proved that when you solved Peter's murder. You've got a good brain. You look at a situation from all the angles, and you consider all the possibilities. You think of things that even the cops don't consider. You're creative, and imaginative. That's all terrific."

"But . . . ?"

He didn't bother with a tiny sip; he took a big drink of the coffee. "But like I said, murder is serious business. You don't need me to tell you that. All right, so I hardly know you. But like I said, you're a decent person, and from what I could tell when I stayed at your place last spring when the electricity was out on the island, you're a heck of a business-woman, too. You came here to escape the rat race of the big city, right? Well, it would be a heck of a shot of irony if that came back to bite you. Truth is, I don't want anything to happen to you. You shouldn't want anything to happen to you. And if you go poking your nose—"

"Somewhere where it doesn't belong . . ."

"That's right." He didn't put sugar or sweetener in his coffee, but apparently he remembered I did because he brought along a couple packets of sweetener and two plastic stirrers from the counter where he'd picked up the coffee. He pointed across the table to my coffee with one of the stirrers. "Drink it before it gets cold."

I wanted to tell him I'd make up my own mind about when to drink my coffee, thank you very much, but the coffee smelled nice and strong—just the way I like it—and he was right about my need for caffeine. With all that had happened back home that morning, I hadn't had nearly as much coffee as I needed. I added creamer and sweetener, stirred and sipped.

I didn't want to defend myself. Heck, I didn't even need to, but I guess the coffee mellowed me because I suddenly felt conciliatory. Even if I wasn't inclined to tell the whole truth and nothing but. "I never said I was going to investigate."

True, because I really had never said it.

At least not to Levi.

"But you did go to see Alice and Margaret this morning."

"What, I don't look like a knitter?"

Since neither one of us apparently knew what a real, honest-to-gosh knitter looked like, Levi chose to ignore the question.

"You know . . ." I leaned forward, wondering if he knew the not-so-secret secret. "The Defarge sisters keep a pair of binoculars right by the front window."

"Do they really?" He sat up, clearly taken by surprise. "I guess I'd better make sure I behave behind the bar. And at home. My bedroom faces the front of the building."

This was something I so didn't want to think about!

"They knew all about what happened to Richie," I said, and damn it, my voice was a little too breathy for my liking. "I wasn't surprised."

Levi lifted one golden eyebrow. "And last night . . . what did the sisters see?"

"Nothing." I hadn't realized how much I'd been depending on the Defarge sisters for information until that very moment. I sighed. "By the time we were all outside watching the fireworks—"

"The shop was closed. So for once, when we needed the sisters to be looking out the window to see what they could see—"

"Margaret was already in the garden setting out the lawn chairs and Alice was out getting cotton candy."

Levi sat back. "So even though nobody said anything about investigating . . ." He took a drink of coffee, the better to give me time to eat my own words. "It sounds like you questioned the sisters."

I folded my hands on the table in front of me. "I didn't

need to. Alice offered the information. Besides, one morning of visiting neighbors does not an investigation make."

"Which isn't to say you're not investigating. You know, one of these days . . ." Again, he pointed with the stirrer, but this time at me. "You're going to poke the wrong person."

"I'll take my chances," I assured him, then went ahead and took chance number one by asking, "What did you see last night?"

Now, this might seem like a perfectly ordinary and reasonable question, but believe me, I knew I was treading on not-so-solid ground. What Levi had—and hadn't—told the police about the night of Peter's murder had landed Levi in hot water for a while. See, that snowy night when Peter was killed, Levi did see something from across the street, but he kept that something a secret. As it turned out, he had his reasons and they were good ones, but they made him look like a suspect and even landed him in jail for a night.

Did that stop me from asking what he saw? Obviously not, and just to prove it, when Levi didn't answer quickly enough I asked again. "You were behind the bar all night, Levi. At least until the fireworks started. And Richie was there all night, too. He helped you before the show, didn't he? I heard he was bringing up cases of beer from the basement, and refilling the ice. Do you think Richie is the one who tampered with the guillotine?"

"I don't think anything, because I don't know anything."

"So you're telling me you never saw Richie go near the stage."

He cupped both his hands around his coffee. "I'm telling

you that Hank was at the bar until the wee hours of the morning and I went over everything with him. A couple times, as a matter of fact. He came by again this morning and we talked about it all again."

"And you're telling me that if you had anything to say, you already told it to Hank."

"I am."

"And while you're at it, you're telling me to mind my own business."

"I'm telling you what I've already told you. I don't want to see you get mixed up in anything you can't handle."

"You don't know me well enough to know what I can handle and what I can't handle."

"Whose fault is that?"

Suddenly, we weren't talking about Richie or Hank or investigating anymore.

And I wasn't one little bit comfortable with it.

I pushed back my chair. "Thanks for the coffee," I told Levi, and headed back toward where I'd parked the car.

Did I say I didn't know much about Levi? I guess I knew enough to expect him to be persistent, because it didn't surprise me at all when he was suddenly at my side. I gave him the briefest of glances before I decided to show him I could be plenty persistent, too.

"Dino says he doesn't know who Richie is," I said.

No comment.

"But after that watermelon got whacked, Dino looked into the audience. Right at Richie."

More silence.

"You have to admit, it's intriguing. If Dino thought

Richie wanted to hurt him, Dino might have decided to strike back."

I guess there's only so long even a Norse god can play the strong, silent type. Levi tossed his hands in the air. "So you're going to . . . what? March back over to your B and B, corner Dino, and beat him with a wet brioche until you get him to talk?"

Apparently I wasn't the only one feeling just a tad sarcastic that morning. "I had planned on talking to him. The brioche is a new thought. Thanks."

"Always willing to help."

"You know, I can be subtle."

"I hadn't noticed."

I didn't spare him a look. But then, I could tell by the tone of his voice that he was smiling, and I preferred not to be caught by the gleam in his eyes.

"Mike Lawrence left the bar early," I said, changing the subject oh-so-smoothly.

"So you think he looks fishy, too."

"I know he was behind the bar when we walked outside to see the fireworks. And I know he left the building just as the fireworks show ended."

"You're wasting your time on that front. Mike called this morning to explain. He said he knew I'd be right back in so he didn't feel bad about leaving. His wife called right as the fireworks show was ending. One of the kids was really sick and she asked him to come home. No mystery there."

"If it's the truth."

I heard him mumble a word I didn't quite hear but could pretty much figure out. "You don't trust anyone, do you?"

Rather than explain that I had my reasons, I stuck to the subject at hand. "Mike has motive galore. He lost his business because of Richie. And his home. And his reputation. Richie gets poisoned, Mike leaves the scene of the crime. You can see where this is headed."

We were back in front of Levi's bar and Chandra was nowhere around. Too bad. This was the perfect opportunity for a graceful exit.

I guess Levi knew I was planning my escape because he put a hand on my arm. Fortunately for both my equilibrium and his safety (I took self-defense classes back in New York when I was being stalked by a crazy guy), he knew better than to leave it there. "Bea, just because there's a mystery to solve—"

"Doesn't mean I should be the one to solve it. That's what you're going to say, right?"

Though it made plenty of sense when I told Chandra the same thing, it grated on my nerves now, and I knew exactly why. It was that darned photograph of Richie, the one taken when he was a kid, and try as I might, I couldn't help but take another look at it.

Though there were plenty of people who probably didn't believe it, I did have a heart, and I swear, just looking at the cute, goofy-looking kid in the picture made it break in two. Like all kids' lives, Richie's contained an endless amount of possibilities. No, he may not have lived up to them. At least as far as anybody knew. But that didn't mean his death didn't send ripples through his community.

I guess that's what I was feeling, those ripples that

flickered over my skin like the touch of a skeleton's hand, cold and dry; I shivered.

I guess that's also why I lifted my chin and defied what I knew to be Levi's unarguable logic with a look that told him that if I wasn't dead-set on investigating before, I sure was now. "Like I said before, nobody said anything about investigating. So who says I'm looking to solve Richie's murder?"

Levi didn't take the bait. In fact, all he did was look in the direction of the grocery store. "When Chandra left here earlier, she was smiling."

"So?"

"So I know Chandra. Of all your friends, she's the one who's bound to bug you the most about investigating. She's an excitement junkie. You know that. Chandra is a drama queen. And in her own way, she's as nosy as the Defarge sisters. But this morning, like I said . . ." He pointed to his own mouth, though I'm pretty sure there wasn't anyone on the island who would have mistaken his grimace for a smile. "Smiling. Chandra was smiling. That means she's not mad at you. And that means she's not upset. And that means you caved and agreed to investigate. And that explains what you were doing over at the knitting shop before you walked over here."

"Maybe you should be the detective."

One corner of his mouth twitched. "Maybe. And maybe you should mind your own business."

"Maybe."

Chandra or no Chandra, I turned and went to the car. I didn't bother to add the rest of what I wanted to say to Levi, but then, the stormy look in his eyes told me he probably caught the subtext.

Maybe I would mind my own business.

Right when Hell froze over.

⟪ 9 ⟫

I would apologize to Chandra later for not waiting around for her.

Then again, she was the one who'd abandoned me in the first place, so maybe I wouldn't even bother.

If I ever made it home.

I grumbled and pounded my steering wheel. With the sailing regatta scheduled to start in just a little while I should have anticipated heavy traffic in the downtown area, and when I left Levi's I should have gone not toward the lake, but away from it.

Talk about symbolism! I'm pretty sure this said something not-so-good about the way the man turned my brain around.

And boiled my blood.

"Poking my nose where it doesn't belong," I muttered. "Minding my own business. He's got a lot of nerve and—"

A couple teenagers stepped off the curb in front of the SUV, and I slammed on the brakes and grumbled a word I only use when I'm alone. They were oblivious to my death-ray looks, so once they were on the other side of the street, I eased my foot off the brake and joined the rest of the traffic that crawled toward the yacht club hosting the day's event. This wasn't just a boat race; it was a daylong extravaganza that included a craft show, musical entertainment, and vendors of all things nautical. Nearly to a street where I might be able to turn to get out of the island equivalent of rush hour, I stopped the SUV to allow three elderly women to cross from the Smoky Joe's Ribs food truck on one side of the street to the Sweet Sushi truck on the other.

As it turned out, it was a good thing I did, or I never would have seen Mike Lawrence near the yacht club entrance, selling ice cream out of a cart.

Parking was another challenge altogether. Fact is, I'd never actually owned a car when I lived in New York, but I'd learned a lot from watching the way many of my neighbors drove. And parked. Within just a couple minutes, I'd managed to go where no SUV had gone before—nor was meant to go—smack dab between a massive motor home and a golf cart.

I exited the SUV before anyone showed up to point out that I had no business wedged so close to either vehicle and joined the flow of the crowd heading to the lake. I was so busy trying to see over and around the people on all sides of me to where I'd last spotted Mike, I practically ran right into Luella, who was going in the other direction.

She put a hand on my shoulder to keep me from going down like a stone. "You look intense. What's up?"

"Mike Lawrence!" I stood on tiptoe so I could see the entrance to the yacht club. Both Mike and the ice cream cart were gone and I grumbled a curse. "I need to talk to him."

In her own way, Luella was as tuned in to island gossip as the Defarge sisters. No doubt, like everyone on the island, she knew the details of Richie's story. She didn't have to ask; she also knew exactly why I wanted to talk to Mike. She wasn't the least bit surprised that I was hot on the trail of a suspect.

"I just got back to port with the group of fishermen I had out this morning, and I'm on my way home for a while before I take another group out this evening. You know I'd offer to help but—"

"I do. Don't worry about it! You go home and get some rest and I'll catch up with you later and let you know what I find out."

Luella smiled her gratitude. "I'll keep an eye out for Mike," she promised, and edged out of the worst of the press. "I can't stand crowds. Give me the lake any day!"

I knew just how she felt. The closer I got to the yacht club, the more I was simply pushed along by the tide of spectators. When we were finally across the street and just a few feet from the lakeshore, I managed to dodge a stroller, sidestep a woman with a walker, and double shuffle around a couple who insisted on walking side by side with their arms looped around each other when there was hardly room for even one person to get by. I slipped to the side, away from the main gate where regatta tickets were being collected.

Fists on hips, I looked around and wished I wasn't so short. The answer to my problem, though, was only a few feet away in the form of a lightpost sunk into a foot-high cement base. I grabbed the post, hoisted myself up onto the base, and took advantage of a completely new perspective on the scene.

An Impressionist painter would have had a field day with the swirl of colors that played out before me. Lake Erie was a brilliant blue, three shades darker than the dome of sky above it, and there was just enough wind to kick up foamy whitecaps that turned turquoise where they broke against the sides of the boats with their sails, billowing and brilliantly white. Sailors stood at the ready, a couple here and there decked out in jewel tones that added colorful exclamation marks to the scene, a splash of green here, a dab of red there.

I'd never been much of a sailor myself, but I'd attended a few of these kinds of events over the years, and I knew the boats that looked to be randomly sailing back and forth were actually plying the waters near the starting line, waiting for the signal for the race to begin.

Onshore, the panorama was just as interesting. The grounds of the yacht club were immaculately groomed, the grass a gorgeous emerald, and the geraniums that lined the walk a crimson as dark as rubies. The folks in the crowd were dressed in every fashion imaginable, from traditional sailors' whites to brightly colored sundresses to denim and T-shirts, the kaleidoscope of colors intensified by the afternoon sun.

Lucky for me, the race started and the slowpokes still

waiting for a good vantage point got a move on. The crowd thinned, and I spotted Mike and his ice cream cart on the other side of the main entrance. I got over there just a fraction of a second after Alice.

"Don't tell me, let me guess, gorgeous. You're here for a chocolate cone!" Even before Alice answered, Mike flipped open the lid of the ice cream cart and started to scoop.

"You know me too well," Alice chirped, then in response to Mike asking about a vanilla cone for Margaret, she added, "I think it's too hot to take a cone back. It will be mush before I get halfway there."

While Mike took Alice's money and made change, she took the time to look around and noticed me standing in line behind her. "Well, isn't this a coincidence. I'm lucky enough to get to see you twice in one day!" She took her cone and stepped aside, and because I didn't want to grill Mike in front of her, I signaled to him that I'd order in just a bit and moved to stand in the shade with Alice. "Are you going to get chocolate, too?" she asked.

I glanced at the list of flavors written on an erasable board and attached to the front of the cart. "I think I've already got my heart set on salted caramel."

Alice grinned and took a lick of her cone. "Good choice. Now don't you go tattling on me to Margaret about this. If she finds out I had ice cream and she didn't get any, I'll never hear the end of it."

I crossed my heart to prove my good intentions. "Margaret's back at the shop?"

Since Alice was mid-lick, she simply nodded. "I know I can't stay long. I just wanted to see the start of the race. But

I've got to hurry back. Good heavens, if anyone comes in and asks Margaret a knitting question . . ." Whatever else she was going to say, her cheeks turned pink and Alice clamped her lips shut.

Call me as nosy as the Defarge sisters, I couldn't help but wonder what was going on.

"Margaret must know as much about the shop as you do," I ventured, trying to draw her out. "You two have owned the shop for how many years?"

"Oh good heavens!" Thinking, Alice closed her eyes. "Going on forty, I think," she finally said, opening them again and realizing there was a chocolate drip about to run down her hand. She licked the edge of the cone. "And of course Margaret knows as much as I do about inventory and orders and payments and utility bills and such."

Don't think I didn't notice that she'd left something out.

"But not about knitting?"

The pink in Alice's cheeks intensified. "You know how it is with sisters," she said, and I had to admit that I didn't; I had no siblings. "Well, it's worse with twins," she assured me, undeterred by my only-child status. "Always sticking up for each other. Always having each other's backs. Of course, that's why I hate to say anything bad about Margaret but . . ." She leaned in close. "Truth be told, she's not much of a knitter."

I would have laughed if not for the grave look on Alice's face. To her, this was serious stuff.

"Oh, she tries," she added, and I guess she thought that took care of the having-each-other's-backs part, because she went on to say, "but Margaret's fingers just aren't as nimble as mine. They never have been. Not even when we were kids and first learned to knit. It was for the war effort, you know, Korea. All the women here on the island got together two nights a week over at the town hall and knitted socks for the soldiers. Such a good memory!" Her smile was soft, but only for a moment. Then her lips puckered. "Oh, I don't mean the war. Don't get me wrong. I'm talking about the friendship between the women. We got together, we talked, some of the women brought the letters they got from sons and husbands and brothers, boys we all knew who were all away fighting the war. And we knit socks. My goodness, did we knit socks! We even got a commendation from the national Red Cross because we made so many pairs." Her slender shoulders went back. "Even though I was a brand-new knitter, I ended up knitting more socks than anyone. That's how easy knitting came to me. Like that!" She snapped her fingers. "Margaret . . . well, she tried, bless her heart. But it was never easy for her. To this day, she can't look at anyone knitting socks without getting heart palpitations. Now don't you go spreading word around about any of this," she warned me with a look. "Margaret's a little touchy when it comes to her knitting skills."

I gave her a wink. "Your secret is safe with me."

That was enough to satisfy Alice. She took another lick of her cone, gave me a jaunty wave good-bye, and headed downtown to the knitting shop.

"You want that ice cream now?" Mike asked me.

I assured him I did, paid for my cone, and bided my time. If there was one thing I'd learned investigating Peter's untimely demise, it was that suspects can't be rushed. At least not without spooking them. Since I couldn't afford to let Mike know I was investigating, I decided to play dumb.

"I don't think I've seen you working for the ice cream company before. Oh!" I put a hand to my mouth. Too dramatic? Since Mike went as still as a statue, his hand inside the ice cream freezer and his face suddenly the color of the crimson geraniums that grew nearby, I don't think he even noticed.

I did my best to sound repentant. "This was one of Richie's jobs, wasn't it?"

Mike slapped the cooler cover closed. "Yeah, well, Richie's a little busy being dead today so the guy who owns the concession called me to fill in."

I took the ice cream cone out of Mike's hand. "So what's your theory about the way Richie died? You must have one. Everyone else I've talked to about it today does."

As if he couldn't believe I cared enough to even ask, Mike snorted. "Drank himself to death. Or maybe it was terminal stupidity that killed him."

He didn't know.

Or he pretended he didn't.

The chill that ran through me had nothing to do with the ice cream.

I watched Mike carefully, hoping to gauge his reaction. "You haven't heard the news."

"I know the idiot is dead, and I say good riddance. Believe me, the world is a better place without Richie Monroe in it."

This didn't seem like an especially good time to start slurping down a salted caramel ice cream cone, but since it was already dripping down my fingers, I gave the cone a quick lick.

"Richie was murdered," I told Mike.

If Mike was surprised by this piece of news, he didn't show it. He wiped a damp rag over the top of the ice cream cart. "Everybody who ever met the guy hated his guts. It was bound to happen sooner or later."

"You don't sound especially sorry."

Understatement, and I guess Mike knew it because he barked out a laugh. "Sorry? Should I be? I mean, really? I know you're pretty new around here, but even you must have heard the story. That jackass ruined my life."

Somehow, eating ice cream and talking about murder didn't seem to go together, but the sun was hot, and my salted caramel was quickly disintegrating.

I licked around the cone, paying special attention to the rim. "Did you like Richie?" I asked Mike.

Surprised by the question, he flinched. "Like him? You mean before he ruined my life or after?" It was a small ice cream cart and no way it needed it again, but he swiped the towel along the chrome top one more time.

"I tried," Mike said, and I knew it wasn't easy for him to admit it; a muscle jumped at the base of his jaw. "You know what I mean? Like everyone else on the island, I felt sorry for the guy. He was so quiet, and anytime I saw him, he was usually alone. Yeah, I tried to like him. And I tried to help him out. I hired him to do lots of odd jobs for me. And I thought, you know . . . I thought maybe if I stopped in at a work site to see how he was doing, and we talked a little bit . . . I thought I could get to know him a little better, maybe sit down and have a beer with him sometime. And just when I figured I'd ask if he wanted to come by the house for a burger and a brew, that's when he'd do something so stupid that all I could think was that I wanted to wring his neck."

"Or poison him."

Mike snickered. "Poison? Really? Who the hell would waste perfectly good poison on a jerk like Richie?"

Ice cream dripped on my fingers, and I grabbed a napkin from the cart, wiped my hand, then took another quick lick to prevent another drip. "You tried to help him out. You gave him work."

"You got that right. And how did he repay me? By screwing up my life. Did I like Richie? You know, now that I think about it, I can tell you one hundred percent without a doubt, I hated the guy's guts."

I made a face. "That's probably not something you should say too loud."

Mike snorted. "What, you think the cops will think I'm the one who offed the guy?"

"Did you?"

He propped his fists on his hips. "Are you accusing me of something?"

"Me?" I managed a laugh. "Honest, the only thing I could possibly accuse you of is selling the best ice cream I've tasted in a long time. Really, Mike . . ." I couldn't afford to make an enemy of the guy, not when he hadn't told me everything I wanted to know. I made sure I kept a smile on my face when I moved closer to the ice cream cart. "I understand how you feel about Richie. If the guy had blown up my house—"

"Yeah. See. That's just it!" Like he'd just thought of something, Mike pointed a finger in my direction. "Now you're talkin'! If anybody has a reason to kill that idiot, it was Peebles, the Used Car King. That place he had over at the other end of the island was worth more than a million. More than a million! And it was just his weekend summer home. Can you imagine?"

I could, but it hardly mattered.

"Dan Peebles is staying at my place," I told Mike. "He checked in this morning. He wasn't even on the island last night when Richie was killed."

"Maybe he says he wasn't on the island last night. Does anybody know that's true? Hey." Mike stuck out his chin. "I watch the cops shows on TV, just like everyone else. I know what I'm talking about. Peebles is a royal pain. Believe me, I know. He's the one who took me to court over what happened to his house. He's the one who sued me for all I was worth, and then some. Because of him, the feds found out I was paying Richie under the table."

And not paying Social Security taxes.

I didn't mention it. There was no use pouring salt on Mike's obviously open wounds.

Instead, I tried to close in on the information I wanted from another direction. "So what do you think?" I asked Mike. "If Peebles won his case, why would he still be mad at Richie?"

"Mad doesn't even begin to describe it. Man . . ." As if

he still couldn't believe it, Mike shook his head. "The day we all had to appear in court and Richie took the stand to talk about what happened, Peebles lost it. He jumped out of his chair and he would have strangled Richie right then and there if the bailiffs hadn't held him back. The judge, he forgave Peebles, said he understood his emotional distress. That's what he called it, emotional distress. But I'll tell you what, I've never seen that kind of hatred in anybody's eyes before or since."

"Not even when you think about Richie?"

Mike grunted.

I guess that was the only answer I needed.

A couple kids came up and got ice cream bars and I waited until after they'd walked away before I said anything else. By that time, I was down to chomping the cone and I took a bite, swallowed, and said, "You were at the bar last night. Did you see anybody talking to Richie?"

Mike's smile was tight. "I was a little busy."

"But you knew he was there."

"Sure. Son-of-a-bitch had the nerve to come up to the bar and order a couple drinks from me. Just to rub it in, you know? Just so I wouldn't forget I wouldn't be working odd jobs if it wasn't for his stupidity."

"So Richie wasn't sorry for what he did and how he cost you your livelihood?"

"You mean was he sorry for blowing up that house?" I don't think Mike had ever considered this before. His head cocked to one side and he was quiet for a moment or two. "He said he was sorry. In court that day. He said it was an honest mistake and it could have happened to anybody."

"Could it?"

"Anybody dumber than a rock."

"Which Richie was."

"All you had to do was talk to the guy. You knew in an instant he had a couple screws loose."

"But you sent him to the Used Car King's house to turn off the gas anyway."

"Yeah, I did." Both his hands flat against the ice cream cart, Mike leaned forward. "Biggest mistake I ever made in my life."

"Maybe. Maybe not. Not if you count the fact that you left the bar early last night."

Mike didn't expect the change of subject. He pushed away from the cart, grabbed the handle, and rolled it down the sidewalk, looking for a new location to set up.

I followed along.

"That doesn't mean anything," he said without looking my way. "My kid was sick."

"It means you were inside the bar with Richie while we were all outside watching the fireworks."

"So?"

"So by the time I got inside after the fireworks show, Richie was already dead. That means you were probably inside the bar with Richie when he died."

He stopped and spun to face me. "You're crazy."

I gave him a one-shoulder shrug. "I've heard that before."

"Well, I'd better not hear anything about any of this again. Because I'll tell you what, I learned plenty from what happened to me last year. All about the legal system, and how sometimes people who don't deserve it get royally screwed. I hear one word out of you, lady . . ." He jabbed a finger in my direction. "I hear anybody say anything about how you're talking like I could have done something to Richie, and I'll sue the pants off you. I've learned my lesson. I'll fight as dirty as I can to make sure I win."

Mike stalked away and I knew better than to follow.

Oh, it's not like I was worried he might actually make good on his promise and sue me and win. Jason Arbuckle, my attorney back in New York, could handle anything. But I knew better than to get embroiled in all things legal. Lawsuits equal nitpicking, and nitpicking draws attention. My whole point in coming to the island in the first place was to get away from that sort of thing and find peace.

Does that mean I'd back off if my investigation led me in Mike's direction?

Obviously not.

But it did mean I vowed to keep a low profile.

That actually might have been possible if halfway back to town I didn't see Margaret coming from the other direction. One look at me in the SUV and she stopped, waved an arm to get my attention, and called out, "Yoohoo! Little Miss Detective!"

She couldn't hear my groan, and even if she had, I bet she would have ignored it.

"I hoped I'd see you!" Margaret, resplendent that day in pink pants and a pink and white top, crossed the street to intercept me and I stopped the SUV and rolled down the window. "I heard you were over at the regatta."

"I didn't stay long." That was probably obvious since the

race had started only a little while earlier. "I need to get home and—"

"And keep digging into the mystery of Richie's death. Yes, of course!" Margaret nodded and looked past me. From this distance there was no way she could see all the way to the yacht club and Mike's ice cream cart, but she nodded knowingly. No doubt, her sister had filled her in on all the details. "What did Mike tell you?"

I tried for a graceful smile. "All I did was buy ice cream from Mike."

"Uh huh. And I just fell off a turnip truck. No matter!" She put a friendly hand on my arm where I had it propped at the open window. "Because I think I might be able to help you. You know . . ." She winked. "About the i-n-v-e-s-t-i-g-a-t-i-o-n."

There was no use denying it. Not to a woman who felt the need to spell out the word when we were the only ones around. "All I did was talk to Mike," I said.

"Yes. Alice told me she thought that's why you were hanging around. But here's something I bet Alice didn't tell you . . ."

Honestly, I thought I was about to find myself in some sort of one-upsmanship knitting competition and get a critique of Alice's skills. That's why I was so surprised when Margaret said, "Richie and his girlfriend . . . they had a big fight yesterday morning."

"I didn't know. That he had a girlfriend or that they had a fight."

"Oh yes." Margaret was very pleased with herself. Her lips pinched. "We saw the whole thing. They were out in front of the hotel and I'll tell you what, she was not a happy camper. I couldn't hear exactly what they said, but I know a woman who's madder than a wet hen when I see one. I thought her head was going to explode, and there she was pointing at poor Richie and her jaw flapping a mile a minute. Alice and I, we tried to get closer, but . . . well . . ." Her blue eyes twinkled. "Even meddlers like us don't like to look too obvious."

"Alice knew about the fight? She didn't say anything when I stopped at the knitting shop this morning. Or when I saw her a little while ago."

"Oh, you have to forgive my sister. She's a little touchy when it comes to love."

This was another surprise, and I guess my expression showed it because Margaret stepped nearer to the SUV. "You see, Alice has never had much of a love life, so when there's talk of boyfriends and girlfriends, it always rankles her just a little. As for me . . ." Her smile was just a tad self-satisfied. "I don't have a problem talking about love. You see, fifteen years ago, I met a man who came to visit relatives here on the island. We fell in love. And got married."

"I didn't know that you were—"

"Oh, not anymore." She didn't wait for me to ask for the details. "After we got married, I actually left South Bass for a while. Tony had a place in Florida, near Sarasota, and we lived there. I came back here a couple years ago, after he died. Started using my maiden name again. Because that's how everyone knows me."

I would have offered my condolences if she'd given me a chance.

"Anytime the subject of romance comes up, Alice gets

all prune-faced," Margaret said. "That's why I knew I had to be the one to tell you about Richie's girlfriend. She could be a suspect, don't you think?"

"I don't know, but I would like to talk to her. What did you say her name was?"

"Name?" As if she'd never considered it before, Margaret twitched. "Well, I don't know her name. But that's no problem. She works over at the hotel. You know, the girl with the crossed eyes."

❖ 10 ❖

"None of it makes any sense."

Kate didn't have to elaborate. We were on my front porch enjoying a Friday early evening glass of wine, and Chandra and I knew exactly what she was talking about.

Richie's murder.

Of course she was talking about Richie's murder.

In spite of the fact that the weekend Bastille Day celebration was now officially in full swing, the island was packed with tourists, and the excitement was cranking up for the next day's big party in the park, Richie's murder was all anyone could talk about.

"Mike did it," Chandra announced, though how exactly she'd come to that conclusion was anybody's guess.

"I think it was You-Know-Who." With one French-manicured finger, Kate pointed up and toward the house.

Big Dan Peebles and Didi had gone inside only a few minutes before to change for dinner. "He's got good reason."

"Yes, and so do Gordon and this mysterious girlfriend of Richie's," I pointed out. "And Dino," I added in a whisper just in case he was anywhere within earshot.

"And that's why none of it makes sense." Our wine wasn't gone, but Kate was particularly proud of the newest Wilder Winery wine—an earthy pinot noir with just a hint of cherry—and she topped off our glasses. "It's like everyone you've talked to has a reason to want Richie dead."

"Well . . ." I sipped, nodded my approval in Kate's direction, and sipped again. "That's pretty much what Mike told me."

"Yeah, just like he told you he left the bar early on Wednesday night because one of his kids was sick." Chandra tossed her head and her blunt-cut, blond hair shimmered in the sunlight that streaked across my front porch. "We all know what he was really doing. Running from the scene of the crime."

"But we don't know that," I reminded her. "We don't know anything for sure. Not yet."

When we heard footsteps on the stairway right inside the front door, we all sat back and drank our wine. With a house full of guests, I didn't know who might be coming or going, but I did know that whoever it was, that person didn't need to know we were speculating about the murder.

Whoever it was, he (or she) didn't come outside, and after a couple minutes of silence, we settled back into our conversation.

"It's unacceptable," I finally said, voicing the troubling thought that had been bouncing around in my brain all that day. "One of our neighbors has been murdered. We can't have that. We've got to do more to make sure whoever is responsible—"

"Mike," Chandra said.

"Whoever," I repeated. "We can't let a thing like this hang in the air. It's bad for the island."

The front door popped open.

"You are obviously speaking about those who are pretending to be me." Gregory Ashburn stepped onto the porch, resplendent as ever in his Dickens regalia. I knew the *me* he was talking about wasn't the real *me* . . . er . . . *him*. He meant Dickens, of course, and he was obviously referring to Timothy Drake, who, as if on cue, followed him out to the porch.

"Good evening, ladies." Drake bowed. "You are coming to the band concert in the park this evening, I hope. I have been told there will be an opportunity for those people pretending to be me . . ." His glance at Ashburn was icy and I knew why. He wasn't talking about the real *me* . . . er . . . *him*, either. "There is word that the contest judges might be about and that we will have a chance to step to the center of the park so that they might get a first look at us. No doubt"— he smoothed a hand over his plaid vest—"they will see instantaneously that there is only one true Dickens among a flock of imposters."

"Yes." Ashburn stepped around Drake. "Only one true Dickens."

"Certainly." Drake stepped in front of Ashburn. "Only one."

"And at least one more," I mentioned, thinking of the

man I'd met in the knitting shop. "Just so you boys know, you've got some competition."

"A shame anyone else would even think to try." Ashburn marched down the steps.

"A pity anyone at all would imagine there might be a chance to compete." Drake waited until Ashburn was all the way out to the street. Then he left, too.

"Crazy," I mumbled, and this time, I wasn't talking about the murder.

"You got that right." I didn't know if Kate was talking about the murder, either, at least not until she added, "Poison. Did Hank ever say what kind?"

I shook my head. "I never heard."

"They're still doing tests," Chandra assured us, and I didn't doubt her information for one minute. When I got home from my interview with Mike at the regatta on Thursday, I noticed Hank's SUV parked in front of Chandra's house. Apparently, while he was visiting, they'd talked about the case—in addition to whatever else they might have been doing. "They'll know soon," she said, "and then maybe . . ." A single tear streaked down Chandra's cheek. "Then maybe we can do something to help Richie's spirit rest in peace."

"Now, Chandra . . ." Kate is anything but warm and fuzzy, and she likes it that way. That didn't stop her from putting a hand on Chandra's shoulder. "You can't keep getting all upset about it. It's just a shame, that's all. Poor Richie—"

"Poor Richie!" Chandra's voice broke over the words. "All everybody ever saw was this weird, crazy guy who never amounted to much of anything, and all they ever called him was 'Poor Richie.' But he wasn't like that. I mean, not a loser. Not always!" Her sigh was monumental. "Back in high school, Richie was a different sort of guy. But things changed. Richie changed. He was a completely different person when he came back from college."

"Richie went to college?" It wasn't like I didn't trust Chandra's memory, but let's face it, ivy-covered walls did not exactly mesh with what I knew about Richie. "Are you sure?"

Chandra didn't answer me. In fact, all she did was hop to her feet and motion us to follow her.

We did.

Down my front steps. Across my lawn. Over the stepping-stone path through Chandra's herb garden and then through the maze of fountains and garden gnomes and whirling, twirling suncatchers that surrounded Chandra's house.

All the way to her sunshiny yellow front door.

Even then Chandra didn't stop. She threw open the door and went inside, and because we didn't know what else to do, Kate and I went right along.

Once inside the tiny foyer, the first thing I noticed was the same first thing I always noticed at Chandra's—the spicy scent of incense that hung in the air and settled on my shoulders like a cloak. She turned to her right and marched down a hallway, and when I fell into step behind her, the scent wafted around me in waves.

"In there!" Still out in the hallway, Chandra stepped back to let us into the spare bedroom that she used for her crystal and tarot readings. There was an Oriental rug on the floor, a low-slung futon along one wall, and a table under a window that was draped with brightly colored gauzy fabric. A bookcase against the purple wall was filled with titles like *Tarot for Every Day* and *Are There Spirits Among Us?* There was a wooden box on the shelf there, too, and Chandra grabbed it and riffled through the contents. She pulled out a photograph and held it out to me.

When it comes to old photographs, I'm no expert, but I sized up this one and decided it was from the eighties. It showed a dark-haired girl in a sapphire blue taffeta dress with a V neck and a deep ruffle around the neckline and shoulders. She stood under an archway decorated with phony flowers and next to her was a teenaged boy with shaggy hair and glasses. He was wearing a tux that was too big for him.

"That's Richie," Chandra said, pointing to the boy. "And that's me. We went to our high school prom together."

"You could have mentioned it before."

We were out on Chandra's patio, surrounded by potted flowers in every color of the rainbow and wind chimes that hung from nearby trees. When a breeze drifted by they sang a chorus, and over the plinking and the clanking and the chiming, I repeated what I'd already said to her when we were still in the house and looking at that picture of Chandra and Richie. "It's pretty important information, don't you think?"

"What difference does it make?" Like she had inside, Chandra shrugged like it was no big deal, and maybe she was right. Maybe it wasn't. After all, the island was full of people who'd known Richie for years.

But not people who'd gone to the prom with him.

"Tell us about him," I urged Chandra. "And about why you say he changed."

She lit a candle in a yellow glass holder in the center of the red metal patio table and when she was done, Chandra blew out the match and plunked down in the green chair next to my blue one. "He was just a regular guy," she said. "Just a sweet, regular kind of kid. Nobody ever thought Richie would grow up to be a rocket scientist, but he had plenty of ambition. He earned money every summer mowing peoples' lawns and he had a great little business going. That's how he saved money to go to college. He loved to fish, I remember that, too, and he loved music and video games. He was a good kid and when he left here to go to school at Bowling Green University, he was still a good kid. But when he came back . . ."

Chandra's words drifted away, just like her focus.

I remembered what Alice had told us at the knitting shop the day before. "When Richie came back from school, that's when his parents died, right?"

Chandra nodded. "I know that had something to do with him changing. I mean, how could it not? But it wasn't just that. He was back here on the island before his parents died, before his first semester at college was even over. I remember that because I remember I ran into him at the grocery store and I asked if he was home for something special and . . ." It was plenty warm, but Chandra shivered. All those years ago, and the incident still struck her as odd. "He mumbled something about being home to stay and the way he looked at me . . . well, it was like he didn't even know me."

Chandra leaned forward and folded her hands on the table. "That's when I noticed how much he changed. He was like a different person. He used to be fun and funny. You know, the class clown. But when he came back here, he pretty much turned into a hermit. He used to be my friend. Oh, not like that," she added, when Kate pursed her lips and gave another look at that prom picture we'd brought outside with us.

"We were never really boyfriend and girlfriend," Chandra said. "It was a small school. I mean a really small school. So we all just paired up to have dates for the prom. It's not like I went with him because I was madly in love with him or anything. And he sure wasn't madly in love with me, either. But I didn't mind going to the prom with Richie. Like I said, he was a lot of fun and—"

Chandra's mouth dropped open.

I scooted forward in my seat. "You thought of something? Or somebody? There was something about Richie—"

"Exactly." The way Chandra's eyes bulged, she looked a whole lot like the cement gargoyle that goggled at me from the stone wall behind her. "I just figured it out! Maybe Richie wasn't Richie."

Chandra might have known what she was getting at, but the blank looks on my face and Kate's sent a message. As if she could clear it and thus, find the words she needed, she shook her head. "Maybe it's like in *A Tale of Two Cities*," she said. "You know, like that Darnay guy and that Sydney What's-His-Name. Maybe Richie went to school on the mainland," Chandra said. "But maybe it wasn't Richie who came back to the island. Maybe it was someone who looked like Richie."

"Really?" Kate rolled her eyes.

I bit my lower lip. It was a farfetched theory, and frankly, I didn't believe it for a minute. But it did bring up something we should have thought of as soon as we heard about Richie's sad end.

"Where are you going?" Kate asked when I popped out of my chair.

"Into town. Who wants to come with me? We're not going to be able to figure out what happened to Richie until we learn more about him, and I think we all know exactly who can help us."

When we walked into the knitting shop, Margaret was on the phone. "Alice," she mouthed and pointed to the phone, then held up one finger to tell us she'd be right with us.

By the time she was, I was ready with the story we'd concocted on the way over. The one about how Margaret and Alice were always so busy, and how since they were Richie's landladies we figured they might need help cleaning out his house.

"It's going to be a busy weekend," I told her after I'd finished up that first part of the story, and even I was surprised I could sound so innocent when I had prevarication in my heart. "So we're not going to have much of a chance to get any cleaning done until next week, but if we could go over this evening just to look around and see what we're getting into, well, then we'll know what we need. I mean as far as storage boxes and cleaning supplies."

"That is the nicest thing anybody ever offered to do for

me," Margaret said, then added instantly, "for us, really, because my goodness, Alice will just be tickled pink when I tell her the news. You sure you girls want to take on a job like this?"

We assured her we did.

Margaret tipped her head to the side, thinking. "Well," she finally said, "the police have been through the house and they're done with it. Hank himself stopped in this afternoon to tell me as much. So I don't see what earthly reason there would be to keep you out." She reached under the front counter near the cash register and came out holding a key ring with a pink enameled tabby cat dangling from one end. "You're sure?" she asked again before she handed it over. "It could be more of a job than you signed on for."

"There are four of us," I chirped, then added, "well, there will be next week when Luella's not so busy with charters. And like I said, we won't even try to start anything tonight."

"Except to make lists," Kate chimed in.

"And make sure the place is locked up nice and tight when we're done," Chandra added.

"By next week . . ." As if the job was already finished, Chandra brushed her hands together. "We'll be done with it lickety-split."

I couldn't argue with the lickety-split. Lickety-split, before Margaret could either change her mind or realize we had more on our minds than simply neighbor helping neighbor, we took the keys and left the shop, and within just a few minutes we arrived at our destination.

The old Defarge family home was situated on the northwest corner of South Bass, about as far from downtown

Put-in-Bay as it was possible to get on an island that is only four miles long to begin with. With the distance to the knitting shop and the thought of a daily commute in all sorts of weather, I could see why Margaret and Alice had decided to move into the cottage behind the store. Still, there was a certain charm to the setting and I imagined the Defarge sisters as little girls, long before the big-ticket summer home had been built across the street. I pictured them playing in the apple orchard next to the white Victorian farmhouse with the date 1867 painted over the front door.

We let ourselves in through that front door, and while Kate and Chandra hung back, clearly put off by what looked like a couple month's worth of accumulated pizza boxes and unopened mail in the living room where we found ourselves, I took a look around.

Brown plaid couch.

Brown recliner.

Flat screen.

Nintendo Wii.

It was all pretty basic.

And none of it was especially clean.

"Ew!" With thumb and forefinger, Kate nudged a paper plate perched on a pile of magazines on the coffee table in front of the couch. There was a piece of petrified pepperoni pizza on it. "Maybe we shouldn't have lied about why we wanted to get in here. Margaret and Alice shouldn't have to deal with this mess. They really are going to need help getting it cleaned up."

"We really do have to help them," Chandra piped in. "We can't let Margaret and Alice—"

"No worries," I assured them, and since I'd been thinking the same thing, I knew exactly what I had to do. I took my cell phone out of my pocket and let my fingers fly over the keyboard. "I'm telling my cleaning crew I've got a big job for them and a big bonus if they're willing to get it done fast."

It was a mighty generous offer on my part, if I did say so myself, but even that wasn't enough to make Chandra look any happier. She sniffled. "But even once everything is cleaned up . . . even when it's all organized and packed in boxes . . . do you think there's anybody who would show up to claim Richie's stuff?"

"Would you admit it if you were related to Richie?" Kate asked, but she didn't wait for the answer. "So . . ." She glanced around. "What do we do first?"

Before I could change my mind (or have it changed for me by the sight of the black garbage bag filled with empty beer cans that I saw next to the couch), I decided on a plan.

"We try to find something that will tell us what Richie's been up to," I said. "Anything that looks strange or unusual or out of place." When both Chandra and Kate gave me you've-got-to-be-kidding looks, I threw my hands in the air. "Well, it's the only thing I can think of," I admitted. "How about if we each take a room. Kate, you go into the kitchen and poke around. Chandra, you take the living room. I'll go upstairs. If you find anything, yell."

Kate took a tentative step toward the kitchen. "You mean like anything interesting, right? Or do you mean anything alive, like a mouse or something?"

Rather than tell her I thought the latter was a real possibility,

I took the steps two at a time and started my own search with Richie's bedroom.

It came as no surprise to me that Richie wasn't much of a decorator. Or a housekeeper, either.

The room at the top of the steps contained a bare mattress with a beat-up acoustic guitar on it, another TV, and a dresser with open drawers. It was dingy, dirty, and all pretty basic. There was a purple Sharpie on the dresser right next to an unopened carton of Dunfield cigarettes. I am not a smoker, never have been, but I'd seen enough ads to recognize the blue logo on the box. Next to the cigarettes was a photograph in a gold metal frame that showed a young boy standing between two women.

"Margaret and Alice!" Surprised by the sentimental memento, I grabbed the picture and took a closer look. No doubt, the boy was Richie and I'd guess he was twelve or so. As for the Defarge sisters . . .

The color of Margaret's trim suit was faded by time and sunlight, but there was no mistaking its pinkness, just like there was no mistaking how the women in the picture felt about Richie. Both Margaret and Alice had an arm looped around the kid's shoulders, their hands touching and the smiles on their faces were identical. The women looked . . .

"Young and pretty," I told myself, glancing over their smooth complexions and the blond hair they both wore in the same beehive style that I'd bet hadn't been popular for at least a dozen years before the picture was even taken.

I remembered what Alice had told us about how she and Margaret had tried to make Richie a part of their family once his parents were gone. He'd never allowed the sisters to get that close, and yet something about the careful way the photograph was displayed told me he would have liked to try.

"Better watch it, Bea," I warned myself, but not until after I'd cleared away the lump in my throat. "Or you'll be getting as sappy as Chandra."

Rather than risk it, I decided to take the photograph and give it to Margaret and Alice. Something told me the sisters might be comforted by knowing that Richie treasured their friendship even if he'd never been able to let them know it.

From the bedroom I moved down the hall to the next room that was obviously used for storage. One look and I knew this room was a job for another day. There were so many dilapidated cardboard boxes jammed in the doorway, I knew I'd never get past them and into the room, and if I did, I feared I would need a trail of breadcrumbs to lead me back to safety.

Instead, I peeked into a middle bedroom where the only piece of furniture, so to speak, was a treadmill draped with dirty clothes. This side of the house faced east, and already the daylight was fading and throwing gray shadows on the walls. I flicked the switch near the door and the ceiling fan started a slow, steady turn. I needed to pull the chain on it to turn on the light, and as soon as I did I caught sight of something on the far wall and pulled in a sharp breath.

"Kate! Chandra! Get up here," I called.

Something told me they were only too happy to get away from their duties downstairs. Or maybe my voice had more of an edge of desperation in it than I imagined. They joined me, as Chandra would say, lickety-split.

"What's wrong?" Chandra asked.

"What'd you find?" Kate said, hurrying into the room on Chandra's heels.

I pointed to the wall to my right, at a flyer that I'd seen all over the island these past couple weeks, one with a picture of the Boyz of Guillotine on it.

Except when I'd seen it before, the picture didn't have a wicked-looking butcher knife stabbed through it.

"Oh." Kate took one look at that knife and her voice wobbled. She pressed a hand to her stomach. "Something tells me this is not a good thing."

"Or maybe it is," I reminded her. "No matter what Dino says, Richie was obviously mad at him. This proves it. I wonder what the cops thought when they saw this."

"Probably that Richie was just being Richie," Chandra said.

"And it doesn't mean Dino's not right," I told them and reminded myself. "If Richie mistook Dino for someone else—" I clamped my lips shut before Chandra could start in on another body-double theory, and while I was at it, I took out my phone and snapped a picture of the flyer.

It is best if I don't describe the bathroom. Trust me. I told Kate and Chandra we'd have to come back another day for a look through the storage room, and the three of us headed back downstairs.

I was nearly to the bottom of the stairway when my foot caught on a frayed corner of the beige carpet. I lurched and threw out a hand to catch myself. Good move as far as defying gravity went, but while it kept me from doing a header down the stairs, I couldn't hold on to that photograph of Alice and Margaret. As if it were happening in slow motion, I saw the framed picture pop out of my hand. It arced through the air and over the bannister, and the metal frame caught the light from a nearby window and flashed at me. Even before the photo hit the table next to the recliner, I had a bad feeling about the outcome.

The sound of cracking glass only served to reinforce my worries.

"Dang!" I made a face and clomped down the rest of the stairs. "I wanted to give that to Margaret and Alice."

"You still can." Kate jumped into action. There was an empty plastic grocery bag on the coffee table next to an open bag of potato chips. She retrieved it and, one by one, carefully picked up the pieces of the broken glass. "We'll buy a new frame and we can even get it matted. What do you think?"

I retrieved the picture and shook tiny bits of glass over the bag that Chandra held open.

"Hey, look!" She pointed to the back of the photograph. "There's something written there. In purple marker no less. Chocolate Alice and Vanilla Margaret. It's amazing, isn't it? Even back then, people were calling them that."

"Were they?" Thinking about it—and that purple marker I'd found up in Richie's bedroom—I turned the photograph over in my hands. "What good would a marker be after sitting around for something like forty years?" I asked no one in particular. "And why would someone keep it?"

"You mean—" Kate's words dissolved on the end of a little squeal. "Did you hear that?" She grabbed my arm with both hands and held on tight, her voice rising along with her panic. "Did you hear that scratching? There's a mouse in here. I know there's a mouse in here!"

"Shhh!" I gave my arm a shake to get her attention. I'd heard the noise, too, and with Kate mewling and Chandra looking like she was about to start, too, it was impossible to pinpoint where it had come from. "Quiet!" I said again when my first attempts fell on deaf ears. "Listen."

We did.

The noise came from somewhere close, but Kate was wrong about one thing. It wasn't as much a scratching as it was a scraping. As if someone had taken a piece of metal and was tapping with it. Like at the door.

I swung my gaze that way just in time to see a shadow darken the window in the front door.

"Shhhh! Quiet." I hoped my harsh whisper was louder than my suddenly hammering heart. "Don't move! Somebody's trying to break into the house!"

❮ 11 ❯

I've been called a lot of things in my life.
   Cautious has never been one of them.

   Oh, it's not like I didn't want to stand there holding my breath and afraid to move, just like Kate and Chandra. In fact, I knew beyond a shadow of a doubt that it was the smart thing to do. My drumming heartbeat told me so. My quick, shallow breaths confirmed it. Grabbing Kate with one hand and Chandra with the other and heading for the back door also crossed my mind.

   But hey, what can I say? Anger poured through my bloodstream like lava off a Hawaiian volcano, and I knew exactly why. Whoever we saw silhouetted against the curtain-covered glass on the front door window was working hard at jimmying the lock in order to violate Richie's personal space, not to mention Margaret's and Alice's. By trying to break in, that person was also threatening me and my friends.

Cautious? I don't think so.

Not when I had the element of surprise working in my favor.

Before I could talk myself out of what I probably shouldn't have talked myself into in the first place, I marched over to the door, grabbed the knob, and yanked.

I'm not sure who was more surprised to see who.

My mouth open, I stared at Boyz 'n Funk's number one fan, Tiffany Hollister.

Her mouth open, she squealed and tucked her right hand behind her back. Yeah, like I hadn't already seen the metal rasp she'd been using to work on the lock.

Since I was pretty sure she was all set to turn tail and run, I grabbed her arm, hauled her into the house, and slammed the door closed behind her.

"You should have checked, Tiffany. The door wasn't even locked. Explain what you were up to," I demanded.

"I . . . but . . . I . . ."

I am not a violent person, but I will admit that the thought of giving her a good, hard slap in the face crossed my mind. Like a scene in a black-and-white noir detective flick. Maybe then, like in those old movies, she'd start singing like a bird instead of flapping her jaws and stammering.

"What are you doing here, Tiffany?" I asked again, and when she didn't answer quickly enough to satisfy me, I adjusted my glasses on the bridge of my nose and stepped forward so that my sneakers were toe-to-toe with her pink jelly shoes. "Why were you trying to break in?"

"Me?" Tiffany squeaked the word and glanced from me, to Kate, to Chandra, and back to me. Whatever else I thought about the woman and her questionable taste in clothing and music, I had to admit that after the initial shock she was pretty fast on her feet. "I . . . I could ask you . . . you guys the same thing," she said, her voice rough with false bravado. "What are you doing here? Why did you break in?"

I reached into my pocket for the kittycat keychain and dangled it in front of Tiffany's nose. It was kind of fun to see her have to look cross-eyed at it. "Permission," I said, and yes, I will admit I allowed myself the superior little smile that should have told Tiffany she was messing with the wrong woman. If she was smart, she'd pay attention. "Permission from the homeowner. Which, since you've still got that file in your hands . . ." Before she could decide to do something with it that she shouldn't, I reached around Tiffany, snatched the metal file out of her hand, and tossed it on the coffee table. "I'm thinking you don't have the same permission."

With her head high, Chandra stepped forward. "We're here helping with clean-up."

"Because we're personal friends of the women who own this place," Kate added.

Not to be outdone, Tiffany lifted her chin. It might have been a more effective and far more defiant stance if not for the fact that her bottom lip wobbled. "I . . . I just had to see the house, that's all. I had to check things out. You know, on account of how Richie Trayton Monroe lived here."

"Trayton. Yeah," Chandra said. "Yeah, that was Richie's middle name. Back in elementary school, we used to tease

157

him about what a weird name it was. He always said it was a family name, that he was named after some great-great-grandfather or something."

Tiffany nodded. "I wouldn't have known it was him. I mean, how could I? I wouldn't have made the connection except that the name was in the newspaper. You know, in the story about how he got murdered. They didn't just say Richie Monroe. That wouldn't have meant anything at all to me. They used his full name, Richie Trayton Monroe. And I mean, really, how many of those can there be in this world?"

She waited for an answer, and when none of us could give her one, Tiffany raised one pad-enhanced shoulder. She was wearing a white T-shirt with a picture of the Boyz on it, and even thirty years ago, fifty pounds lighter and with hair that didn't look like the color had been poured from a bottle, Dino was not my type. Her gesture made his face fold in on itself.

"I'm not getting it," I admitted, and I thought about inviting her to sit down and explain, then remembered this was Richie's place and we might encounter something we didn't want to on the upholstered furniture. "So Richie is Richie Trayton Monroe. So what?"

Her eyes wide with disbelief, Tiffany leaned forward. "So what? You're kidding me, right?"

I guess my blank expression said it all.

She sighed and I expected a wrist flip to go with it. Instead, Tiffany messed with one of the earrings she wore. It was shaped like a record and had five little metal people dangling from it. I can't say for sure, but I think she tugged Paul's leg.

She eyed us with suspicion. "None of you know the name Richie Trayton Monroe? You live here on the same island where he lived and you don't know the story?" She *harrumphed*, and something told me it wasn't as much a criticism of our grasp of the topic as it was a confirmation of something she thought she already knew. "Well, that proves it, doesn't it? That proves my theory. The creep was lying about everything the whole time!"

Which creep and what he'd been lying about remained a mystery.

And my head was starting to pound, besides.

I massaged the back of my neck with one hand. "Maybe you'd better start at the beginning," I suggested. "You heard about Richie's murder."

She nodded.

"And read that his middle name was Trayton."

Another nod.

"And that made you want to come here to his house because . . ." It was my turn to lean forward, silently urging her to finish the sentence.

"Because of the legend, of course!" This time, Tiffany provided the wrist flip to go with what was, apparently, a monumental statement, and when none of us got it, she screeched her frustration. "Come on outside," she said. "That's where I've got the scrapbook. That will explain everything."

I let Tiffany, Kate, and Chandra go first, then locked up the house before I walked out to where they waited near the golf cart Tiffany had parked in the driveway. There was a tote bag on the floor (need I mention it had the words Boyz 'n

Funk written across the front in purple glitter?), and she reached inside it and pulled out a scrapbook with a picture of the band taped to the front. Underneath the picture in black magic marker were the words *Volume 12, The Dark Days*.

"It's all in there," she said, poking the scrapbook in my direction. "Go ahead. Take a look."

I did.

I flipped through the pages, scanning rather than reading, and not sure if I was getting the message I was supposed to be getting, I looked up at Tiffany. "Richie Trayton Monroe, the guy they talk about in some of these old newspaper articles, he's the same as our Richie?"

One corner of Tiffany's mouth pulled thin. "Like I said, unless there are two . . ."

Kate had been reading over my shoulder. "And according to these articles, our Richie claimed he was the one who wrote some song called 'Ali, Ali, Free Bird.'"

"Some song?" We were, apparently, the three dumbest women on the face of the earth. At least that's what Tiffany's expression said. "'Ali' just happens to be the most popular song the Boyz ever recorded. The album it was on went platinum in less than a week, and 'Ali' was number one on the charts for a month."

Call me cynical, I could barely get the question out of my mouth. "And Richie wrote it?"

As if she'd bit a lemon, Tiffany's face puckered. "Richie claimed he wrote it. Don't you see?" She grabbed the scrapbook out of my hands and flipped through the pages, and when she found the one she was looking for, she tapped her finger against a yellowed newspaper article. "That's what the court case was all about. See, Richie and Dino, they were roommates at Bowling Green."

"Then they did know each other!" The words whooshed out of me along with a gasp of surprise. "Dino said he had no idea who Richie was."

"Well, what did you expect?" Tiffany emphasized the question with a click of her tongue. "After Dino's faith in mankind was destroyed by the evil ways of that slug, Richie Monroe—"

"Wait a minute! Wait a minute!" To get Tiffany's attention, Chandra waved her hands. The sun nearly brushed the horizon and it bathed the scenery around us with a soft, pink glow that boded well for next day's weather. Still, Chandra's face was as pale as a marshmallow. "Are you telling us that Richie was some kind of big-time songwriter? That he was . . ." She nearly choked on the word. "Famous?"

"Infamous," Tiffany insisted. "He wasn't famous for anything but being a no-good thief. See, Dino always swore he was the one who wrote 'Ali' during his first semester at Bowling Green. You know, when he roomed with that Richie." Her eyes narrowed to emphasize the *that*. "I mean, really, why would Dino lie about a thing like that? Have you seen the guy? He's hotter than a wildfire. And handsome. And the best singer on the entire planet. He doesn't need to lie about anything."

As much as I wanted to point out the flaws in her argument (the heck with logic, the thing about Dino being the best singer on the planet nearly sent me over the edge), I stuck to the subject. "So Dino says he wrote this song and—"

"And the band recorded it," Tiffany said. "The rest is music history. 'Ali' was an instant hit, and all of a sudden, Richie crawls out from under a rock and says Dino stole it from him." She snorted. "As if! Dino is hotter than a wildfire and—"

"And let me guess," I ventured. It was better than hearing the litany of Dino's superhero qualities one more time. "All this happened the fall when Richie was a freshman at Bowling Green."

"Awesome!" Tiffany gave me a thumbs-up. "Maybe you're not the cultural loser I thought you were. You actually know something about the history of the band."

"I know something about Richie," I said, and I didn't even bother to look at Tiffany when I did. Chandra and Kate were standing to my left and I glanced their way. "That explains why Richie came back from school."

"And why he was so upset when he did," Chandra added. "Even before his parents died."

"He was a changed person," Kate said. "That's what everyone says. He used to be fun and bright, and then when he came back to the island—"

"It couldn't have happened that way," Chandra chimed in. "Not unless something really big happened to change him. Something really bad. He might have been embarrassed if he tried to pull a fast one on Dino. He might have even felt a little guilty. But he wouldn't have become a hermit. He wouldn't have completely given up on life."

"Not unless he was bitter and depressed." I said. "But if Richie was telling the truth, if Dino stole the song that Richie wrote and Richie was disgraced and deeply hurt by what happened . . ." I thought of the guitar I'd seen upstairs on Richie's bed, and of the poster of Guillotine with the knife thrust through it. "No wonder Richie looked so upset when he saw Dino and the other guys get off the ferry the other night. He never dreamed he'd run into Dino again, especially not here on the island. And when he confronted Dino at my place the next day—"

"Dino claimed he didn't know who Richie was," Kate said.

"Well, of course he would say that." Tiffany plunged back into the conversation and slapped the scrapbook shut. "Richie and Dino were best friends back in college. You can imagine how Richie's betrayal broke Dino's heart. He's still psychologically scarred by the whole experience, poor darling. He had to say he didn't know Richie. To protect his psyche. He couldn't face the painful truth."

"That argument only works *if* Dino was the one who was betrayed," I suggested.

Tiffany went as still as stone and her voice was no more than a whisper. "If you're suggesting that Dino is lying, think again. Like I said, the case went to court. Richie lost."

"Beaten by the mega-group that made millions off the song he wrote." No, I didn't know this for a fact—at least not yet—but I followed where the logic led. "That would be no big surprise. Richie was a nobody. He didn't have the clout. He didn't have the pull. He didn't have the money it would take to hire some crackerjack team of attorneys to plead his case." Just thinking about how Richie might have been railroaded sent a chill across my shoulders and I shook it away.

"If you're so convinced that Richie lied and that Dino is as innocent as the driven snow, why do you care?" I asked Tiffany. "Why show up here at Richie's place and take the chance of being caught breaking and entering if you think Richie was just some kind of no-good scumbag?"

Tiffany's bottom lip trembled. "Don't you see? This whole story about Richie and how he tried to steal Dino's work and be as famous as Dino . . . it's been a stain on the Boyz's reputation all these years. Sure, Dino won his case in court, but there are still people who hear the story . . . like you"—she glared at me—"and question what happened. I thought if I looked around Richie's place, I might find something that would prove the truth once and for all, that Richie's been lying all these years, that he would do anything to hurt Dino and the boys."

"Like mess with the guillotine on stage the other night?" I suggested.

Tiffany's mouth twisted. "I wouldn't be surprised. Richie was a terrible person. He must have been. How else could he have even thought to besmirch the reputation of Boyz 'n Funk?"

Believe me, I was tempted to ask if she even knew what "besmirch" meant, and maybe even challenge her to spell it. I bit my tongue.

"If that Richie was the one who risked Dino's life with that stupid guillotine trick . . ." Tiffany's hands curled into fists. "It makes me so mad just thinking about it. Just thinking how, all those years ago, he cast a cloud of doubt over Dino and nearly broke his spirit. I swear, if I'd known Richie

Trayton Monroe was on this island when I got here . . . I swear, I would have killed him myself."

"Obviously when Richie said someone was out to get him, he wasn't kidding." We stayed around Richie's long enough to watch Tiffany drive away, then hung around a few minutes longer to make sure she didn't double back, and now we were back in my SUV. Since I knew it was what we were all thinking anyway, I threw out the comment. "Now we can add Tiffany to our list of suspects."

Kate was in the passenger seat and she tapped a finger against her chin. "She was on the island on Wednesday night. We know that for sure. We all saw her in the park on Monday night when Guillotine got off the ferry."

"And Dino was on the island when Richie died, too," Chandra said from the backseat. "And now we know there was a connection between Richie and Dino, and not a good one."

"And Mike and Gordon both have motive, and they were here on the island, too," I added. I wished I hadn't. All this talk of all this many suspects gave me a headache.

"Speaking of Gordon," Chandra called out. "Look! There he is going into his cottage."

Luckily, I have good reflexes. Though we were already past the little green cottage that Chandra pointed to, I slammed on the brakes, did a U-turn, and cruised to a stop in front of Gordon's. There was a giant wooden fish out front next to the mailbox and an old fishing net draped across the lintel above the front door that we'd just seen Gordon shut behind him.

"What are you going to do? Are you going to interrogate him?" Kate asked, and I didn't know why she was whispering since we were still in the SUV and Gordon was inside the cottage.

"I'm just going to ask . . . you know." I took my time getting out from behind the steering wheel. Since I had no idea what I was going to ask Gordon, it bought me a little time and (maybe) made me look a little less like I was flying by the seat of my pants. Though the League of Literary Ladies technically had no hierarchy—or no formal organization at all, for that matter—Chandra liked to point out time and again that I was "the brains of the operation." Every once in a while, I felt that I actually had to act like it.

Too bad I was no closer to knowing what words were going to pop out of my mouth when I knocked on Gordon's front door.

The curtains on the front window of the cottage were closed tight. So were the windows. At the same time I found myself thinking that was a shame since a pleasant breeze blew over the lake and Gordon was missing out on it, I saw the mini-blinds behind one curtain twitch. A moment later, Gordon opened the door just a crack and poked out his head.

"Ladies! What a surprise to see you." The way Gordon said it, I couldn't tell if it was a good surprise or a bad one. The way he kept the door open just a smidgen, I wondered what we'd interrupted. "You're not going to the park for the high school band concert this evening?"

"We're on our way there now," I said, and it wasn't exactly a lie since I was planning to ask Kate and Chandra if they wouldn't mind stopping at the park on our way back to the B and B. "We saw you as we drove by and we just thought we'd stop in and say hello."

"That's really . . ." Gordon was not an especially small man, yet in one smooth move, he managed to slip out of the door without opening it any farther and closed it behind him. "That's really nice of you," he said, his smile just a little too forced. "I'm going to be heading over to the park in a couple minutes, too."

"We could give you a ride," Chandra offered.

"Even if you're not ready at this moment," Kate said. "We don't mind waiting."

"That's really very generous." Gordon raked a hand through his salt-and-pepper hair. Had this been a normal conversation with just about anyone else on the island (minus that list of suspects, of course), I would have worried that we came across as three pushy women. But this wasn't a normal conversation. And Gordon wasn't just anyone. Like so many of the others on our suspect radar, Gordon had been wronged by Richie, and he'd been rightfully angry. Angry enough to kill? That, of course, was the question, and until I had the answer, I had every right to be suspicious of everything Gordon said and everything he did.

The fact that he looked way too nervous didn't help.

Before he could cook up an excuse to get rid of us, I decided to head him off at the pass. "We were actually just on our way back from Richie's," I told him. "We're helping Margaret and Alice clean out the place."

Gordon shook his head. "Richie. Poor kid. A shame that sort of thing happens to anyone."

I drew a deep breath and plunged right in. "Especially since there was no way he could have had time to pay you for the damage he did to your boat the other night."

Gordon waved away my concern. "That's what insurance is for."

"But you must have been mad." Chandra, never the one to go for subtle. "I mean, Richie was being Richie and, rest his soul, Richie could be the most annoying person on the face of the earth!"

"It wasn't that big a deal," Gordon assured us. "Now if you ladies will excuse me." He stepped back toward the house and put a hand on the door but didn't open it. "I've got to get dressed and get over to the park. We're taking a first look at all the Dickens impersonators tonight, you know. See you there!"

There was no use trying to stall.

That didn't mean I didn't notice that Gordon never even touched the doorknob to go back inside until we were almost all the way to the SUV.

That just happened to be the same moment we saw Dickens imposter number three, Mason Burke, step out of the cottage next door.

We waved, and Burke hurried over. It looked like he was more than ready for his first appearance in front of the Bastille Day crowds that evening; his suit was freshly pressed, his plaid vest was dashing, and the gold chain on his pocket watch winked in the last of the sunlight.

"I do hope you'll be at the park this evening," he said. "I'm on my way there now."

"I've got the car." I pointed even though, since we were standing almost right next to it, I didn't really need to. "If you'd like us to drive your wife to the park, we'd be happy to help."

Burke's expression went blank. It only lasted a nanosecond, then he shook his head and laughed. "Very kind of you. But she's decided to stay back. She's saving her energy—and her ankle—for the big event on Sunday." He tipped his top hat. "Good evening, ladies."

It wasn't until he had sauntered up the road and I turned to get into the SUV that I realized that while we were busy talking to Mason, Gordon Hunter had slipped back into his closed-up, curtains-shut, blinds-down house.

❖ 12 ❖

Here's the thing about checking out Dickens imperson-ators during intermission at a band concert—it's not easy.

I mean with people milling all around the gazebo in the park where the impersonators were scheduled to line up.

And kids tossing Frisbees.

And folks calling to each other and laughing, and a couple college kids carrying on over near the fountain (which Hank put a stop to practically before it got started).

The fact that I'm short didn't help, either.

I stood on tiptoe and craned my neck, and when that didn't work, I told Chandra and Kate I'd be right back (with all the commotion, I don't think either one of them heard me) and elbowed my way through to the front of the crowd.

I mean, really, it's not like the folks who packed the park were hog-wild to see the Dickens impersonators, right?

Right.

Turns out the crush near the front of the gazebo had less to do with Dickens than it did with dining.

Mike's ice cream cart was set up near one of the two entrances to the octagonal-shaped gazebo and a line snaked over to him that stretched out all the way to the public bathhouse.

Not to be outdone, the hot dog seller positioned his cart nearby, and apparently the cotton candy guy caught on, too, to the old wisdom of location, location, location. I had to squeeze by him and the eight gazillion kids lined up in front of his cart before I could even get close to the gazebo.

Why did I care so much?

Well, it was supposed to be a secret, but I suppose it's safe now to spill the beans. See, I was one of the Dickens judges.

Yes, I know, this seems a little out of character for a B and B proprietor, but apparently Marianne Littlejohn, our town librarian, had somehow caught wind of the fact that I'd once mentioned to the League that I was a former English major. When it came to qualifications, that was good enough for Marianne, and I was drafted. As for accepting, it was that or cause something that might be too near a scene and draw too much attention to myself if I dug in my heels and refused to cooperate.

So judge I was. And though I'd already met three of the impersonators, even I didn't know if there were more.

I found out soon enough.

Just as I got to the front of the crowd, Gordon stepped up to the microphone looking far more relaxed and far less edgy than he'd looked back at his cottage. He called Charles Dickens to the gazebo and, one by one, like a scene out of some strange movie or some even weirder dream, the Dickenses materialized out of the crowd.

Ashburn was first. Didn't it figure. Shoes aside, his costume was perfection and his attitude, as annoying as all get-out back at the B and B, was perfect for the occasion. Gregarious and just the slightest bit impressed with himself. I'd read enough about Dickens (the real Dickens) to know he enjoyed his fame, and I had to give Ashburn credit. The smile, the wave, the slight bow toward the ladies . . . he had it all going for him.

But then, so did Drake.

He was the next one to make it to the gazebo and his mannerisms were a perfect mirror of Ashburn's. If I was judging on looks alone—and I wasn't, remember; there was still the big trivia contest on Sunday afternoon—I honestly wouldn't have known which one to pick.

Then there was Mason Burke, of course, looking as dapper as he had when I'd last seen him at the cottage where he was staying over near Gordon Hunter's. His costume was perfection. His style . . . er . . . he didn't have the panache of either Ashburn or Drake, but hey, ask the woman who'd had to listen to them squabble these last few days. Panache isn't everything.

As I suspected, there were a few other contestants, too. One was a woman, and I had to give her big points for pulling off the transformation. From the hair she had rolled into a tight bun and tucked under her top hat to a suit that fit her to perfection and even a silver-tipped cane, she more than passed for a Victorian gentleman.

As for the last two contestants . . . even now, I cringe thinking about them. At the same time I have to smile. Tyler and Max were college students who freely admitted to the crowd that they were there for one reason and one reason alone: extra credit in their college English class. They wore beards printed and cut from paper, and glasses (which, as far as I could remember, Dickens didn't wear) twisted out of pipe cleaners. As for the denim shorts and T-shirts that featured a man sitting next to his severed head and the words, *Mostly, It was the Worst of Times* . . . hey, their outfits might not be authentic, but I had to give them big points for trying.

With our first look at the contestants over, Gordon called the high school band up for the second half of the show, and I turned to head back to where I had left Kate and Chandra. Alice Defarge was right behind me.

"Enjoying the concert?" I asked her.

By this time the sun had long since set and Alice's eyes twinkled like the dome of stars above our heads. "It's wonderful, isn't it? I was just telling Margaret . . ." Though I never caught a glimpse of her, Alice obviously knew exactly where her sister was standing in the sea of people because she looked across the park and waved. "I was just telling her that we need to do this sort of thing more often. An old-fashioned band concert. What fun!"

The band regrouped under the gazebo and Gordon walked by. "Good evening, ladies." His expression was stony. "Nice to see you again, Bea," he said before he dashed off.

"Again?" Alice watched him go. "You two best friends?"

I knew she was kidding so I laughed. "Hardly. But we stopped to say hello to Gordon earlier this evening on our way back from Richie's." I knew I didn't need to explain. Something told me the Defarge sisters shared everything—well, maybe not critiques of their knitting skills or love lives—and I knew Margaret would have already told Alice all about how we'd offered to clean up the house. "He wasn't very friendly."

"Gordon, you mean? Well, of course you do." Alice shook her shoulders. "You couldn't be talking about Richie, could you? Then again, Richie and Gordon . . . well, I guess it's only natural I'd think of the two of them together. I mean, after what Margaret and I . . . after what we saw the other night."

Whatever she was talking about, it couldn't have had anything to do with Richie's murder. Could it? I knew it was impossible. If Alice knew anything that would help with the official investigation, she surely would have told Hank. Still, there was something about the way she said those words—*what we saw the other night*—that sent a tingle of anticipation through me.

Apparently, Alice knew it. She raised her eyebrows and nodded. "We were out for a spin in our golf cart. Sunday night. Late. You know, just to get a little fresh air and because we knew it was going to be a busy and crowded week. How Margaret and I do love the peace and quiet of the island at night! No matter." She clutched her hands at her waist. "We just happened to go by Gordon's and there he was with Richie. They were unloading a van in front of Gordon's place."

"Sunday night? That was the day Richie damaged Gordon's boat, right?"

"Exactly what I thought." Alice put a hand on my arm. "It was dark, and we couldn't see clearly, at least not without stopping the golf cart and gawking. And you know me and Margaret, when it comes to our snooping, we're way more professional than that. So we couldn't tell exactly, but it looked as if they were unloading boxes and carrying them into Gordon's cottage."

"Gordon must have had to get his things off the boat, right? I mean, after it was damaged. They would have needed to clean it out and—"

"Oh yes, I suspect that's exactly what it was." Alice stepped back into the crowd. "Gordon was so angry at Richie for what Richie did to the boat, I bet he made poor Richie move all those boxes and never paid him a dime!"

We didn't hang around for the rest of the band concert. It had been a long day, and I had a lot to think about. I dropped off Kate and Chandra, but the moment I pulled into the driveway of the B and B and saw Tiffany and her gang of Boyz 'n Funk worshipers across the street listening to the not-so-melodic strains of Guillotine coming out of the garage where I'd let the band set up to rehearse, I knew thinking would not be on my agenda, at least not until eleven o'clock (the official turn-off-all-loud-music-and-TV time at Bea & Bees) rolled around.

I parked the SUV and tucked my keys in my pocket. If I was looking for peace and quiet, I wouldn't find it in my own home for at least another hour. Until then . . .

I ambled down the driveway and turned right, away from the house and from the direction of all the activity downtown. A nice, quiet walk and some time to clear my head was exactly what I needed, to a part of the island where there were no concerts, no rock bands, and far fewer weekend partiers.

A minute in, and my heartbeat ratcheted back and my breathing slowed.

Two minutes, and the tightness that I hadn't realized had been building in my shoulders eased.

Three, and I was far enough from the house for the sounds of croaking frogs and chirping crickets to replace the racket of pounding bass and Dino's wailing.

Life might not be perfect, but for these few minutes, it was as good as it could get, and I smiled to myself, enjoying every single moment while I let my mind work over everything I'd learned that day about Richie, Richie's friends, and Richie's many, many enemies.

I was somewhere between considering Mike's motives and remembering how good the salted caramel ice cream tasted when I heard sounds behind me and spun around.

The shuffle of feet.

The snap of a twig.

Someone following me.

Except . . . I peered into the darkness . . . there wasn't a soul on the empty road behind me.

And I was being way too jumpy for my own good.

I took a deep breath, squared my shoulders, and turned around to continue on my way. There was a cross street coming up on my right, and I could head that way, then loop around and behind the B and B and Chandra's house, then on to another road where I could hang another right and then another, and be back home. It would take only another ten minutes or so to complete the circuit, and if I could get my blood pressure to settle down after that split second of thinking I wasn't alone, that was ten minutes I could use to think about the investigation.

Good advice, but still, I picked up the pace a bit and soon found myself in front of a cottage where row upon row of twinkly solar lights outlined the roofline and the windows and the deck out back. Bathed in the gentle glow, I forced myself to slow down and enjoy the feel of the lake breeze against my skin. I'd lived in New York City for years, right? And I'd walked all over the city at all hours, I reminded myself. If I could do it there, I certainly could do it here on South Bass, the Eden of Lake Erie. I could. I would. I—

A hand came down on my arm and I didn't so much scream as I let out a screech that could probably be heard by dogs ten miles away. Everything I'd learned in the self-defense classes I'd taken back in New York kicked in and I spun, pushed against the person behind me as hard as I could, and yelled, "Back off!"

Self-defense maneuvers.

A good thing.

Except they left a skinny woman I'd never seen before staggering back, her mouth open in astonishment and her eyes wide with terror.

Those eyes . . . although I'd already stepped up to get close when I shoved her, I moved even closer for a better look. Her eyes were small and dark. They were also crossed.

177

"Hey!" I remembered my conversation with Margaret on regatta day at the same time I grabbed the stranger's arm before she could collapse in the street. "You're Richie's girlfriend!"

The winking lights flashed against a face that was pinched and too angular to ever be considered pretty. Her nose was long and thin.

"I . . . I . . ." I bet there wasn't much color in the woman's face to begin with, but the white LED lights only made the pallor worse. She reminded me of those pale fish that live way down deep in the ocean. "Sorry." She blinked and hugged her arms around herself. "I didn't wanna scare you."

"Well, you did. And I didn't mean to scare you, either, it's just that—"

"I shoulda said something." It was plenty warm out, but she chafed her hands up and down her arms. "I just didn't know what to say and I knew I shouldn't bother you, but I knew I had to, like, talk to you or somethin'. I was waitin' for you back at your house and then you showed up, but then you walked away and, well . . . I shoulda said somethin'.'"

"It's okay." It wasn't. Not completely. My heart still jack-hammered against my ribs and my brain jumped to those horrible months back in New York when a stalker made my life a living hell. "What can I do for you?"

Instinctively, I knew her shrug didn't mean she didn't know what she wanted. It meant she wasn't sure how to explain.

I guess the fact that I'd come across as a paranoid—and dangerous—New Yorker didn't help.

I offered a smile. "It's been such a busy week already, I just wanted to get some air. You want to walk with me?"

She nodded and fell into step beside me.

"We haven't met," I said.

"But you called me Richie's girlfriend."

"But I don't know your name."

"Rosalee."

"It's nice to meet you, Rosalee. I hear you work at the hotel."

I think she nodded. Since we were already past the house with the soft lighting, it was a little hard to tell.

"Have you worked there long?"

"Last summer," she said. "And the summer before."

"And is that when you met Richie?"

Another nod, and don't think I failed to notice that her chin quivered.

"It's hard." I didn't need to tell her, but she did need to know that I understood a little of what she was going through. "You must miss him."

"We wasn't serious or nothing. I mean, every year after the summer, I went back to Sandusky where I'm from and then me and Richie, we'd hardly ever even talked to each other or anything. But then when I came back up here the next summer . . ."

I let her gather her thoughts while we walked along in silence past rows of well-tended summer cottages.

"We'd hang out. You know?" Rosalee finally said. "Not like all the time or anything. I mean, it's not like we were living together. Richie was just . . ." I gave her a sidelong look just in time to see her raise her scrawny shoulders. "Sometimes it was hard to talk to him."

"Still, you kept up a relationship all this time."

Rosalee shook her head. "He'd get real quiet sometimes. And sometimes he'd complain, you know, about how life didn't treat him so fair. But most of the time, Richie, he was okay. I mean, like when we stopped at a bar, he paid for my beers."

"Do you have a theory about why someone killed him?" I asked.

Rosalee stopped walking and shoved her hands into the pockets of her black shorts. "Richie sometimes pissed people off. I guess you probably know that. But he wasn't a bad guy. He never wanted to hurt anybody, it was just that sometimes, well . . . sometimes Richie had some real bad luck."

So did Mike Lawrence and Dan Peebles and Gordon Hunter. All because of Richie. This wasn't the time to mention it. "Who do you think killed him?" I asked her.

"I dunno." Rosalee turned away as if that would keep me from seeing her brush her hands across her cheeks. "But who killed him, that's what I come to talk to you about. That's why I was waiting for you and why I followed you. The girls over at the hotel, they talk, you know. And they was saying that you and your friends, they told me you solved a murder a couple months ago, and I thought if you could do it then, maybe you could do it again and, you know, figure out what happened to Richie."

"That's what the police are for."

"The police, they don't care. I mean, not really. Richie was just Richie and everybody thought he was a loser. But he wasn't. He was just . . ." Thinking, she pressed her lips together. "Richie was kind of depressed sometimes. He used to say he could have been somebody but that didn't work out because some guy, he stole what should have been Richie's. I never told him, but I always thought that sounded a little crazy."

"Maybe not." I wasn't prepared to tell Rosalee everything I'd learned from Tiffany about the court case that had once pitted Richie against Dino, not until I had a chance to fact check. "Is there anything else you can tell me that might help?"

She hung her head.

"How about explaining that fight you and Richie had outside the hotel the other day."

Rosalee's head shot up. "Who says?"

"Does it matter?"

She propped her fists on her hips. "Hell, yes, it matters 'cause it ain't true, and anyone who says it is, that person is lying. So what, you listened to that lie and now you think I was mad at Richie? That I had something to do with killing him?"

"Did you?"

Instead of answering, Rosalee kicked a stone and sent it skittering to the side of the road. "I came to talk to you to ask for your help," she said. "But you're just like all the rest of them. You figure people like Richie and me, we're not worth helping, that we don't matter."

Before I could tell her she was wrong, Rosalee stalked back the way we came and disappeared into the darkness.

"So much for that line of the investigation," I grumbled to myself.

But don't think I was about to give up. Either Rosalee was lying about the fight she had with Richie, or Margaret was mistaken about what she and Alice saw. Guess which I was betting on?

I added Rosalee to the list of people I'd need to pay more attention to and hung a right to walk down the street that would take me behind the B and B.

"You didn't have a fight, huh?" I asked myself, thinking about what Rosalee had told me. "That was a whole lot of anger for somebody who claims she and Richie were tight when he died."

That will teach me to talk to myself.

If I would have shut up, maybe I would have heard the noise behind me sooner.

Footsteps against the pavement.

I stopped and blew out a breath of exasperation. "Rosalee," I called out without bothering to turn around, "if you're not going to be level with me, don't even bother following me."

"How about if I'm not Rosalee?"

A man's voice brought me spinning around. If my heart wasn't pounding hard enough to deafen me, I would have realized who it was right away.

"Levi!" I pressed a hand to my chest and relief washed over me. At least until I took a second to assess the situation. "Why are you following me?"

In the waxy light of the crescent moon, his hair gleamed like silver. "I came over to the B and B to see you just as you were walking away from the place. And then I saw that woman follow you. I thought—"

"That I can't protect myself from skinny hotel maids?"

I didn't say it to make him smile, and when he did, I

realized my teeth were clenched. "I'm sure you can protect yourself."

"But you followed me anyway."

Rather than explain, he started walking, and since I wouldn't be happy until he explained himself, I did, too.

"You've been poking your nose into Richie's murder," Levi said, as casual as can be.

"Not exactly poking. More like—"

"Poking."

Honestly, I thought about cutting him off at the knees right then and there, turning on my heels and heading back the way I'd come, but I knew I was closer to home in this direction than I would be if I headed back. "This sounds like a conversation we've already had," I reminded him.

"You apparently weren't listening last time."

I drew in a lungful of air big enough to supply all the wind I needed to level him, but Levi never gave me a chance.

"What you're doing is dangerous," he said.

"I'm being careful."

"Not careful enough to realize Rosalee was following you."

"Or that you were following both of us."

My sarcasm was lost on him. We made the right turn at the street that would take us alongside Chandra's house. "It's not smart," he said, and added quickly, "which isn't to say you're not smart."

"Just that I'm not acting smart."

"You said it, not me."

We walked a little more, and rather than debate what I

figured wasn't worth debating anyway, I decided to catch him off guard. "Why aren't you at the bar?" I asked him.

We were nearing Chandra's and the colored Christmas lights that criss-crossed over her patio threw a rainbow against Levi's face. "If I tell you we weren't busy you're just going to tell me I'm wrong."

"Then tell me the truth instead."

"The truth . . ." We made the last of our right-hand turns and we were back on my street now. There was no music coming from the garage, and since apparently the Boyz had called it a day, no fan club panting with every note, and for this I was grateful. "The truth is that the bar is open again, but Mike had things under control. The rest of the truth is that I'd hate to see something happen to you," Levi said.

"And you think that's a possibility because . . ."

"Because somebody killed Richie, and whoever that somebody is, he's not going to like you—"

"Poking my nose where it doesn't belong. Yeah, you said that already." We got to the B and B and I was surprised when Levi headed up the front walk with me. "The cops are looking into Richie's murder. Do you follow them around, too, and tell them what they're doing is dangerous?"

It wasn't much of an argument, but that didn't mean he had to grin. "That's their job."

"And mine is—"

"It's supposed to be running this place. Which sounds nice and normal and safe, and if you'd just do what you're supposed to be doing and not—"

"Poke my nose where it doesn't belong."

"Yeah."

When had we stopped and faced off across the slate sidewalk like two SmackDown opponents? And when had I propped my fists on my hips?

I didn't know, and right about then, I didn't much care. My blood pounded in my temples when I demanded, "You want to explain why it's any of your business?"

Levi stopped himself from replying, but just barely. That didn't keep a noise that sounded like a bear's grumble from rising in his throat.

He didn't say a thing. In fact, all he did was grab me by the shoulders and kiss me so long and hard, my toes curled.

I think when he was done he turned and walked back toward town. Then again, it was a little tough to tell, what with my glasses all steamed up.

« 13 »

I have an excellent imagination.
    This can be a real asset. Especially when I'm trying to
figure out motive and opportunity and who's who when it
comes to murder investigations.

    And when that same imagination keeps me up all night
reliving that kiss from Levi over and over again . . .

    Well, let's just say that when Chandra showed up at my
back door bright and early the next morning, I was not the
happiest—or the most well-rested—of campers.

    "Pokeberry," was the first word that came out of her
mouth, and as strange as it seems, this was actually something of a relief. Had Chandra been witness to what happened between me and Levi the night before, no doubt she
would have led with that, as well as a billion questions about

how it felt and what I thought and what the heck I was going to do now that he'd taken the first step.

Believe me, I didn't need someone asking me the same questions I'd been asking myself all night.

"Pokeberry," she said again when all I did was attempt to shake the cobwebs from my brain and ignore the thrilling, tingling, tantalizing sensations that zipped through my bloodstream when I thought about Levi. Fortunately, while I was trying to get my act together, I happened to look over her shoulder and see Hank's SUV pull away from her house. Thus, her single-word greeting made a whole lot more sense.

"Pokeberry," I repeated. "They finally determined that's the poison the killer used."

Her mouth fell open. "You must be psychic. How did you know—"

I pointed out the window, and when Chandra turned and saw Hank's patrol car, she barked out a laugh. "So I guess you know what we were talking about," she said.

What Chandra and Hank had been talking about was a much safer and potentially less-embarrassing topic than what they'd been doing. I knew it, and I stuck to it. "Pokeberry grows wild just about everywhere, including all over the island. It would have been a cinch for the killer to dig up a root."

"The root . . ." Thinking, Chandra narrowed her eyes and scrunched up her nose. "Hank says it's the most poisonous part of the pokeberry plant. How did you know that?"

I pulled out my all-purpose answer to so many questions. "I must have read it somewhere."

"Yeah! That's it!" Like what I'd said was some great

revelation, she pointed a finger at me. "It was in that FX O'Grady book, the one about the Victorian undertaker who poisons people with pokeberry, then takes the corpses and—"

"That's enough!" I held up one hand to stop her in her tracks. "Wherever I read it, all I know is that all the parts of the pokeberry plant are poisonous, but the root is the most lethal part."

She nodded. "Exactly what Hank said."

"Of course, the killer could have used the berries, too," I said, doing some quick mental calculations. "It would take a lot of them to actually kill an adult, but if the killer gave Richie a drink and used the berries for red coloring, then spiked it further with pokeberry root . . ." It made perfect, if perverted, sense. "Some of the symptoms of pokeberry poisoning aren't all that different from what Richie would have been feeling if he had too much to drink. He probably never knew what hit him until it was already too late."

Chandra shuffled past me and went right for the pot of coffee I'd just brewed. "It's hard to believe anyone could be evil enough to do that, put poison in a drink, then stand back and watch somebody gulp it down."

"That's the whole point. I mean, about poisoners. A poisoner is a hands-off kind of killer. He wants the victim to die, but he doesn't have the guts to just step right up and make it happen. You know, like with a gun or a knife. So he takes the chicken's way out. He administers the poison, then, just like you said, he lets the poison do the work and never gets his hands dirty."

Over her coffee mug, I saw the horror in Chandra's eyes. "You know an awful lot about poisoners."

I waved away the information as insignificant. "Like I said, I read it all somewhere. They say poisoners are highly intelligent. You know, because they have to plan the murder and get the poison ready and somehow slip it to the victim when no one's looking. They're also supposed to be creative and detailed and good at pretending to be someone they're not."

Chandra's lips puckered. "You mean like somebody in disguise?"

"I mean like somebody pretended to be Richie's friend and probably offered to buy him a few drinks. With all the commotion in the bar the other night, it would have been easy for the killer to slip the pokeberry into Richie's drink on the way back from the bar and no one ever would have noticed. Then . . ."

"Yeah, then . . ." Chandra washed away the thought with a long drink of French roast, and since I had a loaf of brioche out for any early risers who might show up before the designated nine o'clock breakfast, she cut off a slice and took a bite. "So what are we going to do?" she asked.

I told her I was going to wait around until nine so I could serve breakfast, then I was going downtown.

Since Chandra's mouth was full, what she said next came out sounding like, "Thwhe wavi?" She took a drink of coffee to wash down the brioche and said, "To see Levi?" Then before I could tell her she was nuts, she added, "Don't deny it! I saw him here last night. After you dropped me off. Obviously, he was waiting for you to get home."

Though she tried to make it look oh so casual, Chandra's eyes were wide and her cheeks were pink when she glanced toward the closed door to my private rooms. Her voice was singsong when she said, "To tell the truth, I was kind of thinking that maybe Levi would still be here."

"You thought wrong. As a matter of fact, he never came inside the house."

She plunked her coffee mug down on the black granite counter top. "Bea, why don't you two just admit—"

"Are you busy this morning?"

Chandra didn't expect the abrupt change of subject, which was the only reason she blurted out that she wasn't.

"Great. Good." I spun around and went right to the back door. "You'll find everything you need in the fridge. You're officially in charge of getting breakfast for my guests."

"But Bea . . ." She followed me as far as the back porch. "What are you going to do?"

"I'm going to go find out if the maids at the hotel take breaks during their shifts," I told her, and hurried down the steps before either she or my memories of what happened the night before could stop me. "And if they do take breaks, I'm going to find out if those breaks are long enough to give a person time to go over to Levi's and put pokeberries in a drink."

The most logical place to start, of course, was with Rosalee's supervisor, and as it turned out, the name tag on her blue scrubs said she was Hilda. Good thing, since she never introduced herself.

"Of course she worked on Wednesday night." Hilda's eyes were as gray as the hair she had scooped into a ponytail that hung halfway down her back. Her arms were beefy and her movements were as clipped as her words. Obviously nothing—and nobody—messed with Hilda's cleaning schedule. Especially when the nobody in question was a nobody who wanted to know about Rosalee's whereabouts on the night of the murder.

Hilda grabbed a pile of clean towels off the cart she'd been pushing down the third-floor hallway of the hotel right across from DeRivera Park and clutched them like there was no tomorrow. "It's summer." She didn't add *didn't you realize that, you idiot?* but then, she didn't have to. If a picture's worth a thousand words, a scathing looking is worth a million. "All my girls work seven days in the summer."

There was no use throwing logic into the mix and telling her I couldn't have known this. "So Rosalee *was* working last Wednesday night?"

Hilda leaned toward me, the effect not unlike a glacier slowly sliding forward and flattening everything in its path. She tapped her forehead with one finger. "Seven days. Get it? They work seven days."

"But not twenty-four seven. I don't care how good a cleaning person is, she couldn't possibly be here every day and work twelve hours or more."

One of Hilda's grizzled eyebrows shot up. The other sank low over her other eye.

"Of course you probably keep that kind of schedule," I said, because I'd obviously insulted her cleaning-lady honor. "But Rosalee—"

"Three to eleven." Hilda rapped her knuckles against the nearest door, called out, "Housekeeping," and stuck her key in the lock to open the door long before anyone had a chance to answer.

When she marched into the room, I took a step to follow her.

She stopped me in my tracks with one laser look.

I managed a smile that I'm pretty sure didn't fool her for a moment. It didn't fool me, either. Hilda made me shake in my shoes. "Rosalee worked three to eleven that night. That's very helpful. I just wondered . . . did she take a break anytime during her shift?"

When Hilda turned to face me, her shoulders filled the doorway. "Of course I let my girls take a break. What do you think I am, some kind of monster?"

By the time I was able to give voice to the lie that I did not, she'd already slammed the door in my face.

"Okay. Good. Fine." I drew in a breath and squared my shoulders, but it took a few moments for me to get myself moving. By the time I made it down to the end of the hallway, one of the room doors popped open and a woman wearing the same blue cleaning-lady scrubs poked her nose out the door.

"Is it safe to come out?" she asked me.

I glanced down the hallway at the towel cart and the closed door. "If you're talking about Hilda—"

"Hilda!" The woman raised her gaze to the ceiling in a silent prayer. "She sees me talking to you, she'll bite my head off and use it for a soccer ball."

I had an easy solution to that problem. I stepped inside the room and closed the door behind me.

This woman wore a name tag that told me she was Lucy. "I heard what you was sayin' to Hilda," she said, and even though we were alone in the room, she kept her voice down.

"You asked about Rosalee and what she was doin' the other night."

"Rosalee told me she worked on Wednesday night. I just needed confirmation, and I wondered if she took a break, maybe between eight and ten o'clock."

Lucy didn't ask why I cared; she simply nodded. She had a head of glossy dark curls and they bounced along to the beat. "We took two breaks that night. You know, so we could go out back and have a smoke."

"We . . ." I considered what this might mean. "You and Rosalee took your breaks together?"

Another nod. "So now you know, and you don't have to worry about it."

I almost asked what she was talking about, but Lucy didn't give me a chance. She grinned. "People talk," she said, "and Hilda . . ." She rolled her eyes. "That woman's so busy being mean, she don't pay attention to nothin' and nobody. But I knew who you were as soon as I saw you. You're that lady from the B and B, and you want to know about Rosalee's breaks because you're investigating. It's just like on TV. You're checking to see if she had time to go over to that bar and kill Richie."

There was no use denying it, so I didn't even bother.

Lucy shook her head, and her curls danced in the other direction. "No way," she said. "No way Rosalee would ever kill Richie."

"She was in love with him?"

Lucy laughed, and when she realized she might have been too loud, she clapped a hand over her mouth. "Richie was hard to love," she mumbled from behind her hand, then slowly moved it away. "But him and Rosalee, they got along good enough. He was someone for her to talk to, you know?"

"Except I heard they'd been fighting lately. Could it have been about another woman?"

Lucy screwed up her face and waved a hand. "You're messin' with me, right? There isn't another woman on this island who would give Richie the time of day."

"So Rosalee wasn't mad at him?"

"When we got to work on Wednesday, Rosalee was talkin' about makin' him dinner on Saturday night. I don't know about you, girlfriend, but I wouldn't cook for no man who was cheatin' on me."

I wouldn't, either.

But that didn't prove a thing.

"So you and Rosalee . . ."

"We was together the whole time we was on our breaks on Wednesday night, and when we finished, Hilda had us foldin' towels down in the laundry room all frickin' night. Me and Rosalee, we were never out of each other's sight. Not all night long. So even if she wanted to kill Richie—and I'm telling you she didn't—there's no way she could have gone over to that bar and done it."

Believe it or not, when I left the hotel, I was actually encouraged. I'd eliminated Rosalee as a suspect and maybe now with one less person to worry about, I could start to line up what I knew about the rest of the people on the long, long list of Richie Monroe haters.

Apparently, the Universe was all about helping me out.

No sooner had I walked out of the hotel than I saw Mike sitting on a bench in the park across the street. I ducked to my right and made a wide arc down the sidewalk and across the street so I could close in on him before he could see me and decamp, but big surprise—when I got over to the park bench and caught his eye, Mike stood up.

And not like he was going to head for the hills.

More like he was being polite.

"I was just about to go over to the B and B to find you," he said.

Call me crazy, but this wasn't what I expected from a guy who pretty much told me he was going to sue the pants off me the last time we met.

Before I said anything like the "Who are you kidding?" that almost fell out of my mouth, I sized up both Mike and the ice cream cart that sat a few feet away in the shade of a tree.

He took a step toward me. "After the last time we talked, I know that sounds pretty weird."

"Yeah." I stood my ground. If there was some sort of make-peace scene about to unfold, I wanted to know it was genuine before I allowed myself to look too enthusiastic.

"Okay, all right." Mike rubbed his hands over his face. "I'm not the kind of guy who says he's sorry, but I know I came on a little strong last time I saw you. All that stuff about taking you to court—"

"You were kidding?"

"No." When my mouth fell open, he laughed. "What I mean is, I'd take anybody to court who went around telling lies about me. But as far as I know, you haven't done that. Not that I've heard, anyway. And really, it doesn't matter, because see, I realized I was going to have to apologize sooner or later, anyway, because . . ." Whatever was on his mind, it obviously wasn't easy to talk about. Mike pulled a face.

"I need your help," he said.

Before that "Who are you kidding?" could come boomeranging back, Mike walked over to the ice cream cart. It was a shiny silver cube about four feet high, and it consisted of the large freezer compartment where the ice cream was kept and another, much smaller compartment where Mike put change and stored the money people gave him for their purchases. He opened the smaller compartment and pulled out a single folded piece of paper.

"I found this," he said, and he handed me the paper. "Before I took it to the police I wanted to show it to you and get your reaction. You know." His shrug made it seem like it was no big deal. "On account of how people say you're pretty good at putting things together. I figured it was something you should see."

I took the paper out of his hands, unfolded it, and flinched. It was a detailed schematic of the guillotine used for Guillotine's not-so-successful magic trick. My head snapped up. "Are you telling me—"

"It was Richie's. And don't start asking why I kept it a secret or anything, because I didn't. I just didn't think anything of it. At least not at first. I was actually just going to throw it away. But see . . ." He came to stand at my side and pointed at the paper in my hands and the words written next to each part of the diabolical machine. "It's all labeled and it shows how everything works and what's connected to what. And I got to thinking that if Richie knew how the guillotine worked, he could have been the one who messed with it. You know, that night at the bar."

Oh, I knew, all right. Even with the gentle lapping of the waves from the lake across the street, the Jimmy Buffett music that bounced out of a nearby bar, and the delighted shouts of a couple of kids playing nearby, I swear I could still hear the sickening sound of the blade as it thunked through the watermelon. If I closed my eyes, I could still see that melon plunk to the stage, its red juice splashed all around.

I shivered and I didn't even care if Mike saw it. "Where'd you get this thing?" I asked him.

He walked around to the other side of the ice cream cart and opened the lid of the compartment where the frozen goodies were kept. "It was taped inside here," he said, and he stuck his hand to the right of the opening of the compartment and knocked against the top of the cart from the inside. "That's why I didn't see it before. I was cleaning the cart last night, and that's when I found it."

It's not that I didn't believe him; I'm just the kind of person who likes to verify this sort of thing for myself. And Mike didn't look especially inclined to back off so I ♥ could get close to the cart.

Good thing I'm small and agile.

I slipped between Mike and the ice cream cart and, following his lead, I stuck my arm into the freezer box and felt along what I guess I would call the ceiling of the inside of the cart. Slowly, I let my fingers work their way over the dimensions of a single sheet of paper, each side tacked down with tape that had left a tacky residue. Stuck up here the way it was, there was no way anyone would have ever seen the guillotine schematic.

"It's the perfect hiding place," I told Mike. "Richie wouldn't have had to worry that anyone was going to see it or—"

My fingers brushed over another sticky spot, and at the same time I wondered if my original theory was wrong and whatever had been taped in there was some weird size that wasn't the shape of a piece of paper. I again traced the outline of what must once have been attached there. No, I hadn't been wrong. There was one outline for the schematic, and a second one just to the right of it. This one wasn't nearly as big as the first. It was small and rectangular, and even if I hadn't seen Mike's face go ashen I would have asked, "What else was in here?"

"Nothing."

Good thing I can move pretty quick because I pulled my arm out of the freezer compartment just a nanosecond before he smacked the lid shut.

I warmed up my right arm by rubbing it with my left hand. "Come on, Mike. It was still all tacky where the tape was. Just like the other patch. Which means they were probably both put there around the same time. And probably both removed around the same time, too. Like last night."

He clamped his lips shut.

Really, I wasn't much in the mood for games. At least not games other people controlled. For my part, I decided to take a chance and go for broke with a little game of my own. Following a hunch and a mental image that sprang to my mind the moment I mapped out the shape of the second hidden paper, I slipped my purse off my shoulder, dropped it on the grass, and dug around inside for my wallet. When I found it, I pulled out a dollar bill and slapped it on top of the ice cream cart.

"Yay by yay," I said, holding apart thumb and forefinger to measure the bill. "Exactly the distance between those tape marks inside the cart. Apparently, Richie thought it was a good hiding place for more than just guillotine plans."

"So what?" Mike crossed his arms over his chest. "So what if there was some money in there? Richie Monroe destroyed my life. When he ruined my business, he didn't just hurt me; he hurt my wife and my kids, too. And maybe you don't understand because you don't have a family, but messing with my family . . . that's serious stuff. So what if I found a few measly thousand bucks in there? The way I figure it, he owed me."

"A few thousand." It was more than I expected and I let out a low whistle of amazement. "How many few?"

Mike bit his lower lip and I just about screamed.

"There's no use trying to stonewall me. You're going to have to tell Hank. You know that, Mike. And if nobody else claims the money and Hank figures out that it's not stolen or anything, you'll get to keep it. I don't know you well, but I've seen how hard you work. That tells me you're the kind of man who didn't sleep very well last night while you tried to convince yourself that you had every right to keep that money. Once you have the blessings of the authorities, you know you can rest easy again."

He puffed out a breath of annoyance. "I thought if I didn't tell anyone—"

"How much?" I asked him again.

Mike spit out the words, "Twelve thousand."

"Cash?"

He nodded. "A big, fat wad. I'll tell you what, you could have knocked me over with a feather, that's how surprised I was to find it."

"Then Richie wasn't just blowing smoke when he said he was coming into money and he was going to leave the island. It was the truth."

"And I'm a real sucker for telling you about it." Mike stuffed his hands in the pockets of his jeans. "My family could really use that money. And now—"

"Daddy!" Speaking of family, two small boys and a little girl squealed and called and ran across the park in our direction, a few feet ahead of the attractive blonde who was telling them to slow down and behave and not interrupt Daddy when he was working.

"It's okay." I turned and waved so she wouldn't worry about the kids.

They clustered around Mike.

"Can we have Popsicles?" the older of the two boys asked.

"Or ice cream?" the other one piped up. "Emma's feeling better today." He gave his sister a little push. "She ate cereal for breakfast and she didn't even throw up. I bet she could have ice cream and if she can, then we can, too."

I smiled down at the little girl who stood next to me. "Were you sick, Emma?" I asked her.

She looked at her dad and when he gave her the go-ahead that apparently indicated I wasn't a stranger to be avoided, she nodded. "I had to stay in bed. One, two, three days."

She held up the requisite number of fingers to prove it. "And when I really didn't feel good, Daddy had to come home from work to sit with me so Mommy could go to the store and get med'cine. But I'm better now and Daddy . . ." I would bet there wasn't a dad in the world who could resist those big, brown eyes. "I'd like strawberry, please!"

With a smile of surrender, Mike flipped open the freezer compartment and I stepped away. After all, my work there was done. In addition to finding out that Mike's alibi about leaving Levi's to go home to a sick child was true, I'd found out a couple other important things, too. Number one: it looked like Richie was the one who'd messed with the guillotine, and number two: he wasn't kidding when he said he could afford to leave the island.

Of course, that brought up a whole other question.

See, if Mike found the money inside the ice cream freezer, that meant Richie hid it there some time before he was killed. That was a no-brainer.

What took a little more thinking about was the fact that on the night he was murdered, Richie said he'd be leaving the island once he came into some money. Which meant he wasn't talking about the twelve thousand dollars he already had; he was talking about more.

And that, of course, left me wondering. Where had all the money come from? And what had Richie done to earn it?

❖ 14 ❖

So all right, I'd eliminated both Mike and Rosalee from my long list of suspects. Don't think that meant I was giving up on the others! Obviously, someone had killed Richie. Not so obviously (even to me), was why I was so hell-bent on finding out whodunnit.

To that end, I kept myself busy the rest of that Saturday. The cleaning crew was in, and I did what supervising was necessary. Since I'd contracted with the best cleaning service on the island and paid them a bundle, that wasn't much.

I ran interference between Guillotine—they were making final preparations for their concert in the park that night—and the throwback fans who kept vigil in front of the B and B, squealing like the teenyboppers they had been oh-so long before each and every time they caught a glimpse of one of the Boyz.

I made sure I had everything I needed for the next day's breakfast, and since it would officially be the end of the weekend and the last day of the Bastille celebration, I went whole hog. There would be lattes all around as well as banana-Nutella crepes. Yeah, I know, not technically French, but plenty showy and a good way to send off a houseful of guests who would (hopefully) be impressed enough to recommend Bea & Bees to their traveling friends.

I talked to Chandra, Kate, and Luella and told each one of them that I'd meet them at the park that evening in time for the big show. I avoided Levi when I saw him cruising down the snack food aisle at the grocery store because, well, heck, I had no idea what to say to the best kisser my lips had ever had the luck of running into. And besides, the way my heart pounded the moment I caught sight of him, I wasn't sure I could talk coherently anyway, and how would that look?

I prepared bills for everyone checking out the next day, helped Didi search when she misplaced the gauzy yellow scarf she wanted to wear to the concert that night (it had floated under the bed when she took it out of her suitcase), and watered all the flowerpots on the front porch. This, it should be noted, was not completely necessary since when I walked outside—with my cute watering can shaped like a gigantic bee in hand—I caught sight of the hindquarters of Jerry Garcia as he leaped over my porch railing. Good ol' Jerry, was up to his old tricks. He'd already watered my flowers for me.

Through it all, what I was really doing, of course, was biding my time.

As for what I was biding my time for . . .

By five o'clock, the Boyz had headed for the park, Dan Peebles and Didi had left for dinner, and Ashburn and Drake were on the front porch, peppering each other with Dickens questions and preening like pro wrestlers when one stumped the other.

As for me, I got ready for what I had planned. I donned a pair of black jeans (it was a sticky evening and far too hot for long pants, but in the name of an investigation, sacrifices must be made), a black T-shirt, and the scuffed sneakers that weren't nearly as bright and noticeable as my brand-spanking-new white ones. Though I wouldn't need it for a few more hours, I grabbed a small flashlight and tucked it into my pocket. As ready as I'd ever be, I went downtown to the park where, as promised, I met up with Chandra, Kate, and Luella. Just as the sun dipped below the western rim of the lake and I figured it was the right moment to slip away, I crossed my fingers behind my back and told them I was going to the ladies room and I'd return in a jiffy.

The park was packed, and with that many people milling around and blocking the view, I probably didn't need the subterfuge, but I walked off in the direction of the ladies room, doubled around, squirreled my way around the equipment piled near the stage where Dino and Gordon Hunter were doing a last-minute check on the sound system, and shot off to the western portion of the island. With the crowd and the traffic, it wouldn't have done any good to drive, and I knew it, so I hoofed it all the way.

And maybe walking wasn't such a bad thing after all. By the time I got to Gordon Hunter's, the neighborhood of vacation cottages was bathed in the last of the soft light—and enough long shadows for me to hide in when the occasional car or golf cart shot past.

I was just about to turn up Gordon's front walk when I heard footsteps behind me. Not Rosalee this time, I hoped, and not Levi, either. This last bit wasn't as much a hope as it was a prayer. I still didn't know how to start a conversation with him that was sure to be all about dodging the only thing worth talking about to begin with.

Hoping to look more like a casual walker than a snoop, I stepped lightly over a fallen tree branch and kept on going without even so much as a glance at Gordon's darkened cottage. The person behind me kept pace. That is, until that person tripped over the tree branch and let out a screech that sounded all too familiar.

I spun around and darted forward, one hand out to keep Chandra from going down in a heap. Which was a good thing. I would have hated to give her the Laser Look of Death while she was lying on the ground.

"What are you doing here?" I demanded, not the least bit guilty about the Laser Look of Death since she was still upright.

"Me?" Chandra slipped off her sandal, hopped on one foot, and rubbed her toe. By the time she was done gyrating and I was done dancing around to keep up with her just in case she lost her footing, we were both looking back in the direction from which we'd come. "I should be asking you the same thing. You lied to us, Bea. You said you were going to the ladies room."

"So you followed me?"

She dropped her sandal and when it landed on the road

with a *thwack*, she poked her foot back in it. "I was worried. I—"

Chandra's words dissolved in a little hiccup of surprise when a second person materialized out of the shadows.

"Kate?" I leaned forward, peering into the gathering darkness just to make sure my eyes weren't playing tricks on me. "You, too? You followed me?"

"No." Kate is nothing if not a stickler for accuracy. I didn't need light to know I got an eye roll. "I followed Chandra."

"And I followed the whole lot of you," Luella said, when she, too, stepped out of the darkness and closed in on us. "If you're trying to be sneaky, you're doing a terrible job of it. You're making nearly as much noise as those crazy fan club ladies in the park. What's going on? And why didn't you tell us something was up, Bea? I thought when it came to our cases, we were a team."

"Unless Bea stealing away from us doesn't have anything to do with our case," Kate suggested, as innocent as can be except for the little teasing lilt in her voice. "She could be meeting someone."

"A cute bartender, maybe?" Chandra said. "You know, he was at her house the other night." She added this like it was news, but I guarantee it was not. No way Chandra could keep anything that almost-juicy to herself for any length of time. "I have my suspicions," she went on. "You know, about what time he got there—"

"And what time he left that night," Kate put in.

"*If* he left at all that night," Chandra concluded.

And I gave up with a monumental sigh.

"All right. Stop!" At this point, even the truth was better than listening to them speculate about my love life (or lack of it). "The only thing I'm here to do is have a look around Gordon's. He was acting so weird the other day, and honestly, I wouldn't have thought anything of it except that he was on the dock the night Richie went into the water."

"And he was angry at Richie because of what Richie did to his boat," Kate said.

"And Gordon was at Levi's the night Richie was poisoned," Luella reminded us, though she didn't have to.

I nodded, then I realized they probably couldn't see me so I said, "It made me wonder what was up."

"And what was up is that you didn't want to include us." No one could lay on a guilt trip like Kate. I didn't have to see her expression clearly to know she was pouting.

I swore I wouldn't give in to what I knew was an attempt to make me feel bad, then immediately felt bad and caved. "I didn't want to include you because I wasn't sure exactly what I was going to do or what was going to happen, and I didn't want to involve you." I looked around at the circle of faces, pale in the moonlight. "Any of you."

Chandra rubbed her hands together. "So you are planning to break in!"

"No!" I didn't bother to add, *not unless it's absolutely necessary*, because there was no use putting ideas in their heads.

I glanced over my shoulder toward Gordon's. "I wanted to check out the house," I said. "The other day when we were here, I thought Gordon was acting—"

"Damned suspicious." Luella marched up the front walk.

"And awfully jumpy," Kate said and followed her.

"And since he's busy back at the park . . ." The intrigue appealed to Chandra and, grinning, she headed to the house, too.

Which left me, the person who had formulated the plan in the first place, standing there like a dolt. I scrambled to catch up with them just in time to hear Chandra say, "You can use a credit card for that, you know. I see it on the cop shows on TV all the time. They slip the card inside the door next to the lock and it flips open like magic!"

"Hold on!" I knew she wouldn't so I grabbed Chandra's arm. I shouldn't have had to say it, but I felt I needed to make myself perfectly clear. "I'm not here to do anything illegal like break into the house."

"How else are you going to find out what's going on?" Chandra asked.

"And figure out if Gordon's connected with Richie's murder?" Kate added.

Luella? She didn't say a thing, but I could feel her eyes on me. She was looking for answers, too.

I hated to admit that I was plumb out.

"I just thought . . ." In the dark, I didn't know if they could see me shrug and I guess it didn't matter. "I figured if I . . ." For a person who'd spent a lot of time thinking about this little foray into spying, I really didn't have much of a plan, and the sigh I let out pretty much told them so. "I thought I might be able to see into one of the windows," I finally admitted, and honestly, it sounded far lamer than it had when I'd come up with the plan back at home. "I just can't help but wonder why Gordon was so evasive the other day."

"Because he's trying to hide something," Chandra decided right then and there. "Which gives us every right to break in. You know, in the name of the case."

I was not convinced, and it was a good thing Kate and Luella weren't, either. They slipped to either side of Chandra and each grabbed an arm.

"Go," Luella said to me, cocking her head toward the house. "It's hard to tell if the blinds are still all closed, but maybe you'll be able to see something through the windows. You brought a flashlight?"

I took mine out of my pocket to show her I had.

On the off chance one of the neighbors was home and not at the park like everyone else on the island, it didn't seem smart to start with the front of the house, so I went around to the side and the windows I assumed looked into the dining room. They were a little higher up than I remembered, but lucky for me there was a bench nearby and I dragged it over, climbed, and shone my light into the window.

The only thing I got for my efforts was a view of the underside of the closed blinds.

"Dang." By the time I climbed back down from the bench, Luella and Kate were there to meet me.

"Nothing, huh?" Luella didn't waste any time; she scooted down the side of the house to the next window and pointed and Kate and I dragged the bench along. "Try this one."

I did. This time, there were no blinds to block my view, but the curtains were closed tight and so was the window.

"On a pretty night like this." When I gave them the news, Luella said what I was thinking.

"You'd think Gordon would want a lake breeze. Maybe he is up to something. But what—"

"*Psst!*"

The sound stopped us cold and we looked toward where Chandra peeked around the back corner of the house. It was too late to ask Kate and Luella why they hadn't kept a better eye on her, so when she waved us over I jumped down from the bench and we all stepped in that direction.

"Come on," Chandra hissed. "This way. While you three were busy wasting your time with the side of the house, I got the back window open."

"We're not going inside." I felt duty bound to mention this before any of us took as much as another step. "I might want to find out what Gordon's up to, but I'm not willing to go to jail for it." Because they were closest, I glanced at Kate and Luella. "Agreed?"

They did, and I zoomed over to where Chandra waited because she had not agreed, and I wanted to head her off at the proverbial pass. "We're not going in," I said, even as I realized we didn't have to.

Here at the back of the house there was a small covered porch and a window just to the right of the back door. That window opened into the kitchen. Chandra explained that just for the heck of it, she'd tried sliding the window open and, lo and behold, there it stood, a gap of a couple inches showing between the bottom of the window and the top of the sill. Here, too, there were curtains pulled across the window, but Kate stood to my right up against the porch railing and held them aside so I could sidle up nice and close and get down on my knees to see through the opening. My breath stuck behind a ball of anticipation in my throat, I shined my flashlight into Gordon's house.

"So, what is it?" The excitement in Chandra's voice shivered through the still night air and she gripped my shoulder with one hand hard enough to make me wince. "What do you see?"

"Boxes," I reported, and even I wasn't sure what it meant or how I felt about it. "Stacks of cardboard boxes."

"Makes sense." Luella stood to my left in front of the door and I heard her shuffle against the wooden porch. "You remember what Alice told us. She saw Richie and Gordon moving boxes the night Richie damaged Gordon's boat."

"He would have had personal items on board," Kate said. "Clothes and probably food and—"

"Boxes," I said again before they could convince themselves that their theory was right. I looked up and over my shoulder from one woman to the next. "Not just a few. Not like the couple it might take to carry some stuff from Gordon's boat." Just to be sure, I stuck my nose as far as I could get it in the gap of the window opening and slid my light around the kitchen. "Dozens of boxes. And if I look real hard . . ." I did, and was just able to make out the doorway that led into the dining room and the dozens more boxes stacked in there. "They're maybe three feet high and two feet long," I reported. "I'm not very good at guessing, but I'd say I can see at least fifty of them. Maybe more." I sat back on my heels and looked up at my friends. "No way these are personal items Gordon and Richie moved off the boat. Not unless Gordon had everything he's ever owned on board."

"What does it mean?" Kate asked.

I didn't know, and I'm not sure how taking another look was going to help me figure it out, but take another look I did. I crouched back down, squinched up as close to the window as I could, and arced the beam of my flashlight over the boxes one more time.

And that's when I saw it.

"Blue logo," I said, more to myself than to anyone else. "There's a blue logo on the boxes and I've seen it before."

Thinking through this new development, I plunked my butt down on the porch. "Richie's house," I finally said, though no one had asked me. "It's the same logo that was on the carton of Dunfield cigarettes in Richie's bedroom next to the purple Sharpie and the picture of the Defarge sisters."

Luella's mouth fell open. "There's been talk among the boaters, whispers more than anything else. About people smuggling cigarettes into Canada. There's a huge black market there for American smokes. You don't think—"

"I don't know." I closed the window, hauled myself up, and brushed off the seat of my pants. "But—"

But what?

But we had to tell Hank.

But we couldn't tell Hank without explaining what we were doing at Gordon's in the first place and how we were peeking in his windows.

But we'd have to say something because if there really was something havey-cavey going on, and if Gordon was involved, it was our civic duty to report it.

But we didn't really know the details, at least for now.

But I didn't have any time to think about any of that, because just at that moment, we heard the sound of a door opening and closing from the cottage next door and saw Mason Burke walk out the back door.

No, I stand corrected.

He didn't *walk* out of the cottage. He *slipped* out, very quietly, even though as far as he knew, there weren't four women on the porch next door, hunched over in an effort to make themselves invisible.

We didn't have to worry.

With a baseball cap pulled low over his forehead and his jacket collar turned up (it was way too warm to wear a jacket), Mason put his head down on his chest, hurried to the front of the house, and disappeared down the road.

"What do you suppose that's all about?" Luella asked in a whisper.

"I don't know," I whispered back. "But there's something awfully familiar about . . ."

About what?

Really, I wasn't sure. I only knew that watching the way Burke shambled off into the night reminded me of something. Or someone. Neither of which I could place.

Rather than waste the brain cells, I concentrated on what I could get my thoughts around and leaned over the porch railing to search darkness. "He's dressed all in black," I reported to them when I stood upright again. "And he's carrying something big and square. Come on." I led the way down the steps, grateful for my sneakers, and shushing my friends with a hand gesture when they whispered among themselves.

Out at the road, we could just see Mason as he disappeared into the darkness.

"He's probably just going to the concert," Kate suggested. But then, of all of us, Kate has the least imagination.

"Or he's headed into town to pick up something for his wife," Luella said. But then, of all of us, she has the biggest heart.

I glanced over my shoulder at the cottage where there wasn't even one light on.

Chandra noticed, too. "Maybe she goes to bed early," she suggested. But then, of all of us, she's the one most willing to believe that people are, at heart, good.

Unfortunately, I didn't necessarily agree. Not about the goodness or the kindness or the fact that Mason Burke, dressed in black and slinking through the night, was doing nothing more than going to hear Guillotine pound the living daylights out of their guitars.

With that little someone/someplace memory still niggling at the back of my brain and beckoning me on, I headed off down the road after Burke and the other Ladies fell into step behind me. Keeping as far back as we could, but still able to keep an eye on our quarry, we followed Mason Burke all the way into town.

He stopped now and then, hoisting the flat, square package he carried and switching it from one arm to the other, and when he did, we stopped, too, stepping into deeper shadows when we could find them, elbowing Chandra when she forgot that this was real life and not TV and started to comment about how much her feet hurt.

We were nearly all the way back to the park when Luella

214

dared to mutter, "The concert. That has to be it. He's going to the concert."

But he wasn't.

Burke bypassed the park completely and turned down the street toward Levi's.

Except he wasn't looking for a drink.

As one, we stopped cold and watched Burke march up the steps to the Defarge knitting shop.

As it turned out, it wasn't the smartest of moves on our part. We stood in the halo of a streetlamp, and after all that time of being quiet and careful, Burke caught sight of us.

"Oh." His surprise was nothing but a momentary glitch. "Good evening, ladies," he called out. "Going to the concert?"

Since he was willing to act like we hadn't just been caught gawking at him, I decided to play along and sashayed over to where he stood. "That's exactly where we're going. How about you?"

"I'll be along in a minute." He was a nice man with a cordial smile. He moved the clumsy package from one arm to the other. This close, I saw that whatever it was, it was about two feet tall and another wide, wrapped in brown paper and tied with string.

"Do you need some help with that?" I asked him.

"This?" Burke looked at the package as if he'd forgotten it was there. *As if* being the operative words in that sentence. He carefully set the package in front of Alice and Margaret's front door. "No, no," he said, and he added a laugh to the statement like that was supposed to somehow prove that the last thing he needed was an assist from a woman who was dressed all in black, just like he was. "It's a . . ." He laughed again. "Well, it's supposed to be a surprise, but I don't think it will hurt to tell you." By now, Chandra, Kate, and Luella had come up behind me, and he included them in the look he shot all around. "It's a gift from my wife," he said. "For Alice and Margaret."

Before any of us could ask why anyone would deliver a gift in the middle of the night, he went right on. "She was so grateful for that yarn I picked up here the other day, I can't tell you. Why, when I left the cottage tonight, there she was knitting and knitting and knitting some more. The woman is a knitting machine!"

Apparently she was a machine that knitted in the dark.

Burke didn't know I knew this. That would explain why he acted as if nothing was wrong. "My wife and I, we happened to see a poster at a garage sale here on the island yesterday," he said, pointing to the wrapped package. "It's a picture of a woman knitting, and I told my wife it reminded me of that drawing I saw inside the shop, the one that hangs behind the cash register. My wife insisted on buying the poster and I went out and got a frame for it and now I'm going to leave it." He made a sort of *voila* gesture toward where the package leaned against the door. "You know, as a surprise."

"That's really nice," I said at the same time I backed away and wished Burke a good night.

"Well, so much for following the guy," Luella muttered when we were far enough away so Burke couldn't hear. "Here we thought he was acting suspicious and he was just being neighborly."

She was right, and I was appropriately shamefaced.

That is, until we turned the corner to continue on to the park and I took the chance of peeking around the side of the nearest building.

I was just in time to see Mason Burke glance around. Sure the coast was clear, he picked up that wrapped package and hurried off into the night with it.

If you ask me, that's a funny way to leave a surprise for the nice old ladies at the knitting shop.

❖ 15 ❖

We have reputations on South Bass.

I mean, reputations as something other than the four nosy women who look into murders they have no business investigating.

Kate has the winery. Luella, her fishing charter business. Though it amazes me every time I think about it, I know that Chandra is busy all summer doing tarot and crystal readings for tourists who apparently have too much time on their hands and too much money in their pockets and too little common sense to know when they're being taken for a magical, mystical ride.

Me? I'm proud to say that in the months since it has opened, Bea & Bees has earned a reputation for its wonderful (if a little over-the-top in some of my guest suites)

Victorian ambiance, the quality of its food, and the friendliness of its innkeeper.

Like it or not, we had no choice. We had to go back to the concert.

If we didn't, we'd look like we didn't support the chamber of commerce.

Believe me, our fellow merchants would notice.

We joined the crowd of partiers just as Guillotine started into their second set. There was no guillotine on stage, I noticed, and frankly, I wasn't surprised either by that or by the pounding bass line, the thumping drums, or Dino's rough, raging solos. In spite of the tight black pants and white shirts with billowing sleeves that were supposed to make them look like they just stepped out of the French Revolution, Guillotine was hard-core tough, the driving music seemed to say. Even if the ladies screaming and swooning in the front row were all dressed in bubblegum pink.

I played my part and listened semi-intently for a couple songs, then casually moved toward the fringes of the crowd. Just as I was hoping I would, I spotted Gordon Hunter and made my way over to where he watched the celebration, a smile as big as all of gay Paree brightening his face.

"It's . . . well! Everyone . . . wonder . . . time." Though I couldn't hear all of what he yelled into my ear, I was able to fill in the blanks.

Because there was no hope of being heard in turn, I nodded.

"We're getting . . . great reaction . . . our visitors."

Another nod.

Kylie Logan

"I just wish that guillotine—"

The song ended, and suddenly Gordon screaming in my ear wasn't such a good thing. I backed away and applauded along with the rest of the crowd (except for the women in the first row who cheered with all the enthusiasm of rabid Scottish soccer fans). I'd hatched a plan the moment I laid eyes on Gordon and now seemed as good a time as any to put it into action.

"Do you have a cigarette?" I asked him.

It wasn't my imagination. Or a trick of the charming made-to-look-like-gas-lamps streetlights that marched up and down the sidewalks that surrounded the park.

Gordon actually did blanch.

He patted down the pockets of his blue blazer, which, as it turned out, was kind of a weird thing to do since he replied, "I don't smoke. Didn't know you did, Bea."

I was evasive. "Just that sort of night. Party atmosphere and all." I knew I didn't have much time before Dino started up again, so I did a quick survey of the buildings across the street. The souvenir shops were closed, but the bars and restaurants were open to take advantage of the crowds. I could see they were packed. A brief and annoying thought fluttered through my head: I hoped Levi's was busy, too, then I wouldn't have to worry that I might bump into its proprietor.

"I could probably buy a pack of smokes at any of the bars," I said, furiously consigning thoughts of Levi to the nether regions of my brain where they belonged. "I never keep any around since I hardly ever indulge. I wonder if anyone around here sells Dunfields."

The next thing I knew, someone somewhere in the crowd was infinitely more interesting than me, and Gordon disappeared. He never even said good-bye.

Where had that little bit of nicotine-laced prevarication gotten me?

Well, to be perfectly honest, not far. But it did make me wonder if it was possible that Gordon really was smuggling cigarettes over the lake into Canada . . .

And if Richie damaged a boat full of those cigarettes and had to help Gordon offload them . . .

And if Richie realized Gordon was up to more than just emptying the boat's refrigerator and getting his skivvies back on dry land . . .

And—

A bolt hit out of the blue.

Or maybe it was just the electric vibrations of the first earsplitting chord of the next Guillotine song that shivered in the air and made my sternum quiver.

"Richie already had twelve thousand dollars, and he said he was going to have a lot more money very soon."

Poor Kate. When I saw her walking by with Jayce Martin, I didn't even bother to explain the train of thought that had brought me to this particular station. I grabbed her by the shoulder and yelled into her ear and repeated myself. "Richie said he was going to have a lot more money very soon. What if Richie knew about the smuggling?" Now that I had her attention, I didn't need to scream quite so loud. "What if Richie was blackmailing Gordon? And Gordon—"

Neither one of us needed me to finish the sentence.

Kate's mouth fell open and she simply nodded to let me

know she understood, and because there was no way the two of us could hope to even begin to explain what was up to Jayce (and probably no way we wanted to, anyway), she vanished into the crowd with him.

Just for the record, I noticed he had a hold of her hand.

As for me, I heaved a satisfied sigh, and it had nothing to do with thinking that maybe Kate had finally set aside her a-little-bit uppity attitude that Jayce, as a ferryboat captain, wasn't good enough for her and realized he was a great guy and he adored her. No, my satisfaction came from thinking that the pieces of the puzzle that was Richie's murder were finally starting to fall into place, the fog was lifting, the day was dawning.

Except . . .

Somehow, I managed to block out the discordant rhythms of Guillotine and concentrate on the case. Song after song didn't exactly float past (they were more of the stomping variety), and I found myself facing the inescapable fact: Gordon was looking like a good choice for most-wanted perp, but there were still others I needed to consider.

As if the Universe was listening and providing me the push I needed, across the park I caught sight of a flutter of gauzy yellow.

Didi and Dan Peebles. Believe me, I hadn't forgotten that of all the people who hated Richie's guts, Peebles had one of the very best reasons. Gordon Hunter might be currently at the top of my list of those-who-might-have-dunnit, but I am nothing if not thorough, and I knew I needed to get my information lined up nice and neat. I zigzagged my way through the crowd and as luck would have it, arrived at the picnic table where Dan was entertaining a group of people just as Dino called out, "Good night, Put-in-Bay! We love you!"

Yes, the word *cliche* crossed my mind.

I waved a greeting to Peebles and his guests and said *no thank you* to a glass of wine which they weren't supposed to be drinking in the park in the first place. Since I knew Dino and the Boyz would be coming back onstage soon for the encore they'd been anticipating and thus practicing all week, I asked Peebles if I could speak to him privately for a minute.

"She's looking for a deal on a car!" Like we were long-lost buddies, Peebles looped one arm around my shoulders and spoke loud enough to be heard in Sandusky, all the way across the lake. "Best used car deals on the mainland," he added, and with his free hand, slapped the nearest man on the back. "You have my promise, and she knows it, too." He gave me an extra squeeze. "Girl is from New York, and even she knows you can't get a better deal on a used car than you can from Dan Peebles. I've got financing, too," he told me with one of his signature, broad winks. "I promise, I can get a nice, low payment, even for somebody like you who must just barely make a living operating a motel like you do."

Good thing my teeth were gritted, or I might have set him straight both about the motel and what he assumed were my reduced circumstances. Too bad. It would have been especially satisfying to point out to the big blowhard that I could buy and sell him a couple thousand times over.

Instead, I controlled my temper and my tongue. At least until we crossed the road and stood just outside the dock where, what seemed a lifetime ago, we'd all gathered to celebrate the start of the big Bastille Day weeklong celebration. That's when I slipped out from beneath Dan's clingy grip and said a little prayer that I hoped Peebles was about to incriminate himself.

Honest, it would have given me a special kind of tingle to see him in prison orange.

"So . . ." He didn't just rub his hands together; he chafed them as if he was sure this was one way to start a rousing good bonfire. "What can I do for you, little lady?"

"You can stop calling me little lady." Since I managed to say this with a smile, he thought I was kidding.

"I was going over the final bills back at the B and B," I said, emphasizing those two initials just a bit and hoping he realized they did not in any way, shape, or form spell *motel*. "I knew you'd be busy tomorrow morning over at the B and B, and I didn't want to bother you then, what with you packing and leaving the B and B. I just wanted to make sure. You arrived at the B and B . . ." Yes, I was laying it on a tad thick. I reminded myself that pride goeth before the not finding out who the murderer was, and told myself to get a grip. "You checked in at the . . . You arrived at my place on Thursday morning. The same day you arrived on the island, right?"

"Checked in to your sweet little place on Thursday." Peebles nodded right before he gave me another anything-but-subtle wink. "But truth be told, little lady, that's not when I got to the island. Nope. Got here on Wednesday."

Wednesday. And Richie was killed on Wednesday night.

This bombshell from Peebles was something I hadn't

expected and I thought it over, wondering what to say next. "Wednesday! Is that so? I was just checking—"

"Just checking to see if I could have possibly killed that no-good loser, Richie Monroe." Peebles slapped my back with so much force, it nearly knocked me off my feet. He held out an arm to keep me from falling over, but he didn't apologize. "Of course you're checking! Everybody on the island says you're some sort of detective or something. That you're looking into the murder. I've been waiting for you to ask me if I killed the SOB."

"Did you?"

Peebles didn't need to turn up the volume so I could hear him over the musical stylings of Guillotine. He was way louder than the band. "I guess I'm the logical suspect," he finally admitted with a snort of laughter. "But I'll tell you what, lately, it never crossed my mind."

"Because . . ."

"Because I'm not that kind of man!" I wasn't sure if it was a particularly drawn-out bass note or Peebles's rip-roaring laugh that vibrated the sidewalk where we stood. "Don't get me wrong," he said, "I thought about it a time or two. I mean, back when the house first blew sky-high. But that was months ago, and I'm over it now. Have been since we went to court and I got justice." There was the wink again. "And damages."

It wasn't that I didn't believe him. Oh wait, it was. "What time did you arrive?" I asked him.

"On the island? Got the five forty-five ferry out of Port Clinton," he told me. "So it must have been a little after six."

Which meant he was on dry land by the time someone laced Richie's drink with pokeberry.

"But I didn't kill the guy," Peebles said. "I was . . ." This time, he didn't bother with a wink. I got an elbow to the ribs instead. "Me and Didi, we were over at the new house site. You know they laid the foundation last weekend. And I wanted to check it out, make sure it was done right. Even planned a little surprise for Didi while I was there. Brought along a little pop-up tent and we set it up right there where the house is going to stand. We kept each other busy keeping busy, celebrating, if you know what I mean."

I did.

As for taking his statement at face value, that was another matter altogether, and I guess Peebles realized it. He raised an arm and made a semaphore wave toward his party in the park. "Didi! Hey, Didi honey!"

Yes, she heard him over Guillotine.

I was pretty sure all of Put-in-Bay did.

In short, short white shorts and a skintight orange tank, Didi shimmied across the street and Peebles didn't waste any time. "Hey, honey, Bea here's asking about us staying out at the house site on Wednesday night. You took pictures, right? Show them to her. I mean . . ." I think the way he lowered his voice to a manly growl was supposed to be sexy, and in Didi's world, maybe it was. She giggled. "Show her the ones you can show her."

Didi pulled out her phone and when her very long and very pink fingernails *clicked, clicked, clicked* to the proper screen, she turned the phone so I could see it. There in living color were Peebles and Didi dressed in matching black shorts and red camp shirts, outside a pop-up tent, champagne glasses in hand. Since he was far taller than her, I imagined he was the one who'd held up the phone above his head to snap the picture. Behind them, I could see a broad cement slab and the beginnings of wood framing, and beyond that, a strip of blue lake.

Scroll.

There they were again, Peebles and Didi, their smiles a little bigger, minus the red camp shirts.

Scroll.

And there they were again, minus just about everything else.

I'm hardly a prude but my cheeks were hot. "Well, then . . ."

"Oh, come on." A poke from Peebles. "We're all adults here. Don't be so shy. And take a good look. A really good look."

I swallowed hard and forced myself to do as I was told.

That's when I saw the date and time stamp on that last picture.

And that proved it.

Dan Peebles was up to a whole lot of something on Wednesday night. But it had nothing to do with poisoning Richie Monroe.

You have my promise.

By the time I crossed back over to the park the concert was over, but the party was just getting started.

Groups of revelers streamed toward the bars across the park and the boardwalk in the other direction. Other people sat and got comfortable, waiting for the fireworks show to begin. They laughed and sang and called out greetings. As for me, I was too busy with my own thoughts to care about any of it.

Peebles was out. So were Rosalee and Mike.

Gordon Hunter was in.

Who did that leave?

"You bet your life I want that other bottle of scotch! Just like it says in our contract."

I was near the stage, and the voice thundered out from behind it, unmistakable to anyone who'd been at the concert for the last couple hours.

Dino.

I froze, my mind racing.

Dino and Richie.

Theirs was a relationship that went back decades, and if what Tiffany had told us about the song that made Boyz 'n Funk famous and Richie's and Dino's dueling claims about who wrote it, animosity was the name of this game.

I slipped behind a small mountain of amplifiers that Paul, Scotty, Nick, and Jesse were just beginning to wrangle, stepped over a spaghetti tangle of wiring, and got to the space between the back of the stage and the motor home that had been parked parallel to it to allow the band a fifteen-foot by ten-foot green room of sorts. I arrived just in time to see Dino down half a tumbler of amber liquid and hear Gordon promise he'd have the other bottle of scotch for him in a jiffy.

When Gordon hightailed it out of there, Dino caught sight of me and stepped back, his chin high, his arms raised, his face flush with the excitement of being back in the spotlight. Or maybe it was the scotch. "Huh? So?"

I wasn't sure what I was supposed to say, so it's a good

thing Tiffany zipped past me to snap a few dozen photos of Dino.

"Huh? So?" This time Dino asked Tiffany.

"Fabulous!" She chittered like a fledgling, darting left and right to get more pictures. "I'll have these up on the fan page in just a bit," she told Dino. "Along with a little video clip. Only a few seconds," she added with a gulp when it looked as if he might object. "Just a couple lines from 'Come Down the Road,' that second song in the set after intermission. Just enough to make people crazy to hear more."

"Well . . ." He pretended to think about it, then gave in with a smile that apparently carried a higher wattage over where Tiffany stood than where I was; she melted. I pretty much stayed my ol' regular self, unmelted and just as curious as ever.

" 'Come Down the Road.' Did you write that one, Dino?" I asked.

His shoulders inched back. "You bet I did, and I'll tell you what, it's going to be big. Mark my word. Bigger than big. As soon as people have a chance to hear it, they're going to be all over us for more."

The way I remembered "Come Down the Road" . . . well, truth be told, I didn't remember it. Each one of Guillotine's songs blended into the next, until my overall impression of the concert was one of noisy discord.

This was not the time to mention my opinion to Dino, so instead I said, "Writing songs. That's exactly what I wanted to talk to you about."

He spit out a laugh. "Not everyone's got the talent, honey. So if you're thinking of giving it a try—"

"Oh, not me." There was a table nearby strewn with the remains of a sandwich platter. I brushed aside a scattering of potato chip crumbs and perched myself on the edge of it. "Actually, I was talking about Richie."

"I didn't say anything!" Tiffany blurted out, even though just the fact that she felt she had to blurt—and the bright red color that rose in her cheeks—pretty much proved she did.

Dino crossed his arms over the white shirt with the ballooning sleeves. "If you know the story," he told me, "then you know that scumbag . . ." His spite was tempered by a hiccup. "That Richie Monroe—"

Okay, whatever I expected, it wasn't that Dino would get all choked up.

He coughed behind his hand and acted like it was no big deal. "It was a long time ago," he mumbled. "Back then, me and Richie were friends."

"And these days, Richie rigged the guillotine to cut off your head."

"Did he?" Dino belted out a laugh. "That son-of-a-bitch! Leave it to Richie to do something that crazy."

"You're not mad?" I asked him.

"I would have been if he cut my head off."

I didn't bother to point out the flaw in his argument, but then, I didn't have much of a chance. Dino came and sat down on the table next to me.

"We were friends," he said, and this time I knew it was the scotch talking because his words were slurred. "A long . . . long time ago, me and Richie were friends. We were roomies. Sure I was mad when it all went down. But . . ." He burped and pounded his chest. "I didn't want the guy to die."

Which is different than saying *I'm not the one who poisoned his drinks.*

"When Richie showed up at my place the other day, you told me you didn't know him," I reminded Dino.

He reached for the bottle of Johnny Walker. There wasn't much left in it, but then, Dino's glassy red eyes and his slurred speech were pretty much proof that the glass he was drinking out of on stage wasn't filled with water. No matter, he emptied the bottle into his glass and slugged it down. "So I didn't want to bring up ancient history. What difference does it make?"

"I think it made a lot of difference to Richie."

I can't say if Dino believed this or not. He pulled out his phone, and a couple seconds later, shoved it under my nose. The screen showed a website called Richie's Telling the Truth.

"You see this?" he asked. "It's brand-new. Showed up on the web earlier this week."

I hadn't seen it, and I gave it a quick once-over. The website was neither well-written nor artistic, but it did convey a message. *Years ago,* Richie said in a rambling, misspelled message, *I wus cheated, but I won't be cheated again. The world needs to no the truth.*

I glanced at Dino. "What is the truth?"

"Tell her, Dino." Tiffany advanced on us even before Dino could open his mouth. "Tell her how you wrote 'Ali,' and how Richie tried to say it was his. Tell her how all these years, you've had to live under the dark cloud of Richie Monroe's lies. People have thought less of the Boyz," she said, clearly for my benefit. "Because of the lies. But tell them, Dino . . ." Tiffany scrambled over to stand in front of her hero. "Tell her how you wrote the song that made Boyz 'n Funk famous."

Dino still had the phone in his hands, and he stared down at the picture of Richie that looked back up at him. Richie, looking grungy and disheveled, and in spite of his fifty years, still young around the eyes.

Dino clicked off the website. "What difference does it make?" he asked no one in particular.

Which is different than saying *of course Richie lied and I'm the one who wrote that song*.

I knew it, and so did Tiffany.

"He besmirched the band's name," she said, her voice tight. "Tell her, Dino. What difference does it make if the jerk is dead? Tell her the truth!"

With a grunt, Dino got up and lurched to the other side of the little enclosure. He scrubbed a finger under his nose. "I dunno," he mumbled. "Maybe . . . maybe there was a little bit of truth in what Richie said."

I bounded to my feet.

A far less dramatic response than Tiffany's, which consisted of her jaw opening and shutting but no sound coming out.

I found my voice first. "Dino, are you saying—"

He whirled around and slashed a hand in the air. "I'm not saying anything!"

But I had news for Dino; he already had. Okay, so it might have been the scotch talking, but even silence can speak volumes.

"I can't believe it." Tiffany's arms hung at her sides. Her

shoulders drooped. "All these years I thought Richie Monroe was the bad guy. And now you're saying . . ." Tears splashed down her cheeks and she swallowed hard. "You're telling me . . ."

Her head snapped up and her face, already pale, turned ashen. "Oh my God!" She hyperventilated. "Oh my God! If it's true . . . if Richie really did write that song . . . if all this time I thought he did what he did to hurt the band . . . Oh my God! What have I done?"

And before I could ask what, indeed, Tiffany raced out of the enclosure.

Which is different than saying *I did it, I killed Richie Monroe,* but I had to admit, it looked mighty fishy.

« 16 »

Whatever remorse Dino may or may not have felt over his broken friendship with Richie, Richie's death, and maybe Richie's murder, didn't stop him and the other Boyz from dragging down to breakfast late, turning green at the sight of the banana-Nutella crepes, and demanding so many pots of coffee, I caught myself wondering how much it would cost to put Juan Valdez on the payroll.

By the time they went back up to their rooms to sleep off the combined effects of those couple bottles of scotch and the celebrity that came from being the center of attention in the park the night before, and I cleaned up and made sure everyone's bills were slipped under their doors, I didn't have much time to get downtown. There was a parade scheduled at noon, and after that the big Dickens trivia contest. I'd promised Marianne Littlejohn I'd be there early to look over the questions she'd prepared.

The important word there is *parade* and I guess I hadn't been paying much attention to the chamber of commerce bulletins that arrived in my email, because I had no idea the word *extravaganza* also applied. The closer I got to downtown, the more congested the streets were. Roadblocks, high school marching bands, Marie Antoinette (complete with huge powdered wig) in the horse-drawn cart that would take her to the guillotine, and costumed peasants running behind to throw insults at her . . . Everywhere I tried to drive or turn or get by was a dead end, and I ended up looping around downtown and heading off to the far side of the island in the hopes of finding less congestion and easier access to the park from the other direction.

No such luck.

And in the long run, that turned out to be a good thing.

See, my circuitous route took me right past Crown Hill Cemetery, and there, a flash of flamingo color caught my eye.

I wheeled into the cemetery, and a minute later I was out of the SUV and walking toward where Tiffany Hollister stood with her head bowed and a bouquet of flowers in her hand.

It wasn't until I was right up next to her that she realized I was even there, and it wasn't until I was there that I saw that she was staring at a bit of newly disturbed earth between a mausoleum and a tall obelisk with an urn at the top of it.

"Buried in an unmarked grave." Tiffany's words escaped her on the end of the sigh that sounded as if it had been ripped from her soul. "Such a sad ending to so noble a life."

I would have been excused for saying, "Huh?" Instead I settled for, "Who?"

When Tiffany turned my way, I saw that her cheeks were streaked with tears. Her eyes were a color three times as deep as her pink shirt, and her melancholy was even bigger than her shoulder pads. "Richie, of course." Her words were soaked with tears. "This is where they buried Richie yesterday."

I couldn't believe I'd been so busy that I'd actually missed the funeral.

"Not to worry." Tiffany must have known what I was thinking because she patted my arm. "That was the way he wanted it. No funeral. No mourners. No big to-do. The man from the funeral home told me. Richie . . ." Her voice wobbled and the hand she touched to her cheek trembled. "Richie left instructions for them years ago about his cremation and what he wanted done with the ashes. He told them he wanted to be as anonymous in death"—she fished a tissue from her pocket and blew her nose—"as anonymous in death as he was in life."

I can be forgiven for being caught flat-footed by all this. After all, this was the woman who was numero uno when it came to the I Hate Richie club. And when I saw her the night before after the concert, I remembered she'd mumbled something about Richie before she fled the park.

"Did you kill him?" I asked her.

Tiffany's tears, the trickling kind before, erupted into the Niagara Falls variety. "Of course I didn't kill him," she wailed. "Why would I kill anyone as heroic and wonderful and talented as Richie Monroe?"

I looked at her hard. I'd once seen a dog trainer pull the same stunt on a particularly ill-behaved Jack Russell, but alas, the strategy worked no better on Tiffany than it had on the dog. When all else fails, I'm a believer in logic. Or at least in honesty.

"Tiffany," I reminded her, "you hated Richie Monroe."

I don't think I'd ever actually seen anybody wring their hands. "No! No! I never hated Richie. I hated the man I thought Richie was."

In its own weird way, this was starting to make sense.

I backed up a step, the better to give myself a little space to think. "So what you're telling me is that you hated Richie—"

"Because I thought he tried to lay claim to Dino's song. And he took Dino to court. And he did his best to besmirch—"

This I knew, so I waved aside the rest of her explanation and got down to the meat of the matter. "And now?"

"Now?" She sniffled. "You heard Dino last night. You came right out and asked him point-blank if Richie really wrote 'Ali, Ali,' and Dino . . ." The waterworks started up again. "He didn't deny it. Don't you see? Dino . . ." She hiccupped and added a little hyperventilation just for dramatic effect. "I think Dino's been lying all these years. Richie really did write 'Ali, Ali.' And I . . ." Forearm to forehead. "I've spent my life standing up for Dino and telling anyone who would listen that Richie was the bad guy. And all this time . . ." She hung her head.

"Poor, poor Richie," she said, talking now to the patch of barren ground. "Your name was dragged through the mud and you were cheated out of the fame and fortune that should have rightly been yours. I'll never forget you, Richie." She laid her bouquet of daisies and carnations on the small mound of freshly dug earth. "I'll tell the world your story, Richie. I swear."

I waited for the *as God is my witness* part, and when it didn't come, I figured it was safe to talk again. "Tiffany, yesterday Dino showed me Richie's website, the one Richie started up to tell the world his side of the story. You said when you saw it, you did something to retaliate."

"Yes, but I didn't kill him." She shook her head. Then nodded. Then did a weird sort of combination of both that left me feeling as if we'd been transported from South Bass and set down along the San Andreas Fault. "If that's what you were thinking, don't. What I did . . ." She pulled out another tissue and dabbed it to her eyes. "I'm ashamed to admit it. Ashamed to think I was taken in by the likes of Dino. All these years . . ." The tears came tumbling down. "All these years I've been president of the fan club, and this is what I get in return. My heart broken." She pounded her chest. "My faith in mankind crushed."

"So you . . ?"

"I . . ." She heaved a sigh. "I started up a website, too. It was all about how Richie's was a pack of lies. I talked about how Dino wrote 'Ali' and that Richie was nothing more than a poser. But don't worry!" She said this with all the conviction of a woman who thought I really might. "I've already started to make amends. I stayed up all night last night taking down the old page and starting a new one. You know, as a tribute to Richie."

"That's nice." It was, in its own twisted way. "But it still doesn't explain what happened to Richie. Do you think Dino could have—"

"Killed him?" Tiffany's voice ricocheted off the mausoleum and echoed through the cemetery. "Richie was a walking dead man all these years. Ever since his song was stolen and he lost faith in his talent and his friends. Don't you see? Dino ripped out Richie's heart. He robbed Richie of his ability to trust. I just don't think Dino killed Richie; I know he did. All those years ago."

I was hoping for something a little more definitive but knew it was not forthcoming, so I left Tiffany to her mourning and her new obsession and continued on to the park, my mind playing over the possibility of Dino as killer. Dino and Gordon. At least I was narrowing down the field. The trick, of course, was to figure out which was which, and which had (so far at least) been clever enough to pull the wool over all our eyes.

By the time I was close to downtown and actually found a place to park, the parade had started. I wound my way through knots of gawkers, TV cameras from the stations on the mainland, and the tables that had been set up for a craft fair, zipped by Levi's (eyes straight ahead and refusing to glance around), and came up almost all the way to the Defarge Knitting Shop when I realized Mason Burke was standing outside.

Again.

Since he had his nose pressed to the glass in the front door, he didn't notice me right away, but I noticed that he wasn't carrying the big, flat package we'd seen him with the night before.

Kylie Logan

"So, how did Margaret and Alice like the poster?" I asked him.

"They're closed." As if to prove it to me, he gave the doorknob a tug. "I haven't had a chance to give the ladies the picture yet. I decided it would be more fun to present it to them in person than just to leave it here for them. You know, so I could see the excitement on their faces."

It explained why he left with picture in hand the night before. "And maybe when you give your gift to Margaret and Alice," I suggested, "your wife could be with you since the thank-you gift is really from her."

"Wife? Yes, of course." Burke laughed a little too loudly and hurried down the shop steps. His chin on his chest, he disappeared into the crowd.

"Chin on his chest." I watched him go and mumbled to myself, my brain nibbling at the image, reminding me I'd seen it some time before last night when we'd watched Burke sneak into town with the poster under his arm.

Funny thing, though; it's hard to hold on to thoughts when you're surrounded by a few thousand people pushing for a peek at the parade, and soon, I wasn't as worried about Burke's chin or his chest as I was about making it over to the park across the street in one piece.

I was waiting semi-patiently for a high school marching band to . . . er . . . march past, when another flash of pink (it must surely be the color of the day) caught my eye.

This time it was Margaret Defarge, resplendent that day in pants and a matching top in a shade that reminded me of blushing roses. She'd just walked out of the candy shop near the antique carousel and I thought about going over to say hello, but hesitated when I saw her dart to the side of the building, behind the lines of folks jockeying for position at the parade and away from the windows of the shop. She had a blue bag in her hand about the size of a evening purse, and she glanced around to be sure no one was watching, then reached inside, grabbed something, and popped it in her mouth.

When I turned around and darted across the street, I was laughing. No doubt Alice was somewhere nearby and Margaret didn't want her sister to know she was indulging in candy. Or maybe she just didn't want to share?

Another smile brightened my expression. Leave it to the Defarge twins to make a gentle competition even out of eating candy!

By the time the parade was over (and just for the record, it was a mighty long parade), most of the congestion and the noise died down. Let's face it, there are only so many people who are interested in a Charles Dickens look-alike and trivia contest. While most of the island's visitors headed off to water sports or bars, the diehard few gathered in the seats that had been set up in front of the gazebo.

Gregory Ashburn tipped his tall top hat to me when I passed.

If the smile above that unruly goatee of his meant anything, Timothy Drake looked confident.

Tyler and Max, the kids with the paper beards and pipe cleaner spectacles, were anything but nervous. In fact, they'd attracted something of a following in the way of a half dozen girls who giggled and hung on their every word, and they took full advantage, regaling the girls with stories about "that Dickens guy" that sounded way more like fiction than fact to me.

Charles Dickens would have been proud.

Our female contestant—as it turned out her name was Eva DeNato—sat in the shade under a nearby tree, a notebook open on her lap.

Mason Burke . . .

I glanced around the park.

The contest was set to start in less than thirty minutes, and Mason Burke was nowhere to be seen.

"Why the worried look?" Marianne Littlejohn zipped by carrying an armful of books and a manila file folder stuffed with typewritten pages that she handed to me, the questions for the contest. "You look like you've lost someone."

I gave the area another quick scan. "Just one of the contestants, Mason Burke. I saw him a little while ago over near the knitting shop, and come to think of it, he wasn't dressed in his Dickens costume. That explains it, of course," I added, feeling relieved though I didn't know why. "He had to go back to the cottage to get dressed."

"Well, kick-off time is in exactly . . ." Marianne checked her watch. "Oh my, I've got to hurry and make sure everything's set up. Look over the questions. I've included a lot of the ones you emailed me." She grinned. "This is going to be so much fun!"

And actually, I believed her.

That is, until Levi showed up.

Yes, yes, I know . . . the arrival of the island Adonis

should have cheered me, not chilled me. And it would have. Honest. If only I didn't suddenly feel as jumpy as a high school student at her first mixer.

"Hey." Levi, it should be pointed out, did a pretty good job of acting like a high school kid, too. One of those cool boys who is oh so not flustered by the rapidly beating heart of every girl around him.

Or was he?

When I opened my mouth to respond with I don't know what, I saw that his hands were poked into the pockets of his jeans. He refused to meet my eyes.

Whatever I had expected from him, it wasn't bashfulness, and in a twisted sort of way it gave me courage. "Hey." I stepped up nice and close, the better to catch his eye and force him to look at me. "You left in a hurry the other night."

"I did." He did not sound especially proud of this, which is why I would have cut him some slack if he didn't add, "It was a mistake."

I wasn't sure I wanted to hear the answer, but I had to ask so I swallowed hard and plunged right in. "Leaving? Or kissing me?"

Levi lifted his chin. "We need to talk."

"Sure. And when you answer my question, we'll be talking. Which was the mistake, Levi, leaving so fast or kissing me in the first place?"

"Both," he admitted.

It's not like I thought one kiss—as spectacular as it may have been—was some kind of commitment that was going to change my life. I'm way too much of an adult for that. But hearing him dismiss the incident so out of hand, I felt

243

as if a fist had just introduced itself to my solar plexus. I may have even gasped, which is a terrible thing to even think about, and because I didn't want to, I simply whirled around and rushed over to take one of the three seats to the left of the microphone in the center of the gazebo.

"Ah, so you're one of the judges." When Gregory Ashburn stepped up and smiled as if he thought being a guest at the B and B would somehow give him an edge in the contest, I'm pretty sure I didn't smile back. I was trying too hard not to burst into tears.

Levi slipped into the chair next to mine. "That came out wrong," he said.

I gave him the briefest of glances and clung hard and fast to the minutiae of the occasion. Better that than giving in to the mortification that left me feeling inadequate and the inadequacy that mortified me. I lifted my chin. "These chairs are for the judges."

"You didn't tell me you were a judge."

As statements went, it was pretty noncommital. But I was past the objective stage. Anger bunched in my stomach. "So, first you don't think I'm smart enough to investigate a murder, and now you don't even think I can handle judging a trivia contest. I guess that proves you *are* right. What happened the other night *was* a mistake."

Oh, how I love it when they squirm!

Levi ran a hand through his hair. "That's not what I meant."

"About me being smart? Or about the other night?"

Since Marianne zipped over to stand in front of us, I couldn't be sure, but I think Levi's response was either a curse or a growl.

"Questions," she said, and she handed Levi a manila folder like the one she'd given me.

My mouth fell open and I spun in my seat to face him, and yes, the question came out a bit too loud. "You're a judge, too?"

"What, you don't think I'm smart enough to be a judge?"

I wasn't in the mood to handle the cocky smile that went along with his question, so I turned in my seat so I was facing the audience again. "I'd like to think I have a little more class than that," I said, and gave myself a mental pat on the back. Way to go putting him right in his place!

Before I could get too carried away congratulating myself, Marianne took the chair on the other side of me and Gordon Hunter stepped up to the microphone to introduce each of the Dickens impersonators and ask them to step up to the gazebo. While he was at it, I took another quick look around and noticed Margaret sitting in the back row nibbling out of that blue candy bag.

But still no Mason Burke.

Maybe he got cold feet, I told myself.

Maybe his wife had a relapse and, devoted husband that he was, he opted to stay with her.

Maybe he couldn't find his top hat, or lost his pocket watch, or wasn't happy with the way his cravat was tied.

Maybe—

". . . good-looking."

The word Levi whispered snapped me out of my thoughts and I automatically glanced his way. Good thing I didn't assume he was talking about me and say something stupid like, "Oh, this old outfit, it's just something I threw on," because I saw that he was watching Eva DeNato.

"That suit, and the silver-tipped cane," he rasped when he realized my mind had been a million miles away and he needed to repeat himself. "It's a good-looking outfit."

It was, and as it turned out, Eva DeNato did it proud. She was as smart as a whip. One by one, we went through our questions, following the ground rules that had been established for the contest:

Each judge took a turn asking one question.

Each contestant could get two questions wrong before being disqualified.

Each contestant had to stay in the Dickens persona the entire time.

Needless to say, that pretty much disqualified Max and Tyler from the get-go, but hey, they were nothing if not good sports. When they were dismissed, they smiled and waved and bowed like rock stars.

That left Drake, Ashburn, and Ms. DeNato, and that's when things got interesting.

Not to mention cutthroat.

"Who is Phillip Pirrip?" Marianne asked, and when Drake, whose turn it was to answer, hesitated for just a moment, Ashburn clicked his tongue.

Drake shot him a look, pulled back his shoulders, and in his very best—and loudest—British accent—said, "'. . . my infant tongue could make of both names nothing longer or more explicit than Pip.' The answer to your question, madam, is Pip, *Great Expectations*."

There was a smattering of applause from the crowd, not for knowledge, because let's face it, this was a pretty easy question, but certainly for style. Ashburn did not join in. It was his turn to answer and my turn to ask.

"Why did Mrs. Bardell take Mr. Pickwick to court?" I wanted to know.

The way Ashburn rolled his eyes sent the very clear message that my question was not in his know-it-all league. "For breach of promise," he said.

"Ah, love."

This from Levi who at my side, breathed the words more than said them so as not to attract attention.

I pretended not to hear him, and held my breath while he asked the next question.

And so it went with each of the three contestants easily handling anything we threw at them, even when we got down to the nitty-gritty.

My turn to ask and Drake's to answer. "What," I asked, "is the connection between Charles Dickens and the famous line from literature, 'It was a dark and stormy night.'"

"Dickens never wrote that," Drake blurted out, then remembered himself and stammered, "That is, I never wrote that."

"Aha!" Ashburn pointed a finger at his opponent. "He didn't stay in the character of Dickens."

"Dickens?" Drake whined. "You should have said, 'He didn't stay in *my* character.' He should have said *my* character, am I right?" He turned pleading eyes on us, then a smile as venomous as a snake on Ashburn. "*Hasta la vista*, baby!"

"*Hasta la vista!*" That pointed finger of his quivering, Ashburn jumped up and down. "That disqualifies him! That disqualifies him!"

"That . . ." Because Marianne sat there with her mouth hanging open, I jumped to my feet. "That disqualifies both of you." I poked my thumb over my shoulder. "Outta here, fellas."

They stuttered and huffed and puffed and hesitated, but in the end, Ashburn and Drake knew they'd blown it. But that didn't automatically make Eva the winner. I explained that she still needed to answer the question Drake had missed and then (as laid out in the rules) answer a final question that each of the three judges would agree upon.

She took a deep breath. "There is a connection between 'It was a dark and stormy night' and myself," she said, glancing to where Drake and Ashburn sat in the audience, red-faced and regretful. "Edward Bulwer-Lytton, who wrote that famous line, was a friend of mine, and in fact, my youngest son, Edward Bulwer-Lytton Dickens was named for him."

We applauded, but just when we were going to put our heads together and decide on a final question, Levi spoke up. "I've got one," he said, consulting his notes. "You ladies mind?"

Marianne assured him we didn't, though I wasn't quite so sure. It all depended on what he wondered if I minded.

"So here goes," Levi said, raising his voice so he could be heard clearly all the way at the back of the crowd.

"Dickens believed in something unorthodox," he said. "Something that may . . . or may not be factual." Here, Levi's gaze slid to me briefly before it returned to our contestant. "Can you tell us what it was?"

I flipped through my mental Rolodex of Dickens trivia, but try as I might, I couldn't come up with anything about Dickens that justified that sly little look I'd gotten from Levi.

No matter.

Eva DeNato didn't have the same problem. Or the distraction of sitting so close to Levi, his thigh touching mine.

"Krook in *Bleak House* dies this way," she said, but alas (in keeping with the Victorian theme), I was at a loss. At least until she added, "SHC, Spontaneous Human Combustion."

Right about then, I was a believer, too, because I was pretty sure when Levi grinned at me, my cheeks caught fire.

Thank goodness no one but Levi noticed. They were too busy applauding and congratulating Eva.

"Told you that would be fun!" Marianne beamed with all the enthusiasm of a bookworm who had, in her own small way, helped spread her love of reading. "I just wish I would have had a chance to ask one last question." She'd left a book on the floor of the gazebo next to her chair, and now she lifted it and showed me the cover. "It's a reproduction of a first edition of *A Tale of Two Cities*," she said, and she lovingly ran her hand over the cover before she flipped the book open. "It even has the original illustrations. Look at this one." She pointed. "Isn't it wonderful?"

Wonderful, yes.

And familiar.

The pen-and-ink sketch showed a man in Colonial clothing standing behind a wooden counter. There was another man in front of the counter, also in knee breeches and a tricorn hat, and a woman sitting behind it, a mobcap on her head and her attention on her knitting.

"It's the drawing that hangs behind Alice and Margaret's cash register," I said, and automatically looked around for Margaret, but she and her bag of candy were already gone.

"It's Madame Defarge! Wait until I tell them, they'll be tickled."

Marianne trilled. "Oh, maybe it's worth a fortune. You know, there's a story about the original drawing, they say it's been lost for years and that there are treasure hunters all over who—"

"Treasure hunters?" Funny how these thoughts hit. With all the wallop of an atomic bomb.

Mason Burke, that wrapped poster of his, and the way he hurried through the dark, his chin on his chest.

"Like the man who hopped off the boat next to Luella's the night of the party on the dock," I cried, and raced out of the gazebo.

Poor Marianne didn't have much of a chance to say more than, "What are you talking about?" and no way she could keep up.

Levi had no trouble at all.

"You want to explain?" He matched me step for step when I hurried to the knitting shop.

"I do. I can. I mean, he said his wife sprained her ankle when they were packing up the boat, right? But when he got off the boat the night of the storm, he was all alone. He should have been helping her. He shouldn't have been running because he should have been walking with her. What kind of man would leave his injured wife on a boat in the middle of a storm?" Levi had no answer, and I knew it so I went right on. "The same kind of man who says he's bringing Margaret and Alice a gift, when maybe what he's really doing is trying to replace a valuable picture with a reproduction."

We turned the corner and put on the brakes.

Even from here, I could tell that the front door of the knitting shop was wide open.

Though he was at my side, Levi was already one step ahead of me. He got out his phone and called Hank.

❈ 17 ❈

I didn't want to, but Levi clamped a hand on my arm and held on tight, making me wait right there in the middle of the street until Hank and a couple of patrol officers arrived on the scene. When they rushed into the knitting shop, I squirmed away from Levi's steely grip and followed right along.

With Levi at my heels (grumbling something about how I refused to be corralled), I toed the line between the front stoop and the open door of the shop and watched the ugly truth dawn on Mason Burke, who was standing near the front counter. As soon as he got a gander of the boys in blue, his eyes grew wide. His jaw dropped and his face went ashen. All telling signs, I thought, but not nearly as interesting (or as damning) as the fact that there was string and torn brown paper on the floor around his feet and he was holding an exact duplicate of the drawing from *A Tale of Two Cities* that hung behind Margaret and Alice's front counter.

"You want to explain?" Hank asked.

Was that another grumble I heard from the honey-haired hunk who stood at my shoulder?

Indeed, and I'm pretty sure it had something to do with Hank's question being intended not for Mason Burke, but for me.

I took this as a sign that I was welcome both in terms of the investigation and into the knitting shop, so I stepped inside. At this point, I probably don't need to mention that Levi did, too.

"There's a legend about that drawing. It's an illustration from *A Tale of Two Cities*, and that one . . ." I pointed to the drawing that hung on the wall. "Well, of course it's impossible to know for certain without authentication, but I have a feeling that it might be the original."

"So . . ." Leave it to Hank to sound like this was no big deal. His thumbs hooked in his belt, he strolled nearer to Burke. "So what do you have there in your hands, Mr. . . . er . . ."

"Burke." I supplied the information for him. "Mason Burke. He's staying at a cottage over on the west side of the island, and he claims he's here with his wife who sprained her ankle just as they were getting on their boat on the mainland to come over here."

"Claims?" Hank rubbed a hand over his chin. "You want to explain that, Mr. Burke?"

Burke swallowed hard, and when one of the patrol officers slipped on latex gloves and took the picture out of his hands, he didn't put up a fight. "Of course I'm here with my wife," he said. "And as far as that picture . . ." Now that he'd had a few minutes to compose himself, he recovered pretty quickly and laughed. "This is just one big mix-up, officer. I told Bea yesterday, my wife and I found this knitting picture at a garage sale." He pointed at the drawing now being held by the police officer. "I brought it over here to give to Alice and Margaret. As a gift. Honestly, all I wanted to do . . ." The gaze Burke turned on Hank was so open and so darned honest, it almost fooled even me.

"The shop was locked up tight earlier," Burke said, "but when I tried the door now, well, you can see it opened right up. I assumed the sisters would be around, but as far as I can see . . ." As if we didn't know what he was talking about, he looked all around. "There's no one here. All I wanted to do was surprise those nice old ladies. Honest. That's why I came here today."

"Except this morning you told me you wanted to give them the picture in person," I reminded Burke. "So if they're not here, what were you going to do with the picture?"

His jaw went stiff. "I changed my mind. About giving them the picture in person. But then, it hardly matters, does it? I didn't realize the picture we found at the garage sale . . . That is, I didn't remember the one hanging here as well as I thought I remembered it. You can imagine how shocked I was when I realized the picture we'd bought was the same as the one already hanging here. My wife's going to be so disappointed. She wanted a special way to thank Margaret and Alice for helping me pick out some yarn so she had a way to pass the time while she's laid up."

"Not true," I said for Hank's benefit. "Because Mr. Burke isn't here with his wife. He's on the island alone."

With his eyebrows traveling toward his buzzed hair, Hank glanced at Levi before he looked at me. "And you know this . . . how, Bea?"

"Because of the storm the other night, of course," I said, and threw my hands in the air. That is, before I realized that what was so crystal clear to me was still mud to Levi and Hank. I drew in a breath to calm my pounding heart. "When we were at the party on the dock the other night and the storm kicked up, Mr. Burke got off his boat. Alone."

Hank pursed his lips.

"Don't you get it?" I asked, and then was sorry I did. Something told me that wasn't the sort of thing a person asks a cop who has a potential felon on his hands. I backed off the comment with a wave of my hands. "If there was a Mrs. Burke," I said, "and if she'd sprained her ankle as they were packing up the boat on the mainland like Mr. Burke said she did, he wouldn't have jumped off the boat and hurried away from the dock by himself. He would have had to help her."

"Okay." Hank gave me that much, but tempered the comment with a, "So?"

"So when Chandra and I stopped in here the other day, Mr. Burke was here, too. He said he was picking up some yarn and needles for his wife. You know, so she'd have something to do while he was here to be in the Dickens contest. Only he didn't show up at the Dickens contest today, so that got me to thinking."

"That doesn't mean there's not a Mrs. Burke waiting back at the cottage," Hank said.

"Except if she is, he leaves her in the dark every time he goes out." I met Burke's look head-on, challenging him to dispute this, and when he didn't, I suggested to Hank, "Maybe you could send someone out there to the cottage to check. You know, just to be sure."

"No." Burke stepped forward, then froze in place when the nearest cop—a young guy with big biceps and a square chin—pulled back his shoulders and laid a hand oh so casually on the taser clipped to his belt. He mumbled something under his breath, and when Hank leaned nearer because he couldn't hear, Burke huffed. "Bea's right. You won't find Mrs. Burke at the cottage. There is no Mrs. Burke."

Since he seemed to be in the mood to tell the truth, I figured I might as well go for broke. "And you were here to steal Alice and Margaret's drawing."

Burke bit his lower lip. His audacity washed out with the tears that streamed down his cheeks. "They bought it at a garage sale," he whimpered. "Did you know that? Those old ladies, they told me the story. They went to a garage sale and Alice, she liked the picture, and she bought it for seven dollars."

"She told Margaret it cost five," I added for Levi's and Hank's benefit.

"It's just . . ." Burke pulled at his hair. "It's maddening. Impossible. The original illustrations in Dickens's books were made from etchings, of course. But the artist, Hablot Knight Browne, made sketches before he produced the final etchings. The other drawings and all the etchings are accounted for. Every single one of them. Private collections, museums, libraries. Browne signed his pieces *Phiz*, and all the original Phiz illustrations and etchings are well documented. Except for this one." Burke turned to look with reverence at the drawing on the wall. "*The Wine-shop.*"

While all this made perfect if somewhat skewed sense to me, it wasn't straightforward enough to appeal to Hank's cop senses. He scratched a hand behind his ear. "So what are you, Mr. Burke, some sort of burglar? You take the chance—"

"He didn't have to take a chance," I told Hank, and I knew I was right. From Burke's point of view there was only one way his plan would have worked. "I'd bet anything Mr. Burke has been on the island before, probably more than once. I guarantee you that's why he was one of the contestants in the Dickens contest this weekend. You'd been to the shop before, right, Mr. Burke? You must have been, because you would have wanted to check out the picture and try to determine if it was what you thought it was. You asked questions, you poked around. And when you realized how close you were to the Holy Grail of Phiz illustrations, you knew you had to come back and do the ol' switcheroo. The picture you brought had to be an exact replica, down to the hanging wire on the frame. Otherwise, someone might notice. You couldn't take the chance of Alice or Margaret recognizing you as the man who'd stopped into the shop before, so you needed the top hat and the goatee and the old-fashioned clothes. As a disguise."

Burke didn't confirm or deny. He didn't need to. Instead, he simply shook his head, slow and steady, the gesture filled with both disgust and disappointment. "There have been so many stories about *The Wine-shop* over the years," he said. "So many tantalizing little clues. I've spent the better part of my adult life following each and every one of them. The original illustration was owned by a family in England, then it went to France, then it came to this country, then . . ." He threw his hands in the air and they landed against his thighs with a slap. "It disappeared. Just disappeared. That is, until I was able to track it to an island in the middle of nowhere and find out that a little old lady bought it for five dollars."

"Seven," I corrected him, but I don't think he much cared.

"So you see, Officer . . ." Burke looked Hank's way. "I'm not a burglar, I'm a treasure hunter. And this treasure . . ." When one of the cops turned Burke around and slapped the cuffs on him, he found himself looking right at the Phiz drawing. "This treasure was the chance of a lifetime."

Hank and one of the other officers took Burke away. The other policeman was sent out to look for Alice and Margaret since there was no sign that anyone was home at the cottage. When he motioned toward the door, Levi and I stepped back out into the late afternoon sunshine.

Never let it be said that the island grapevine isn't efficient. No sooner were we outside than Chandra, Luella, and Kate came racing around the corner.

"What's going on?"

"We just saw Hank putting that Mason Burke in a patrol car. What happened?"

"Bea, you've got to tell us!"

I did have to tell them, but not in the middle of the street. When Levi invited us into the bar, I balked, but I was out-voted by the other Ladies who were all carrying shopping bags (craft show, remember) and complaining that they were hot and their feet were tired.

My pride might be hurt. My ego might be crushed. My spirit might be flagging. But I know a losing cause when I'm in the middle of one. My own feet dragging, I followed my friends into Levi's where he offered us a (relatively) quiet table in a (relatively) quiet corner, and a bottle of pinot grigio he had delivered to us compliments of the house.

Not that one bottle of a modest domestic pinot grigio was going to get him off the hook for anything.

Sure, Levi and I had just been in on the nabbing of an art thief together, and yes, the wine . . . I sipped. The crisp, acidic flavor of the wine was just what I needed after a close encounter of the felonious kind. But even nice wine can't wash away certain memories.

Like a guy I know coming right out and saying that kissing me was a big ol' mistake.

"What? The wine's no good?" I guess my expression gave away something of what I was thinking, because Kate gave me a look and sipped her own wine. She pronounced it fine with a little nod, folded her hands on the table in front of her, and said, "Okay, spill the beans."

She was not talking about what had just happened over at the knitting shop.

Which is precisely why I pretended she was, and told my friends what happened with Mason Burke.

"Brilliant," Luella said when I'd finished. "You put the pieces of the mystery together like an author plotting a novel."

I wouldn't go that far, and I told her so.

"This calls for a celebration," Chandra announced, and she dug inside her shopping bag. She pulled out a blue bag from the candy shop and offered it to me. "Fudge?"

I wasn't hungry. But there are times when sugar is a very good thing. Especially when it comes to sweetening a sour mood. "What flavor?" I asked her before I made up my mind.

Chandra grinned. "You don't go to the candy shop much, do you? The chocolate fudge comes in a blue bag, the vanilla fudge comes in red, the peanut butter fudge comes in green, and so on. It's a system Glenda over at the shop came up with so her summer workers at the cash registers would know how much to charge for what the workers behind the counter packed."

Chocolate then. I dug right in and Chandra passed the bag around.

"So that Burke guy was nothing but a two-bit thief." Luella munched and shook her head.

"Only something tells me two-bit has nothing to do with it," I said. In my months on the island, I had been virtuous and avoided the candy shop completely. Darn, one bite of the chocolate fudge studded with pecans and I knew the next time I walked by, my resolve would poof away completely and I'd load up on more fudge. "I bet that drawing's worth a fortune. Wait until Margaret and Alice find out! They were talking about refinancing the building, right? If they sold the drawing, they probably wouldn't need to. Heck, they might be able to retire someplace nice and warm and live like queens."

"That will be quite a relief to Margaret." Luella finished her piece of fudge and reached for one of the paper napkins in the holder at the center of the table. "Not having to refinance, I mean. She's never been as dedicated to the knitting shop as Alice is, you know. A couple weeks ago, when I talked to Margaret about the refinancing . . . well, she wasn't exactly enthusiastic. Said she'd rather go back to Florida than stay here and have to listen to Alice criticize her knitting skills."

"Something tells me she might change her tune when she finds out that picture she didn't want Alice to buy is worth a mint." Pinot grigio after chocolate is not the best idea, so I took one sip of wine to wash away the fudgy flavor, and another to make sure it stayed gone. "I wouldn't be surprised if this story gets the twins plenty of publicity and a lot of attention from the media. It's like something right out of an Indiana Jones movie."

"And wait until the newspapers find out how much you had to do with figuring it out." Chandra offered another piece of fudge and I declined.

Good fudge.

Bad idea.

I'd have to make sure to stay far, far away from any publicity Alice and Margaret might garner thanks to the Phiz drawing.

As if the ideas racketing around in it were too heavy to be held upright, Chandra tipped her head to one side. "Mason Burke and the missing picture." She nibbled chocolate fudge. "It's terrific, really, how you figured it out, Bea. But here's what I don't get." She shimmied forward in her seat, planted her elbows on the table, and glanced around at each of us.

"What does what just happened with Mason Burke have to do with Richie's murder?"

Good question. I plumped back in my chair and admitted to them what I didn't even want to admit to myself. "I have absolutely no idea."

The idea struck in the middle of the night, as so many ideas so often do.

Not that I'm complaining or anything. I wasn't sleeping, anyway, and thinking about murder beats thinking about stolen kisses and the resulting disses.

After a week of taking care of guests, I was alone in the house, and I'd drifted off on the couch in the parlor, a book open on my lap. When I sat up like a shot, the book slapped against the floor. I rubbed the sleep out of my eyes, checked the tall case floor clock in the corner, and cursed whatever muse it was who was responsible for the idea—and the bad timing.

Two forty-five.

Too early to call Kate, who never got out of bed until the sun was up.

Too late to call Chandra, who kept night owl hours but never this late.

Too rude to call Luella, who I knew was recovering from a week's worth of fishing charters.

Too crazy to call Hank, who, for all I knew, was at Chandra's anyway. Besides, I'd need more information before I presented my theory to him.

I had no choice but to wait for the sun to peep over the

horizon, and when it did, I planned to be ready with as many dates, times, places, and incidents as I could remember.

Once I had my facts lined up, then—and only then—would it be time to call the League of Literary Ladies to action.

❖ 18 ❖

"What are you doing here?"

Okay, so it wasn't the most gracious way to greet Levi first thing the next morning, but it's not like I could help myself. Just as the sun came up, I called Hank and told him what was on my mind. And Hank? Well, he didn't exactly buy right into the theory. Maybe he hadn't had a cup of coffee yet. Maybe he wasn't a morning person. Maybe he was too much of a cop, and I had read too many books with convoluted plots and seen too many shows on TV where the truth had been staring people in the face—literally—and it was so plain and so simple and so apparent, no one ever figured it out.

Maybe that's why I was so discombobulated when I saw Levi waiting for me outside his bar, where I'd arranged to meet with Hank.

Or maybe it was something else.

"Got an official invite from our friend Hank," Levi said. It was obvious that unlike Hank, Levi *was* a morning person. This early, Put-in-Bay was nearly deserted, and the cardinals and robins were trying out their songs, but he was as bright as a new penny. Jeans, blue golf shirt the exact shade as his eyes, cocky smile. If I'd known what I'd be dealing with, I would have had a second cup of coffee just to fortify myself.

Sans more coffee, I had to rely on my own brainpower. "I don't know why Hank would want you in on this," I said.

"Maybe he's just looking for an impartial witness."

"Because he thinks I'm nuts."

Levi's smile inched up. "Do you think you're nuts?"

"He told you, didn't he? Hank told you what I've been thinking."

Levi leaned back against the closed front door of the bar. "He mentioned you had a theory."

"And he said the theory was a little out there. No, he said it was a lot out there."

His one-shoulder shrug made it hard to know if Levi agreed with Hank or not.

"It is a lot out there," I admitted, my voice teetering on the edge, just as my composure was. But hey, I hadn't gotten much sleep. That was one excuse. Levi was excuse number two. And number three?

"I've been over and over it, Levi. I made long lists last night." To prove it, I waved the legal pad I carried in front of his face. "I went over times and dates and incidents. I hate what I came up with." My voice caught on a sudden knot of emotion in my throat. "I really hate it."

"I know." He pushed away from the door and stepped

forward, and I knew if I gave him the slightest encouragement, he'd give me a hug.

I needed the hug.

But not the hugger.

I held the legal pad to my chest like a shield and forced the tremor of emotion out of my voice. "Hank is picking up the FBI agent from Cleveland?"

Levi checked the time on his phone. "He's at the airport even as we speak. They won't know anything definitively—"

I knew this. Of course I knew this. That's why I cut him off with a shake of my head. "Not until they can study the drawing. They'll start by testing the paper so they know how old it is, and the ink, too. They'll look at that Phiz signature a few gazillion times to determine if it's authentic. Even with the FBI art experts involved, it will take a while."

"You know a few things about art forgery."

I did, for a lot of reasons I didn't want to explain to Levi. It was simpler to say, "If you were Chandra or Kate or Luella, I'd tell you it was because of my late husband, Martin. You know, the antiques dealer."

"The one who never existed." I can't say for sure, but I think Levi found this amusing. That would explain that darned blue glint in his eyes. "You should be honest with your friends," he said.

"As honest as you are with yours?" Oh yes, this was a low blow, but I figured he deserved it. We were friends. Sort of. And he had left me hanging with that stinging comment about how kissing me had been a mistake.

"I'd like to be," he said.

"So would I," I shot back.

"So we each have our own reasons, and our reasons are—"

"Our reasons."

Thank goodness I saw Hank's SUV turn onto the street or we might have gone on this way even longer. Hank and the FBI representative were here and it was time to get down to business. If my brain hadn't told me that, the funny, fluttering feeling in my stomach would have.

We met them in front of the knitting shop and Hank introduced us to Special Agent Sheila Rafferty, a middle-aged woman with short-cropped hair and a no-nonsense attitude. I let them lead the way into the shop.

"Well, good morning!" I saw that Hank had done as I'd asked and called the Defarge sisters so the shop would be open. Alice came around the counter and her bright smiled dimmed when she realized Hank had brought reinforcements. She looked from one of us to the other, but her gaze stopped on me. "What's wrong?" she asked.

"You know about Mason Burke and the break-in." I knew the local cops had interviewed her the day before, so this was a given. "We just need to tie up a few loose ends."

"Yes, of course." There was a steaming mug of tea on the counter and Alice went over to retrieve it and offered to make coffee. We all declined. I couldn't speak for anyone else, but I wasn't in the mood. Not with what I knew I had to say.

"The police explained to you about the drawing, didn't they, ma'am?" Special Agent Rafferty asked. "There's a chance that the one you have hanging here on your wall is—"

"An original!" Alice clasped her hands together. "Whoever would have thought! And my goodness, to think I bought it at a garage sale!"

"It's too bad you didn't know more about the drawing before you and Margaret decided to refinance," I mentioned.

Alice's smile froze. This was something she hadn't considered. "You mean, it might be worth—"

"Millions." Honestly, I doubted the drawing would fetch that much at auction, but I threw out the figure, anyway, just to watch Alice's reaction.

It was predictable.

When she set down her cup, the tea sloshed out on the counter. Alice didn't bother to blot it up. "My goodness." Like her hands, her voice trembled. So did her smile. She swallowed hard. "Wait until I tell Margaret. She'll be so surprised and so sorry she made fun of me for paying five dollars for the picture."

"Except you paid seven, right?" I looked toward Hank, who gave me the go-ahead with a barely perceptible nod, and I took a few steps closer to Alice. "You lied to Margaret about the picture. But then, that's not the only thing you've been lying about, is it, Alice?"

Her eyelids fluttered and her chin quivered. "I'm sure I don't know what you're talking about."

I brandished my legal pad. "Exactly what I thought you were going to say. That's why I made a list."

"Really, Hank!" Alice turned an earnest little-old-lady look in his direction. "I'm sure I don't know what Bea's getting at, but whatever it is—"

"Whatever it is . . ." Hank planted his feet and crossed his arms over his chest. "We need to hear her out."

I had the floor, so I adjusted my glasses on the bridge of my nose and consulted my notes. "I honestly thought Gordon was our guy," I said. "Because he's been smuggling cigarettes over to Canada and—"

"What?" Levi stepped forward.

"I'm on it. Bea and I have already talked all about this," Hank assured him. "Go on, Bea."

"The day Richie damaged Gordon's boat, he helped Gordon offload what was on it. You told us about that, Alice. As it turns out, what was on it was a load of cigarettes bound for Canada. Hank's already gotten a confession out of Gordon." Hank nodded. "But Gordon insists what Richie saw had nothing to do with Richie getting murdered. He swears he didn't do it."

"Well of course he didn't." Alice tisked. "Gordon is a nice man."

"That's just it, isn't it?" I asked no one in particular. "When people are nice, we don't suspect them. We take them at face value, and we never stop to think that it's the nice that's fooling us. That's what it all comes down to. Nice. And *A Tale of Two Cities*, of course."

Alice glanced at the wall behind the front counter. "Certainly you can't think my picture had anything to do with Richie's murder," she said.

"It didn't," I admitted. "But in *A Tale of Two Cities*, there are two men, Sydney Carton and Charles Darnay. And they look enough alike to fool a lot of people. You know, just like twins do."

Alice went as still as if she'd been flash frozen. "I don't know what you mean."

"Maybe Margaret will." I strolled toward the back door. "How 'bout we get her in here."

"Hank!" Alice appealed to him again. "I don't know what this girl is getting at, but she's not making any sense. She's not even from around here. She's from New York. They're all crazy in New York. She doesn't know us. Not like you do, Hank. I've known you . . . Margaret and I, we've known you all your life."

"You knew Richie all his life, too," I said. "After his parents died, you tried to make him part of your family. Look." I'd tucked that photograph of Margaret, Alice, and Richie that I found at Richie's place into the back of the legal pad, and I pulled it out and showed it to Alice.

"Easter," Alice said. "I remember we went to church with Richie and his parents, and then Margaret and I hosted a brunch. He kept it all these years. Poor Richie. If only he could have let down his guard a little and let us get past that wall he'd built around himself."

"Oh, I think he did let down his guard." I flipped over the photo to show Alice what was written on the other side, and since Levi and Special Agent Rafferty couldn't see it from where they stood, I read the words written in purple Sharpie out loud. "Chocolate Alice and Vanilla Margaret. That's how everyone on the island's known both of you for years, right, Alice?"

"Well, yes. Of course." She let go a long breath. "But what does that have to do with poor Richie? Dear boy," she said with a glance toward Agent Rafferty to explain. "He had a big heart, but not much of a brain."

"I don't know about that!" Since I knew he would need it as evidence, I passed the photograph over to Hank. "See, as it turns out, Richie had plenty of brains. In fact, he once wrote a song that would have made him famous if someone else didn't steal the song and claim it as his own. Richie was no dummy. That's why he pulled out this old picture of you and Margaret. That's why he wrote on it in purple Sharpie. Chocolate Alice and Vanilla Margaret. When did he figure it out, Alice, one day when he was selling ice cream?"

She clutched her hands at her waist. "I'm sure I don't know what you're talking about."

I'd made a quick stop at Chandra's before I got downtown that morning. Chandra, of course, was dying to know what was up, and I swore I'd tell all later. What I needed, I told her, was to borrow something, and I pulled that something out of my back pocket.

It was a blue bag from the candy shop.

"The chocolate fudge comes in the blue bag," I said.

Alice fluttered. "Of course it does. Everyone knows that."

"Just like everyone knows that Margaret hates chocolate with a fiery passion."

"Well, of course," she twittered.

"Except on Sunday during the parade, I saw Margaret eating fudge out of a blue bag," I said.

"That isn't possible!" Alice insisted.

"Why?" I countered. "Because Margaret hates chocolate so much? Or because that wasn't Margaret I saw?"

Alice's jaw went slack. So did her shoulders. She would have crumpled to the floor if Levi didn't rush forward to loop an arm around her shoulders. Agent Rafferty reached over and dragged the rocking chair closer, and when Levi piloted Alice into it, she dropped her face in her hands.

Kylie Logan

"You can't know," she whimpered. "No. No. There's no way you can know."

"But you did know!" This was from Levi, and call me crazy (go ahead and try and see what happens when a Manhattanite is called names), but I think there was more admiration than there was doubt in his question. "How, Bea?"

I'd explained it all to Hank in that way-too-early phone call, but I went through it again, anyway. "It's been staring us in the face all this week," I said. "And I should have thought of it, I mean, what with reading about Sydney Carton and Charles Darnay. You see, Alice and Margaret look alike, too, and the more I thought about it, the more I realized that all this week, though I'd seen each of them plenty of times, I'd never seen Margaret and Alice together."

"That doesn't mean anything," Alice insisted. "Just because we're twins doesn't mean we're joined at the hip."

"It sure doesn't. In fact, Margaret even got married and moved away for a while. And when her husband died and she came back, that's when you started talking about refinancing, wasn't it, Alice? And that's when Margaret—"

"Margaret!" Alice popped out of the chair, high color in her cheeks. "She never loved the shop. Not like I do. She never cared what happened here. She wanted to sell it. Hank!" Her eyes wide, she turned to her old friend. "Hank, she actually wanted to sell the shop. She said she had every right to do it since she owned half the place. She was going to take her share of the money and go back to Florida. And where would that leave me? What did she expect me to do?"

"What you did was get rid of her, and all you needed to do was wait a couple weeks until the refinancing papers went

272

through, right, Alice? Then my guess is you'd tell everyone that Margaret had left the island and gone back to Florida and no one would have been the wiser. But then Richie got in the way. You see, Richie," I said for Agent Rafferty's sake, "told me that he was going to have a lot of money very soon, and when he did, he was going to leave the island and never come back. And I found myself wondering where he was going to get that money. He already had a down payment on it, didn't he, Alice? Twelve thousand dollars. You would have been better off using that money to start your renovations than caving in to Richie's blackmail."

"Richie. Richie!" Alice tore at her hair. "I made one little mistake. One little slip. And leave it to Richie, he was on it like a hawk on a baby bunny. I was wearing one of Margaret's stupid pink sweaters, and I stopped for ice cream and I asked for chocolate. I'm not a complete moron," she added, her voice rising an octave. "I covered and made a joke about it. But Richie—"

"Richie started thinking," I said. "That's why he brought out that old picture of you and Margaret, and that's why he wrote on the back of it. That's why at the gazebo on Monday night, when Richie was dripping wet and you brought him tea, he asked if you were Alice or Margaret. He wanted you to know that he hadn't forgotten, that the twelve thousand dollars you'd already given to buy his silence wasn't nearly enough. That's why you lied about the fight you said Richie had with his girlfriend, too, to send me off looking in the wrong direction. Poor Richie!"

Alice's face twisted and she spat out the words, "He asked for it."

"Did Margaret ask for it, too?" I wanted to know.

Alice's bottom lip quivered and she grabbed a fat skein of pink yarn from the counter and pressed it to her heart. "She's making all this up, Hank," she insisted. "Ask Bea. Ask her. That day she was here, she heard Margaret talking to me from the cottage. Chandra heard it, too. Just because Margaret doesn't happen to be around right this very minute—"

Believe me, I'd thought through this part of the problem carefully. I remembered the morning Chandra and I had stopped in and how Margaret just happened to call out as Alice was putting yarn under the front counter. I slipped behind the cash register and felt around below the counter. The remote control that operated the recorder back in the cottage wasn't hard to find.

"Where's the peanut butter?" Margaret's voice called out.

Only I was pretty sure it was really Alice who'd made the recording.

"She wouldn't listen." Tears streamed down Alice's wrinkled cheeks. "She wouldn't listen to reason. She wanted to take the shop away from me. She wanted to take my knitting. I couldn't let her do that. Don't you see? Margaret was never as good a knitter as I am. I couldn't let her do that."

"Are you serious? She actually buried Margaret out at Dan Peebles's new house so when they poured the foundation . . ."

Kate didn't finish her question. She didn't need to. It was Monday evening and the League of Literary Ladies was gathered for its weekly book discussion meeting. This week, we'd opted for my front porch instead of the library, and I sat back in the wicker rocker, a glass of Wilder wine in one hand. "They're going to start digging up the foundation tomorrow," I told the other Ladies. "Poor Dan Peebles, another house of his gone."

"Oh, I don't think he'll mind so much," Chandra said. "After what you told us about him and Didi christening the property . . . this will just give them another chance."

We all laughed, and thank goodness, that lightened the mood. We'd spent all day regretting the fact that we hadn't done more for Richie, and that we hadn't seen what was right in front of our eyes sooner.

"Just like in the book." Luella patted the copy of *A Tale of Two Cities* on her lap. "People getting people mixed up with other people. People switching identities and getting all mixed up."

Kate nodded. "Margaret and Alice."

"And Guillotine really being Boyz 'n Funk," Luella added.

"Charles Darnay and Sydney Carton." Chandra sighed.

I was glad she brought up the book because it gave me a chance to ask the question that had been bugging me all week. "You didn't actually read the book, did you, Chandra?"

Since her face turned the same color as the rosé we were sipping, I didn't really need an answer.

"There's an animated version," Chandra admitted, then burst into a laugh. "I know the story because I watched the cartoon!"

If nothing else, we had to give her credit for ingenuity. We clinked our glasses together.

"Oh!" I sat up. "And I forgot to tell you what I heard this afternoon. Either Richie's death hit Dino really hard or there's something about the air on the island. Dino made a huge contribution in Richie's name to Mike Lawrence and his family."

"A change of heart and a change of fortunes. That is something to celebrate!" Luella said. Again, we raised our wineglasses and I found myself thinking that in spite of two murders, sitting here with the other Ladies, watching the smooth swell of the lake across the street, listening to the birds cheep and a golf cart whirr by . . .

I watched the cart buzz past and was just in time to catch a glimpse of Jerry Garcia's butt when he slipped over the porch railing.

Even that wasn't enough to sour my mood.

See, this really was the best of times.

Turn the page for a preview
of the next book in Kylie Logan's
Chili Cook-off Mysteries

DEATH BY
DEVIL'S BREATH

Coming August 2014 from Berkley Prime Crime!

The way I figured it, I had about three minutes.

The seconds tick, tick, ticked away and before I could waste another one of them, I squirmed in my seat, cocked my leg at a funny angle, and stretched the toe of one stiletto toward the evening purse that was on the floor in front of to the empty seat to my left.

Success!

Or not.

My shoe snagged the sequin-covered purse just as my thigh muscle protested. I winced and morphed the expression into a smile when Jorge LaReyo, the man who ran the tamale stand at the Chili Showdown and who was sitting on my right, happened to glance my way. I counted on that smile to distract him and gave the purse a little nudge. Lucky for me, the floor in the theater of Creosote Cal's Cactus

Casino and Hoedown Hotel was faux hardwood. The purse slipped, skittered, and slid to a stop directly in front of me.

Head up and gaze never leaving the stage three rows ahead of me, I dipped and grabbed, then sat back, unsnapped the little golden clasp at the top of the purse, and dared a look down. That's when I grumbled a curse. The stage was brightly lit, but out here in the theater seats, the lights were dimmed. Teeth gritted, I pretended to be interested in the proceedings up there in the spotlight at the same time I slipped my hand into the purse and felt around.

"It's an ordinary deck of cards!" Up on stage, the man billed as "The Great Osborn" waved a deck of cards still in its box above his head, then showed it to my half sister, Sylvia, who he'd called up from the audience to help with the trick. "I'm going to take the cards out of the box." He did. "And then I'm going to make one of them magically disappear. But not until my lovely assistant here . . ." He wiggled his eyebrows at Sylvia and got a laugh from the audience. "Not until she chooses five cards and, without looking at them, places them facedown on the table."

The Great Osborn was middle-aged, and his belly hung over the royal blue cummerbund he wore with a black tux that was a little threadbare at the elbows. When he looked from the brightly painted prop table to Sylvia, his eyes gleamed.

But then, Sylvia was known to have that sort of effect on weak-minded men.

It was her fairy-tale-princess looks that did them in, of course. The honey-colored hair that was pinned into a knot at her nape, the elegant line of her neck, the high cheekbones and perfectly bowed lips. The pink dress dusted with sequins didn't hurt, either.

Of course, the sparkly dress was exactly why she'd been invited to help The Great Osborn with this particular trick in the first place. From the magician's vantage point on stage, it was impossible to miss a woman in the audience who twinkled like a drag queen on steroids.

Lucky for me.

Sylvia's moment in the spotlight gave me the three minutes I needed.

Three minutes that were quickly slipping away.

"Lose something?"

I didn't have to glance to my left to know when Nick Falcone slid into the seat next to mine. But then, the temperature in the auditorium shot up a couple dozen degrees at the same time an army of goose bumps popped up on my arms and a shiver cascaded through my body.

Ex-cop. Now head of Showdown security.

Deliciousness personified.

Attitude.

How could a girl have any other reaction?

This girl, it should be noted, kept her cool in spite of it all.

Hand in purse, I cast an oh-so-casual glance in Nick's direction, biting back my disappointment when all I felt inside the purse were the essentials: wallet, tissues, contact case.

"Just looking for my lipstick," I told Nick, then I pretended to be interested when The Great Osborn looked at each of the cards on the table and asked a man sitting in the front row to write down the names of the cards as he called them out. Finished, he slipped the cards back in the deck and had Sylvia take the list and search through the deck for the original five cards she'd chosen.

"But there are only . . ." No one could do wide-eyed wonder like Sylvia. How she made herself blush a color that perfectly matched her outfit—and on cue—was anybody's guess. She went through the entire deck one more time before she surrendered and put a hand to one cheek. "Only four of my cards are in the deck!" she gasped.

"That's because . . ." With a ta-da sort of motion, The Great Osborn opened the box the cards had come out of and extracted the missing card. "It's here!" he said, and smiled and bowed when everyone applauded.

Except for me, of course. But then, clapping would have been a little hard since one of my hands was still in the purse.

And Nick. He didn't clap because he was too busy leaning in nice and close. His hot breath brushed my ear when he whispered, "It might help you find your lipstick if you looked in your own purse."

He never had a chance to notice the frigid smile I shot his way in response. That's because the trick was over, and The Great Osborn kissed Sylvia's hand and shooed her back to her seat.

Nick got up and sidled out of the row. Sylvia waited until he'd exited and, flush from her triumphant stage appearance, sashayed back to her seat.

That left just enough time for me to replace her evening bag exactly where she'd left it.

"So?" Funny how she could twinkle even when the lights weren't trained on her. "What did you think? How did I do?"

"Shhh!" I said, even though it didn't matter. The Great Osborn took his final bows and Creosote Cal himself strolled to the center of the stage and told everyone it was time for intermission.

"But don't you go far," he said, his pseudo-cowboy twang in keeping with the boots, the jeans, and the ten-gallon hat that fit in with the Wild West theme of Cal's hotel in Vegas where we'd be opening another Chili Showdown the next day. "Y'all are gonna get your booth assignments in a few minutes, and then we've got a real treat in store for you. Hang on to your funny bones, pardners, because Dickie Durbin is up next."

I popped out of my chair, but dang, I couldn't get away from Sylvia fast enough. Not when Jorge and the other folks to my right were being slowpokes about getting out to the aisle.

She knew I was stuck, and Sylvia pounced on the moment. "The Great Osborn said I was a natural," she purred.

I'm not a big believer in batting my eyelashes but this seemed as good a moment as any to give it a try. "A natural what?" I asked her.

I guess the way she puckered her lips made them need freshening up, because she got her lipstick out of the purse, the one that only moments before had been in my hot little hands.

From the other side of the aisle, I saw Nick raise his eyebrows.

I ignored him.

I was getting pretty good at it. The ignoring part, that is. In spite of his deliciousness and all. Nick and I had actually been thrown together a time or two only a short while before, when a Showdown roadie was murdered and I (yes, that's right, little ol' me) solved the crime. Nick wasn't happy. About me investigating, and especially about me taking credit where credit was certainly due. But then, if there was one thing I'd learned about Nick in the weeks since I'd joined the Showdown to take over my missing father's chili and spice truck, it was that Nick was never happy.

Far be it from me to try and be the one to bring some sunshine into his life.

"There're my two favorite girls!"

Tumbleweed Ballew was one of only two people in the world I'd let get away with that kind of happy-family horse-hockey when it came to talking about me and Sylvia. The other was his missus, Ruth Ann, and when they closed in on us, they were both grinning like prom queens.

Tumbleweed and Ruth Ann were the administrative heart and soul of the Showdown, and they'd been family friends for years, since back before I was even thought of, when my mom showed up looking for work at Texas Jack Pierce's Hot-Cha Chile Seasoning Palace and stole the job—and Jack's heart—from Sylvia's mother.

"We've got booth assignments!" Ruth Ann and Tumbleweed wore matching outfits: jeans, denim shirts, vests with long leather fringe on them. Ruth Ann had an envelope in her hand and she waved it in front of me. "Bet you can't wait. You checked out Deadeye when you got here, didn't you? Isn't it a hoot?"

The simpering smile that I'd thought was a permanent fixture on Sylvia's face melted around the edges, her lower lip protruding. "I think *tacky* is a much better word. Honestly, Tumbleweed," she turned to the seventy-year-old, "how did you get talked into this whole fake western thing? It's going to make us look—"

"Like we can actually get into the spirit of things and have a little fun?" I refused to wilt beneath the acid stare that came from my half sister. That didn't mean I ignored her. It was plenty fun to goad Sylvia. In fact, it was one of the joys of my life. "Get with the program! This is Vegas! Everything's supposed to be over the top. And it's all for fun!"

"Fun." She rolled her baby blues. "A wing of the building that's meant to look like a western town."

"Yeah, the town of Deadeye," I reminded her.

A shiver snaked over Sylvia's slim shoulders. "Sweet. And what's the point of Deadeye, anyway, except to make more work for us? If we've got to move all our merchandise and supplies out of our trucks and into one of those hokey little booths—"

"There's a sheriff's office, a blacksmith shop, a general store. Even an undertaker." When Tumbleweed chuckled, his belly shook. "These next few days are going to be more fun than a pillow fight! Visitors will get to walk down the main street and stop into each of the little shops to do business with our vendors."

"And there's this. . . ." Once again, Ruth Ann waved the envelope in her hands. "Here's your assignment."

In Sylvia's world, time was money, and she didn't like to waste either. She plucked the envelope out of Ruth Ann's hands and opened it. When she read the single piece of paper inside, her jaw dropped. "The bordello? You've actually assigned Texas Jack's stand to the bor . . . the bor . . ."

"Now, now, honey." Tumbleweed put a hand on her shoulder. "It ain't like we're casting you two girls in a bad light or anything. It's just that we looked the place over. You know, earlier in the week when we got here." He leaned closer. "It's the biggest space in Deadeye," he confided. "And the nicest. We wanted to make sure you girls got the best spot."

"Well, I think it's hilarious and who knows . . ." Because I knew it would annoy her, I poked Sylvia in the ribs with one elbow. "Maybe we'll end up getting a little action. Hey, what happens in Vegas—"

I didn't get the chance to finish; Sylvia had already walked away.

"Seriously." I shook off the bad vibes of Sylvia's annoying Sylvia-ness. "We appreciate the plum spot. I can't wait to see it."

"There's a bar along one wall where you can set up your spices," Tumbleweed said.

"And even a red velvet fainting couch!" Ruth Ann grinned. "You're going to love it, Maxie, honey. And Sylvia . . ." She looked toward where Sylvia was making her way toward the ladies room. "She'll come around."

"Yeah, like in about a million years." This didn't bother me especially. After all, it wasn't news. Sylvia was and always had been a stick-in-the-mud. You'd think a woman who had been arrested for murder back in Taos and owed her freedom to me finding the real killer would relax a little and get over herself. But then, we were talking about Sylvia.

I decided right then and there that it didn't matter. The night before the opening of every Showdown was always a party and I wasn't going to let thoughts of Miss Tighter than a Tick spoil my evening. Especially not in Vegas. "You ready for tomorrow morning?" I asked Tumbleweed.

His grin traveled from ear to ear. "Devil's Breath chili judging first thing in the morning! I've got to admit, having it be event numero uno was a stroke of genius."

"And your idea!" Ruth Ann wound an arm through her husband's and smiled up at him. She was a dozen years younger than Tumbleweed and as stick-thin as he was beefy. When I was a kid and fantasized about the perfect family that I did not have, I always thought of Ruth Ann and Tumbleweed. Unlike my own parents—divorced going on twenty years—they'd stayed together through thick and thin. I always thought they were the perfect couple, and over the years nothing had made me change my mind.

"Karl Sinclair is here, you know," Ruth Ann purred. "That ought to attract plenty of attention to the Showdown."

Sinclair was a showman extraordinaire. He billed himself as the champion of hot chili and had a legion of followers from all over the world. Well, tomorrow's event ought to prove if he had the chops to go along with his reputation. Four regional winners coming together to earn a national title that was as hot as . . .

Well, as hot as Devil's Breath.

See, in the chili community, Devil's Breath is an all-encompassing name for the hottest of the hot. I, for one, was thrilled that this special category had been added to the cook-off for the weekend show, along with the usual divisions: traditional red chili (made with any meat and red chili peppers but absolutely no beans or pasta), chili verde (made with any meat and green chili peppers but absolutely no beans or pasta), salsa, and homestyle (made with any combination of ingredients including beans and pasta). The Devil's Breath contest was garnering us plenty of publicity and putting us on the map here in Vegas, where, let's face it, you have to be over-the-top to get noticed. Since I love chili—the hotter the better—and since after the contest, attendees could donate money for charity and get a taste of each of the finalists' recipes, I couldn't wait.

"What a weekend it's going to be!" Tumbleweed beamed. "Why, we're even going to have a wedding."

"You mean *weddings*," his wife corrected him. "And speaking of that . . . oh, Reverend!" Ruth Ann waved toward a woman who made her way through the crowd toward us. "Reverend Linda Love," she told me as an aside while we waited for the minister to come over. "She owns the largest wedding chapel in Vegas and on Sunday, she's going to officiate at a ceremony that will get her in the record books. The largest mass wedding ceremony—"

"Ever performed in Nevada at a Western-theme hotel on a Sunday afternoon."

I had to give Reverend Love credit—when she finished the sentence for Ruth Ann, she smiled in a way that told me that even she knew how crazy it sounded. But like I said, this was Vegas, and you didn't get to be the proprietor of the most mega of the wedding chapels in the town that wild and crazy built without having a little bit of attitude and a lot of circus ringmaster going for you.

I could tell Reverend Love had plenty of both.

She was a tall woman of sixty, slim, and wore her chin-length, blond hair stylishly mussy. The hairdo added a little bit of casual pizzazz to what might otherwise have been a forbidding persona: black power suit, sparkling diamonds at neck and wrists, a watch that no doubt cost more than the worth of Texas Jack's entire enterprise.

She shook hands all around. "I hope you'll all be here for the ceremony," she said, taking each of us in with a glance. "Tumbleweed and Ruth, like I told you when we made the arrangements, you could always renew your vows."

"That's a great idea!" I said.

That made Reverend Love turn her attention to me. "And how about you?" she asked. "If you've got a special someone in your life, Sunday would be the perfect day to make it official."

"Oh no!" My hands out flat, I backed away, both from the woman and the thought of such a thing. "Been there, done that," I told her, which wasn't technically true because Edik and I were never married. "Not going to make that mistake again."

The reverend's smile never wavered. "Love is never a mistake," she said. "No matter the outcome. It's that moment of commitment that matters. The way it shines through the universe and touches the world with love."

Maybe.

Or maybe Linda Love had never had her credit cards scammed and her bank account emptied by a rock band's lead guitarist who she thought she loved.

The old memories came crashing down and a shiver

snaked over my shoulders. I twitched it away and changed the subject as much as I was able, scrambling to remember any little bit of info I'd heard about the weekend ceremony. "One of the performers from here at the casino is going to assist you, right?"

"Absolutely!" Reverend Love glanced around at the crowd, obviously looking for the performers. Like The Great Osborn, each of them—except for Dickie Durbin who was slated to be up on stage next—had already done an abbreviated show for the gathered vendors. "Each of the regulars here is going to perform one more show this weekend, and whoever sells the most tickets, well, that's the performer who will help me out with the ceremony and be immortalized along with me in the record books."

"I hope it's that magician fellow we just saw perform," Tumbleweed said, rocking back on his heels. "He was mighty good. Did you see the way right there at the end he made that card magically move from the table back into the box?"

I didn't have the heart to point out that even I could have gotten away with that trick. That one card had never left the box to begin with.

"Or that wonderful singer, Hermosa," Ruth Ann piped up.

Again, I kept my mouth firmly shut. Hermosa (just Hermosa, one name, like Cher but without the looks or the talent) had treated us (and oh, how I use those words in the broadest sense) to a medley of songs right before the magician came on stage.

"Or Yancy. Don't forget Yancy. He's a perennial favorite here at Creosote Cal's." With a nod, the reverend indicated the elderly African American man who chatted with a group of people on the other side of the room. I'd come in late and had missed Yancy Harris's performance, but I remembered seeing the poster that advertised his act when Sylvia and I checked in. Yancy was blind, had been all his life, and according to what I'd heard about him, he could wail on the piano keyboard like no other man around.

"And then there's Dickie, of course." Was it possible? Did I actually see the reverend's eternally pleasant expression droop at the mention of the comedian's name? It sure didn't last long. But then, a middle-aged balding guy in an orange-and-brown-plaid sport coat came up behind the reverend and wound an arm around her waist and whatever expression had been on her face, it was lost in a tiny screech of surprise.

"Talking about me, aren't you, sweetie?" Dickie Durbin himself. I recognized him from the posters out in the lobby. His publicity photos had obviously been taken by a skilled professional—or thirty years before. They didn't show the bags under Dickie's eyes, or the blubbery jowls. They definitely weren't scratch and sniff, either, because if they were, I would have caught wind of the musky aftershave Dickie must have applied with a soup ladle.

"You are going to stay around for my act, aren't you, Reverend?" Dickie asked, then gave me a broad wink. "She'll stay. I know she'll stay. Reverend Love here, she's a real doll!"

One more squeeze and Dickie hurried onto the stage.

It was our cue to get back to our seats.

I slipped into mine just as Sylvia came to hers from the other aisle.

She smoothed her skirt. "Busy mingling, I see."

"Maybe." We'd just gotten off the road a couple hours before and parked our RV and the food truck we hauled behind it, and I hadn't bothered to get dolled up like Sylvia had. I was wearing skinny jeans and a skin-hugging top that was nearly as dark as my short, spiky hair. Vegas, remember, and I wasn't about to be intimidated by the likes of Sylvia because I went for casual (and pretty sexy, if I did say so myself) rather than for her sober good taste.

I smoothed my hand over the legs of my jeans. "Mingling is good for business."

"Business is good for business," Sylvia shot back and I braced myself. If she started into another lecture about price points and profit margins, somebody was going to have to call the Vegas boys in blue because I was going to go off on her.

Good thing she didn't have the chance.

The stage lights dimmed and a single spotlight turned on Dickie Durbin.

We clapped politely.

And I settled back, all set to enjoy a little comedy.

At least until Dickie opened his mouth.

"Hey, did you see who's here? It's the Lee family!" The comedian pointed down toward the front row and like everyone else in the audience, I craned my neck to see who he was talking about. Turns out it was Tumbleweed and Ruth Ann.

"Ug and Home!" Dickie announced with a flourish. "Get it? Ug Lee and Home Lee."

A couple people actually had the nerve to laugh.

I was not one of them.

"Not here." Just as I was about to pop out of my seat, Sylvia's hand came down on my arm. "You'll embarrass us," she said.

"I'll pop that idiot in the nose."

As if this was exactly what she expected, Sylvia was ready with an answer. "That's what he wants. It's how he gets attention. Dickie picks on everyone and everything in the room during one of his shows, and the madder they get, the more he picks. Look, Tumbleweed's laughing."

He was, but not with a whole lot of enthusiasm.

Ruth Ann, it should be noted, was not.

"And that Reverend Linda Love!" Both hands to his heart, Dickie went into a pretend swoon. "Have you heard about the big wedding on Sunday here at Creosote Cal's? That's going to be something, huh? And I'll let you in on a little secret. . . ." As if it was actually what he was going to do, he leaned toward the audience. "You know, the one who sells the most tickets to his show in the next couple days is going to help out Reverend Love with her ceremony. Come on, folks! You know where you're going to be on Saturday night. My show. My show!" He pointed a finger at his own chest. "If you're not, you're idiots. Or you've got lousy taste. But then, I'm guessing you must not be the brightest bulbs in the box, anyway. Otherwise you wouldn't be traveling around with this crazy cook-off show! I don't even think any of you are Americans. I think you must all be from Chile. Chile! Get it?"

Somebody must have; there were a few laughs.

"Hey, as long as you're all here." Dickie glanced around

the audience. "I figure you're all experts, and I've been meaning to ask you, where do you find chili beans?"

Someone in the back row thought Dickie was serious and called out the name of his own stand to which Dickie replied, "Idiot. You find chilly beans at the North Pole."

He actually got a couple laughs out of that one.

"So, back to that wedding ceremony. You know, the one Reverend Love is going to perform. Reverend Love, she's a real doll." He put a hand to his eyes and scanned the audience. "Where are you, Reverend Love?" he asked and waved when he saw her. "A doll," he said. "A real doll. And since I'm going to sell the most tickets this weekend, I'm going to be the one who's going to help her out with the ceremony. She's going to be marrying a whole bunch of people, all at the same time. Hey, Osborn!" He leaned back and looked into the wings. From where I was sitting, I could see that The Great Osborn was watching the show. "Bet you're not gonna be one of them, huh?"

It was an inside joke so it was no wonder nobody laughed. Especially not Osborn, who threw a look at Dickie that could have incinerated asbestos.

Water off a duck's back. This time, Dickie aimed his sights on Yancy Harris.

"You see who's over here." From the stage, he pointed down to where Harris sat, all the way down at the end of the same row I was in, sunglasses on and a white-tipped cane in one hand. "Hey, Yancy, you see what I mean by all this, don't you? I mean, you *see* what I mean, don't you?"

Yancy shook his head and I couldn't hear him, but I saw a muscle bunch at the base of his jaw at the same time his lips moved. Something told me the words weren't a glowing review of Dickie's shtick.

"And then there's Hermosa! You all saw her here earlier this evening, didn't you, folks?" Dickie pointed to the back of the theater and we all turned in our seats when he waved Hermosa toward the stage. It took a moment for the spotlight to find her, but when it did, it followed along. She was a chesty woman with a big head of bleached hair, and she was squeezed into a green dress that fanned out at the bottom, like a mermaid tail. She took tiny, mincing steps up to the front of the theater.

"She's something, isn't she, folks?" Dickie clapped and the audience joined in. "Hermosa has an unforgettable voice. And have you seen the way she sways left and right when she really gets into a song?" Dickie swung his hips back and forth. "You know why she does that, don't you? It's harder to hit a moving target!"

I didn't even bother to groan. But then, I was pretty busy watching Hermosa curl her lip, toss her head, and turn on her heels to march out of the theater.

Me? I was pretty much with Hermosa. I'd had enough of Dickie Durbin. I got up out of my seat to leave.

"Hey, where you going, sweetheart?" Dickie called after me and checked his watch. "We had it all planned. You're not supposed to meet me in my dressing room for another fifteen minutes. Hey, that would be something, wouldn't it? That little chickie and me." He whistled low. "Talk about a hot tamale! And believe me, when it's all over, I'm going to talk about it plenty!"

By the time I punched open the door and walked out into

the lobby, I wasn't even mad, just disgusted by stupid Dickie and his stupid jokes.

Come to think of it, I guess I wasn't the only one. There hadn't been very many laughs packed into Dickie's performance, but there had been plenty of people—Tumbleweed and Ruth Ann, Hermosa, The Great Osborn, Yancy Harris—who looked like they would have liked nothing better than to commit murder.